# the
# s-word

*For Chris*

# the
# s-word

# one

LIZZIE WASN'T THE first person to kill herself this year. Five months prior to her final ascension Gordy "Queerbait" Wilson hanged himself in his basement. Rumor has it he used the belt his father beat him with. For two hours he hung there, feet hovering above the ground, before Daddy came down the stairs in search of a cold one.

I guess that's the difference between Gordy and Lizzie.

Lizzie didn't go quietly.

I'm Angelina Lake. I was Lizzie's best friend. We were inseparable, until she hooked up with my boyfriend at the prom. Maybe you've heard about it? Every jackass in the blogosphere had a field day with the story: *Little Miss Perfect Steals Prom Queen's Beloved.* My Lizzie with my Drake. The whole school came to my defense. And while Drake got off with a boys-will-be-boys slap on the wrist, Lizzie became the Harlot of Verity High.

It started with a single word, painted in the corner of her locker. I was coming out of English when I saw it. It was the Monday after prom, and Mrs. Linn had asked me to run some papers to the office. I'd barely taken three steps when Lizzie's locker caught my eye.

SLUT

The word was unmistakable. Even in tiny black writing, the marker stood out against the beige. I stepped up to it, running my fingers over the word.

SLUT

Why had they written this? *Heartbreaker* would have been a better word. *Backstabber.* But *slut*? Lizzie never touched anybody before Drake. She was Princess Prude.

Still, there it was.

SLUT

For a second, I thought about erasing it. I slid my nail across the *S* to see if it would chip. It didn't, but I had plenty of pens in my bag. Three seconds and the word would be blotted out. Hidden, and even the vandal would forget. But if I left it there, and everybody could see it . . . well, how long before another one appeared?

Yeah, even then, I knew the word would multiply. I don't know how. I could just *feel* it at the base of my neck, like fingers scratching me there. Warning me of what was going to happen.

The bell rang.

People poured into the hallway. My locker had been next to Lizzie's all year, so no one batted an eye at the sight of me hovering there. Besides, most of us were still suffering from that two-day, post-prom hangover funk. Walking on shaky legs. Stumbling. Then everything went quiet, like all the oxygen had been sucked out of the hall. I knew people were watching me, even though my body blocked the graffiti.

I turned.

The hallway pulsed with bodies, but it didn't matter. Lizzie's were the only eyes I could see. It was the first time I'd seen her since prom night. The first time I'd looked at her since her limbs were entangled with Drake's. Here she was dressed in a sweatshirt and jeans, quite the departure from baby-blue satin and ivory lace. She didn't look like a princess anymore. Her eyes caught mine and we were frozen, both of us staring across the crowded hall, mesmerized by the wreckage of our friendship.

Everyone was watching.

My skin felt hot, and I didn't want to move away from the locker, to reveal what was written there. Would she think I'd done it? Should I care? In the two days since I'd stormed out of the hotel room, leaving Drake to zip up his rented tuxedo pants while Lizzie tugged at the broken strap of her dress, I'd checked my phone a thousand times, waiting for her to explain.

*Drake* had called. *Drake* had apologized. *Drake* had begged for my forgiveness.

Drake had blamed Lizzie.

That's when I told him to fuck off. It takes two to tango, and these two did way more than that. But my God, at least he'd called.

So there I was, mouth open, lips trying to form the word: *Why?*

Why hadn't she called?

Why wasn't she sorry?

I searched Lizzie's face, trying to separate the image in front of me from my darkest memory. But everywhere I looked, I saw *him*. I saw his fingers tucking a strand of pale hair behind her ear. I saw him staring into her eyes, telling secrets. Did his lips trail in a semicircle around the curve of her chin, teasing and teasing until she gave in? Did they think of me at all?

I closed my eyes.

The movement hurt. My eyes stung, but it went deeper than that. I could barely swallow, my throat felt so sore. And Lizzie just stood there, pretty pink lips—kissable lips?—pursed in a frown.

*Are you sorry?*

I took a step forward. The crowd parted to let me pass.

*Do you care?*

Lizzie opened her mouth, as if to speak. But she must've thought better of it, because those kissable damn lips closed.

*Or was I just the girl you used to get to Drake?*

I tried to turn.

But I couldn't. I was waiting for something. Maybe just for Lizzie to say my name. For godsakes, this was the girl who'd slept over at my house every Saturday since we were five, who'd held me when I cried over my parents' divorce.

I tried to catch her eye. She studied the floor.

*Lizzie, look at me.*

*Tell me you're sorry.*

*Tell me you don't hate me enough to hurt me this way.*

Lizzie said nothing. When the tardy bell rang, she walked away. And as all the dramatic tension oozed out of the hallway, the onlookers left as well.

So did I.

Over the next few days, I checked my phone less and less often. My stomach didn't drop quite so hard when I opened my locker to find no notes. A week went by, and still, Lizzie said nothing.

And when the second scribbling of SLUT appeared on her locker, I said nothing too.


IN THE WEEKS that followed, things got significantly worse for Lizzie Hart. Our once Untouchable Saint was now the Slut. And that word did exactly what I thought it would do. It multiplied, making little S-word babies. It spread to Lizzie's notebooks, her book bag, even her car. It burrowed its way under her skin like a disease, poisoning her from the inside.

You could see it.

I could see it.

I said nothing.

Then someone created that playing card. You know, the one of Lizzie wearing *nothing* but a crown of stars? People passed it around and added little details. Some genius even came up with a title:

Lizzie Hart, Queen of Sluts.

That name followed her everywhere. I thought she'd never get away from it. But Queen Lizzie found a way. She did the one thing we never expected.

She died. And the S-word died with her.

Until today.

It's the Monday after Lizzie's funeral, two weeks shy of graduation, and someone's written SUICIDE SLUT all over the senior lockers.

And the weirdest thing? The words are in Lizzie's looping scrawl.

# two

BY FOURTH-PERIOD LUNCH, everyone's talking about the ghost of Lizzie Hart. A couple of girls from the Cheer Bears have gone home sick. Not that I blame them. They weren't exactly sugar sweet after Lizzie got busy in the bedroom with my boyfriend. Dizzy Lizzie, Tizzy Lizzie . . . weird no one ever said "Busy Lizzie." Maybe because the words don't look like they rhyme.

My classmates aren't exactly geniuses, you know?

Needless to say, I'm certain the deranged graffiti artist can be tracked down without the help of a ghost whisperer. I knew Lizzie better than any of these people; if she was going to rise from the grave, the last thing she'd do is make an appearance outside of English. I mean, seriously. Besides, I don't believe in ghosts or gods or any of that imaginary-friend crap. (I'm not like her preacher daddy.)

A flesh-and-blood person is pretending to be her. Just like flesh-and-blood people ruined her life.

So let's start with the obvious suspects, shall we? The ones I should've questioned when SLUT first appeared.

The easiest to track down will be Kennedy McLaughlin, head of the Cheer Bears and vixen extraordinaire—the only girl in our class to be branded with the S-word prior to seventh grade. Rumors have speculated that Kennedy would've been crowned Prom Queen if not for Lizzie's prom-night tryst with Drake. According to some (Kennedy's followers, no doubt), people only voted for me out of pity. Of course, with that logic, she should blame the school board too. All that funding poured into abstinence-only education, and they go and put prom in a hotel ballroom.

Half the senior class rented rooms.

Miss Popularity is found on the bleachers of the football field, positioned perfectly so the boys below can see all the way up her long, long legs, past the hem of her skirt, and then . . . nothing. Her legs cross at the thigh, cutting off the view just when it gets interesting. We girls learn early what to show and what to hide, to walk that tightrope between useless prude and usable slut.

Hooray for choices, right?

Kennedy's surrounded, per usual, by her loyal subjects. Little gnats in cheering uniforms. Not to worry, I'm wearing mine under my jacket. It is Monday, and there is such a thing as tradition. Or maybe I'm just playing a part these days.

Kennedy dismisses her girls as I approach. The sea of red skirts parts to let me through. Some of the girls have on red-and-white-striped kneesocks. Others wear petticoats beneath their skirts. Once cheering season is over, we get pretty creative with the uniforms. I call this look Circus Freak Chic.

"We need to talk," I say when the wave of girls recedes.

"No shit, honey bear." Kennedy stands, smoothing her skirt, and I feel like I should bow or something. After all, the girl is gorgeous. With her bleached-to-high-heaven hair and candy-apple lips, she looks like a vampire who'll suck the life out of you and make you like it.

Plus, she's got that ass people rap about.

"You want to get out of here?" she asks, holding out a hand. I don't take it. "You look like you need a drink."

"What I need is a lobotomy."

"That's cute, Angie. Everyone's really falling for the act. A little white makeup and you'll be on the train to Teenage Gothica." She tugs at my hair as we walk down the bleachers. Last weekend I dyed it inkblot black. I even gave myself Bettie Page bangs. And no, I didn't ask the girls' permission. So even though I've got legs up to my neck and blue eyes people describe as "startling," I've gone and committed Cheerleading Sacrilege.

"Hope you're not planning to strip me of my pom-poms," I say with a gasp.

Kennedy sighs.

Together we snake through the park surrounding Verity High. I can see my breath on the air. Spring may have sprung in the southern parts of Colorado, but here in the Rockies it still feels like winter. I wrap my jacket tighter around me as we leave the campus behind. Nobody tries to stop us. Half the seniors have early release, and besides, security sucks at this school.

Even after everything that's happened.

We've walked for two blocks in silence when the sight of the staircase, nestled cozily between buildings, makes me feel warm. We go down the stairs and into the dark. Inside the hidden café, fake candles emit a pathetic orange light. I'm pretty sure this place has used the same dingy cleaning rag since the seventies. But that's okay, because they let you smoke inside, and you can set your flask in your lap and they pretend not to notice.

We order two mochas and sit in an all-wood booth. The place is pretty much deserted. Kennedy offers me her flask but I decline.

"Suit yourself." She sets to work making a poor-man's Spanish coffee. "I take it you've seen the writing?"

I peer at her through my lashes. Guarded, like I'm some sort of detective. (Yeah. Right.) "What do you care?"

*Real smooth, Angie.*

She gives me a look. "So I didn't love the girl. I'm not heartless."

"No one expected you to love her."

"Sure they did. Everyone's supposed to love fairy princesses." Kennedy ties back her hair with a ribbon. God forbid a strand should slip into her coffee and soak up some alcohol. Miss McLaughlin makes every drop count.

"Is that why you treated her the way you did?"

Kennedy scoffs. "I was nothing but cordial to your little friend."

"You were icy at best. And after prom, you acted like . . ."

"Like what?" She narrows her eyes. In the light of the low-hanging chandelier, those hazel irises look golden, like she's lit up from the inside. "Like she hurt my friend?"

*Like she was already dead.*

But I don't say it. I can't say it.

"You acted like you hated her," I say instead.

"I was angry with her," Kennedy corrects.

"Angry enough to brand her a slut?"

She leans back, making room for the accusation. "The entire school did that, last I checked. Or maybe just Drake Alexander."

At the mention of his name, my eyes close. Yes, I thought I loved him. Yes, I invented a future for us in my head. So what? I'll get over it eventually. I have no choice.

"I need to know who's responsible," I say, and I hate how desperate my voice sounds. These days, I could cry at any moment. It's humiliating. "Do you know who went after her—"

"Went after her?" Kennedy cuts me off. "Were there torches involved?"

"You know what I mean." I shake my head. "The S-word could've showed up on her bedsheets for all I know. Can you imagine?"

"Yeah, I can actually. I got tits when I was eleven. That automatically labels you as easy." She smiles smugly. "But you know that."

I cross my arms over my chest. "It was worse for her."

"Only because she was a late bloomer."

"So you're not the one who wrote it?"

"No. Wait—before or now?" Her eyes are narrowed into slits.

I shrug, all nonchalance. "Either."

"Are you serious?" She jerks forward. "You think I'd do it *now*?"

"What's the difference? It was mean before, and it's—"

"Awful now. Sincerely fucked up, Angie. Only a deranged psychopath would write it now. In *her* handwriting."

I lean back. It's impossible to get comfortable in this booth, but I want to give her the illusion of space before I ask my next question. My eyes trail to the darkened room, the dust hovering above our heads, the lights that flicker if you look at them the wrong way. But I turn and catch her gaze when I say, "So you know what her handwriting looks like?"

She doesn't even bat an eye. "Anyone who sat close to her could have mimicked her writing. She was always scribbling in that little diary." She rolls her eyes. It's so dismissive I want to scream. "God knows why she brought it to school."

"She didn't want her dad to see it," I say without missing a beat.

Kennedy pauses, dropping her gaze. It's like it never occurred to her that Lizzie had a family. "Well anyway, her handwriting was no secret," she says more softly.

"So anyone could imitate it?"

She nods.

"But only a psychopath would?" I ask.

"Yeah."

Finally, I lean in. "What about before? Before she—"

"Before is different." Kennedy brings her cup to her lips. "Like I said, now it's deranged. Back then it was just . . ."

"Life ruining? Suicide inducing?"

She fishes for the dregs with her tongue. "High school."


NEXT MORNING I get a big fat dose of high school when Mrs. Linn sends me on an errand during first period. I'm heading back from the office when I see the piece of paper stuffed into my locker grate, just below a fresh scribbling of SUICIDE SLUT. I pull it down and skim the writing. I skim it again. I'm skimming and skimming and I know people will be coming into the hallway soon, but I don't tear my eyes from the page. Even in poor copy, the script is unmistakable.

The looping little *l*s.

Fairy wings around the occasional *i*.

Pretty enough to have been written by an actual fairy.

Lizzie's perfect handwriting.

Lizzie's diary.

This year is going to be different.

(I know. I've said this before.)

But now I really mean it! No more cowering in the dark. I'm coming out of the shadows—and I'm ready to be seen!

Ready to be loved, if love is ready for me.

I've spent so much of my life keeping my affections a secret. Keeping myself a secret, afraid of what people would think of me if they knew the real Lizzie Hart. Would they hate me? Would they push me aside?

I can no longer afford to wonder about these things.

I'm seventeen. This is my senior year, and I'm going to enjoy my time here no matter what people think.

(That's the spirit when walking into a lion's den, right?)

So here I am, world, not the prettiest picture, but a hundred percent unique. My heart is open, and I'm ready to be invited into the light. And into someone's arms . . .

Whose?

Well, that too will be revealed when the time is right. After this year, I might lose the chance to tell you how I feel. So I'll do it. I have to do it. Regardless of the consequences, I'll never forgive myself if I don't.

There are just a few things I need to get in order before I do:

First, I must present myself to the world in an appealing fashion. (How I'm going to do this remains to be seen.)

Second, I must find a person, at least one person, who accepts me for who I am.

And third, I must make amends with the one girl in the entire school who has every right to hate me.

The girl I betrayed.

# three

THE BELL RINGS.

I look up from Lizzie's entry. People are flooding the hallway, passing around me in little streams, barely glancing my way.

*They have no idea what I'm holding.*

The page slips from my hands. Back pressed against my locker, I slump down to the floor, landing in a heap. Lizzie's entry follows, fluttering to my lap. The movement takes so much time, a part of me wonders if those words will rearrange into a different story when they land.

They don't.

There they are, as clear as day: *The girl I betrayed.*

"Who did Lizzie betray?" I murmur as people crowd around me. To their credit, they're not laughing and pointing yet. But they are whispering and staring, some of them crouching down to get a better look at the page.

To them I ask: "Was it me?"

Lizzie's words make no sense. No matter how many times I

read them, they make no sense. This entry is from September. She didn't go after Drake until April.

*Didn't she?*

I look up, above the heads of my audience. I need to give my eyes a break. My vision is getting blurry.

Still blurry.

No, that's just the mural on the wall. After Gordy Wilson died, a group of art students created the Unity Murals: four massive paintings depicting "student unity" on each of the main halls. Each hallway got a different color scheme: red for freshmen, gold for sophomores, violet for juniors, and blue for seniors. But they didn't realize that painting humans in a range of blues makes them look like they're drowning. The kids in the sophomore painting look like they're catching fire. The junior hallway is nice—that soft violet hue gives the impression of floating.

I won't set foot in the freshman hallway. On the wall, as in life, those kids are bleeding.

My eyes trail from the senior mural, where bodies flail in an azure sea, to the line of still-beige lockers underneath. There, Drake is moving as if through water, reaching up slowly and pulling a page from his locker grate.

My heart seizes.

*I could stop him*, I think. *I could run screaming through the hallway. I could tear that page out of his hand and shred it to pieces.*

But I don't. I'm rooted to the spot, stomach churning, both horrified at the thought of him reading Lizzie's secrets and mesmerized by the idea of how he will feel.

If he knows how she felt about him, will it make a difference?

Will he regret using her and then throwing her away?

These questions are rhetorical. I'll never know the answer to them. I never want to speak to him again. Besides, I have more pressing concerns, as two pretty little Cheer Bears yank me to my feet.

Elliot Carver and Cara Belle. The girls we toss into the air. The ones so light and airy they disprove the theory that real women aren't as skinny as models. For this reason, people find them easy to hate, but I used to like them.

Now I wonder if their sweetness is an act.

"We're getting you out of here," Elliot whispers, red hair tickling me. She's pressed so close she might as well climb into my lap. On the other side, her dark-haired partner in crime plucks Lizzie's entry from my hand, linking her arm through mine. They're wearing the same damn dress—one in black, and one in red—to complement each other's hair.

*Sisters from another mister, I guess.*

I almost laugh as they guide me down the hall. These idiotic musings are the only things keeping me sane. Elliot's full Irish, and Cara's Italian and Japanese, but they do that twin thing whenever they can. Today they look like witches, with long fingernails and kohl-rimmed eyes.

Rumor has it they mix love spells into their lip balm.

They all but shove me into the bathroom. That's when I break free from their grip. Stumbling across the room, I lock myself in a stall. Still, I've got too many questions to sit quietly.

"What did Lizzie mean?" I study the graffiti scribbled across the stall door. Phone numbers. Words of hate. Same as always. "How did she betray me?"

Silence. On the other side of the stall, a faucet is dripping. But the girls aren't talking, and I need them to, right this minute.

"Did you guys know about this?" I plead, my voice dangerously close to desperation. "I need to know."

Still nothing.

Finally, as if through the vast recesses of time and space, Elliot speaks. Her voice is pinched. "Maybe prom night wasn't the first time . . ."

My eyes flutter closed. Her words shouldn't bother me after everything that's happened. But the idea that prom night was just the tip of the iceberg is almost too much for me to handle.

"Did you . . . hear something?" I manage, voice cracking.

"Nothing!" Elliot squeaks. I wonder if she's going to cry. God, what a pair we make. "I'm just guessing."

"Don't guess." That's Cara, and her voice is cold. I peer through the crack in the stall so I can watch them.

And it's a good thing I do. They're putting on quite the silent little movie out there. First, Cara glares at Elliot, pushing Lizzie's entry into her hand. Then, Elliot nudges Cara in the ribs.

*No*, Cara mouths.

I step out of the stall. For a minute I just stand there, holding on to the frame for support. "What do you know?"

"We don't know anything," Cara insists.

I step forward. "I saw you," I tell Elliot, who's rolling up the entry like a wand. "I saw you arguing through the stall. Why did you nudge her? What do you know about this?" I rip the entry from her hand.

"We don't know anything!" Cara exclaims, stepping in front of her friend. Protecting her from me. Isn't that sweet? "I promise, Angie. I just *hate* talking about this. It *kills* me."

"That's a funny choice of words."

She goes white as a sheet. *White as a ghost?* It's like all the blood has drained from her face. "Please," she begs in that mesmerizing voice. "You have to give us a break. We haven't slept. We aren't eating."

*When are you ever eating?* I want to snap. But that's counterproductive, now, isn't it? And I've got more important things to get at.

"Why are you so upset?" I place my hand on Cara's arm, like maybe I'm comforting her, or maybe I'm dangerous. And I could be either. I haven't decided yet.

Now she's crying. "You know why," she whispers, blinking up at me. It's hard to look away. "We weren't nice to her. We wouldn't let her be our friend."

"She even tried harder this year," I agree, thinking of the times Lizzie sidled up to Kennedy when she thought I wasn't looking. At the time, I thought she was trying some weird social project—bridging the gap between the outcasts and the elite.

Now I think she just wanted my friends to be her friends.

"You rejected her," I say. "You rejected her earlier this year, and I rejected her after prom. None of us would give her a chance." I hold Cara's gaze. "So if you know something, now would be the time to get it off your chest."

Cara's shaking, and Elliot won't look me in the eye. But they say nothing.


I'M ON MY way to being very late to second period when I pass the office. I start to get this tingly feeling on my neck, like maybe I should go in. The office staff knows me pretty well; being Mrs. Linn's TA has its perks. How hard could it be to get ahold of the student locker list?

*Try it.*

*Just try.*

*Come on, Angie. Everyone's doing it.*

I pinch my cheeks and slip into the office. Compared to the multicolored hallways, this room is stark. They've slapped these cutesy motivational posters onto the bright white walls:

*Hang in there!*

*Math is cool!*

*Eat an apple!*

Nothing useful. Nothing real.

Ms. Carlisle beams when I approach the desk. "Back so soon?"

"Unfortunately." I cover my self-induced blush with my hand. "I totally screwed up those copies I made for Mrs. Linn last period. I'm such an idiot."

"Don't you dare." She touches my arm. She's got this long, gray hair that defies old-lady convention and she always offers up little doses of feminist mysticism when I need it. I kind of love her. Which means I'm kind of an asshole for tricking her.

But I can't stop now.

"Can I use the copier again? You can send me a bill for the extra copies, I swear."

"Oh, stop." She chuckles. At least I can entertain her while I lie through my teeth. "Use it all you like."

"It'll only take a minute," I promise. "Oh, I almost forgot. Another one of Mrs. Linn's freshmen forgot her locker combo. Annabel Leary, I think." I narrow my eyes like I'm thinking super hard.

Ms. Carlisle nods and sifts around for the student locker list. I head into the copy nook, pulling Mrs. Linn's study sheet from my bag. In all the diary commotion, I failed to bring her copies back to English class. The copier's so old it practically jams itself. I hardly have to wrinkle the paper to get it to make that annoying beep.

"Paper's jammed," I call to Ms. Carlisle with a laugh. She doesn't get up. I know she thinks solving my own problems is "empowering." But she'll come to my aid if I start to have a meltdown.

All that's left is to set the alarm on my phone, and then I pretend to fuss with the copier for another minute. Meanwhile, Ms. Carlisle's getting more and more frustrated in the next room. I don't have to see her. I can hear her huffing. Pretty soon it gets to be too much and she calls out, "Honey, are you sure you've got that name right?"

"Yes," I call back. Then, more quietly, "No. Maybe. You don't see it?"

She looks for another minute. "Are you sure Annabel didn't transfer? Or maybe I'm thinking of Abigail Lark."

Actually, they both transferred: Anna because her dad got offered a job out of town, and Abby because she got pregnant. No one would own up to being the father, so my brilliant classmates declared *anyone* could be the father. After the hundredth "Who's your baby daddy?" joke, fifteen-year-old Abby bailed.

"You're thinking of Abigail. I can double-check with Mrs. Linn," I say, smacking the copier loud enough for her to hear. "Damn it."

"Hey, now."

"Sorry. This thing is so ancient. Can you help?" A bit of a whine enters my voice. "Please?" I hit copy again, and of course the copier just beeps; I haven't cleared the jam, after all.

I shake the machine.

"Hey, hey!" Ms. Carlisle sweeps in, her long skirt trailing the floor. "Out of the way." She starts pushing buttons, lifting levers and all that. I watch her in faux-fascination until my phone starts to ring.

"Shit. I mean—sorry." I open the phone and stop the alarm. Then I hold it to my ear. "Hello?" Ms. Carlisle just shakes her head. "Hey, slow down," I say to the dead air. "What do you mean someone wrote something?" Here's where I start to shake, and Ms. Carlisle can't help but take notice. She touches my arm but I jerk away. "Kennedy, please tell me what it says. Please. I need to know. I—"

I look up, eyes widened in surprise. "She hung up!"

Ms. Carlisle tilts her head. "Angie?"

"Oh God." I'm shaking badly now, trying to do that lip-tremble thing that actresses do so well. "Oh God, oh God."

"Calm down, sweetie."

I look at her with unblinking eyes. Soon they start to sting and moisture appears. I've never been the cry-on-command type, but this is good too. "Someone wrote something on my locker."

Her eyes darken. "What do you mean?"

"I mean, someone wrote something! Kennedy saw it on my locker and she won't tell me what it is!"

"Calm down, now, it's okay." Her voice is strained but I can tell she's trying to be soothing. "I'll just give Jack a call—"

"No!"

"He's maintenance, Angie. It's his job."

"I don't want anyone else to see it!" I stretch my eyes to their limit. "Please, will you just look and tell me what it says? Please?" A tear forms and drops.

"All right." She nods, watching me. I'm clearly stricken. Better safe than sorry. "I'll go take a look." She yanks my study sheet from the copier and resets it on the tray. Then she presses the big green button. "You just watch over this and I'll be right back."

"You're the best," I say as copies shoot out the other end.

And she is. She's gone just long enough for me to copy the locker list and put it back on her desk. When she returns, I've got my original copies for Mrs. Linn stacked on top of the copier.

I tuck them under my arm and approach tentatively. "Well? What did it say?"

"Don't you worry about that." Her eyes won't settle on me. Her skin looks blanched. "I've gone and taken care of it."

"Really?" I sniff. There's a dark blotch on her hand, just below her thumb.

"Sure thing." She forces a smile and pats my back. "Hurry on to class."

"I'll ask Mrs. Linn about the name," I say, putting on my brave face. "I won't let you down." But of course I will. I'm clearly a ditz, too frazzled for my own good. I can't be expected to remember my own name, let alone someone else's.

I ought to buy her some major secret-admirer candy to make up for this.

I SPEND THE next few periods familiarizing myself with the locker list, but nothing interesting happens until fifth-period Math. There, Marvin Higgins—Latin classification *Mathus geekus*—is hunched over in the front of the class, studying some pages that look all too familiar.

*Fantastic.*

Marvin's pretty far down on my list, below the Beauty Queen, the Drama Queen, and the boy who broke my heart. Still, he's on there, so it looks like I'll have to talk to him next.

Halfway through the period, Mr. Farmington asks us to break up into little groups. I plunk down next to Marvin in the front row—a first in Math class. My place is in the back, where Farmington's voice is faded and the distance allows for easy texting under my desk. Then again, I'm not all that into gossiping with my friends these days, so it's not really a major loss.

Marvin looks at me like I'm going to smack him. "Yeah?" he asks. He's slid the diary pages under his math book, barely hidden.

I snatch them up. "Interesting reading?"

"They were just sticking out of a locker." He's blushing up to his ears.

Oh, Marvin. That awful mama's-boy haircut. That dirty peach-fuzz mustache. Why do you do these things to yourself?

I put the pages in my bag. "*Your* locker?"

He blinks at me behind the same glasses he's worn since sixth grade. "Could have been."

"Oh, I forgot. We have communal lockers at this school." I think of the day the senior guys stuck Polaroids of their junk into Lizzie's locker. They really did treat her like she belonged to them after prom.

His scowl softens. "She was my friend."

"She was everyone's friend, apparently. Now."

Yet, not too long ago, my classmates tripped over themselves to make her life miserable.

Marvin's eyes stare back at me, pleading. "You know I cared about her."

*Like you care about your blow-up doll,* I want to say. *If you cared about her at all, you wouldn't be reading her private thoughts.*

But I hold my fire. Truth is, if I got my hands on Lizzie's entire diary, I wouldn't be able to stop myself from reading it.

"Did you even know her that well?" I ask.

Marvin smiles dreamily. "We've lived next door to each other since we were kids."

*No shit. Why do you think you're on my list?* But I don't tell him that. "I never saw you. Were you hiding behind the curtains?"

He frowns but doesn't deny my accusation. "I knew her as well as I know myself."

Eye roll. "So you knew she was going to swap fluids with my boyfriend on prom night? Gee, Marvin, and you didn't tell me?"

He locks his jaw. I picture him lying in bed at night, grinding his crooked teeth into dust. His answer surprises me. It's got a little bite. "He's not your boyfriend anymore."

I snort, and Mr. Farmington looks up from his desk. Better open my math book for good measure. All around us, people are hunched over their worksheets, but I can tell they're listening in. They're just more subtle than I am.

"Not that I blame you for dumping him," Marvin says. "That asshole deserves what he got."

"So you're mad at Drake?"

"I'm mad at everyone." His fingers curl over the edge of his desk. For a second, I glimpse that possessiveness he always showed around Lizzie. "Everyone who hurt her," he adds, loosening his grip. "She was perfect, and they made her like everyone else."

"Who are 'they'?"

He shrugs.

I soften my voice. "Tell me what you know. Things you heard, things you saw."

"And?" He nods to my bag.

"And maybe I'll let you read a little more." *Yeah. Right.* "Deal?"

Marvin shrugs again and begins working out the first of our study questions. He finishes within seconds. When he looks up, his eyes are guarded. "Just not here."

I used to sing for you all the time. Remember? At the park, when the three of us played trolls and fairies. In the kitchen, when we learned to make cakes. Your eyes lit up at the sounds I could make.

In those moments, I actually believed you cared about me. In those moments, I felt loved.

But somewhere along the line my voice dried up. Was it middle school, when the shame of unknowing became the shame of desire? Was it high school, when I learned to wear invisibility like protective armor? I was so terrified of you glimpsing my feelings that I closed myself off to you, to everyone.

Now I wonder . . .

What if you could hear me sing again? Would your heart hear what your eyes refuse to see? Would you come running to me? Or even walking?

Walking I would accept, at this point.

Today Jesse Martinez told me the Verity Players are putting on a spring production of <u>A Midsummer Night's Dream</u>. There's a scene in the play where the Queen's fairy attendants sing. So I'll sing at my audition and if the judges are pleased with the sound of it, they'll allow me to dance around on clumsy legs in exchange for my voice.

A mermaid-meets-the-sea-witch kind of exchange.

And you'll come to watch the play. The school's MVPs always do. Cheerleaders and football stars mingling with the artists. The one time the beautiful people join hands with the freaks and geeks. Then, maybe for one brief moment, you'll take my hand and feel what I still can't speak.

So, say it with me:

Lizzie

Break

A

Leg

February 14th


I'M IN! I'M IN THE PLAY. And somehow I'm a
lead!!!

I can't believe it.

How could this have happened? I'm shaking in my
boots—HA-HA—the tall black ones passed down to me
from you-know-who. I see boys watching me when I
wear them. Sometimes, it makes me wish I could want
something I'm supposed to want. Something that
isn't forbidden . . .

Listen to me, I'm rambling! My mind literally
will not focus on one thing! I auditioned for the
play on Wednesday. Feeling bold, I performed
Titania's longest monologue in its entirety—sang it,
actually, assuming it was the only way they'd
consider me. They didn't even clap when I finished.
Just sat there staring. I thought, at the time,
they were so stunned by my stupidity that they
didn't trust themselves to speak. But now I
wonder . . .

Do I dare?

Do I dare?

They actually liked me! More than liked, if they

cast me as the lead fairy, right? Fairy Queen. Lord knows, if I were to expect a lead, it might've been Helena, crawling on my hands and knees after Demetrius. Dragging myself through life like a stray mutt, begging for love's scraps.

Pathetic? Indeed.

But I didn't expect a lead. Honestly, I expected nothing. Not even a fairy attendant to fulfill my twisted dreams of wooing you. Am I wrong for wanting to woo? Am I wrong for trying to be happy?

Am I wrong for taking this chance?

Today, on the feast of Saint Valentine, I feel like the universe is guiding me. For not only am I cast as the Fairy Queen, but Madame Swarsky in her infinite wisdom (and beauty, and strength, and wonder—Oh, how I adore her right now!) has requested the aid of the musically inclined Mrs. Barlow so that I might SING MY LINES!

In fact, all the fairies are to sing periodically, as Madame Swarsky now realizes "the fairies are wont to do"! I have "opened her eyes to the missing element of the play." Could I be happier?

Surely I could.

(I think you know what I mean.)

But for now, I'm as giddy as a babe walking on clouds, finding that butterflies spring up from her hands. I'm one step closer to revealing my True Self to the world, I've succeeded in something I

couldn't have dreamt of, and I have, according to
Verity's leading drama expert, brought a delightful
new twist to a classic play.

Yay, me!

Of course, there is the Slight Complication: I've
taken the part from its rightful and glorious owner:
Miss Shelby McQueen.

Shelby McQueen, president and founder of
Verity's Sisterhood of the Nubian Princess, star of
every production since the start of her freshman
year, a veritable goddess of the stage, is

Nothing

Short

Of

ENRAGED.

# four

SHELBY MCQUEEN. WHEREVER will I find Shelby McQueen?

Oh, yes. Lucky for me, Miss Who Am I Going to Play Today happens to share my seventh-period Drama class. This'll be too easy.

So I think, but Shelby's in rare form today, smoking an imaginary cigarette and lounging on the piano like she's preparing for her solo. Great, multipaneled dividers fan out from the piano like wings. The entire room looks like a set tailored to flatter her: mahogany walls draped in velvet, antique chandeliers dangling from the ceiling.

The kind of beauty that has to be donated or it wouldn't exist.

Shelby greets me with a husky "Hello, sugar. What's your poison?"

"Reality," I quip, and climb onto the piano beside her.

"That's what they all say." Shelby bats her pretty brown eyes.

So she wants to play Hide Behind the Character. So what? Drama class is a veritable free-for-all at the end of the year and I've got nothing but time.

She can play the dame. I'll play the old-timey detective.

Whatever gets the canary to sing.

"Nice to see ya, sweet cheeks," I say, tipping an imaginary hat.

Shelby's smile spreads across her face. She's wearing a purple 1950s-style cocktail dress. The hem dances just past her knees, all propriety. But her attitude says floor-length, slit-up-the-thigh red satin.

"What can I do for ya, daddy-o?" she asks.

"Got some questions for ya."

She leans back on her elbow. "Ask away." She's got that dark hair twisted into finger waves. She must get up at five in the morning to perfect this look.

I launch right into my attack. "How did you feel when one Elizabeth Hart clinched the role that many believed to be yours?"

Shelby's eyelids flutter. For a second, I think she's considering dropping the act. Given such a serious topic, she has one of two choices: forgo creativity and face up to the truth, or hide from the ugly facts.

Shelby's an actor. So she hides.

"Casting is not a democratic process," she says in that manufactured sultry voice. "I did my best."

"Gonna give me a song and dance, eh?" I slide off the piano and begin that classic detective circling bit. It's difficult, with these dividers in the way. But I do my best, weaving in and out of view, giving her moments to hide, and to be seen. "You've been the lead in every production since you first set foot in this school. Having that role snatched from you must have been infuriating."

Shelby huffs, entirely unfazed. "Titania is hardly the heftiest role in the play."

"Fair enough. But she is the most regal."

"Oh, sugar, what do you know about it? Elizabeth won the role fair and square." Her cheek twitches. "She even added her own flair to it, if you recall."

"I heard something about it."

"And I was nothing short of appreciative of Lizzie's talents. An actress is always diplomatic."

"Hmmm. Not according to Lizzie."

She touches her chest. "Excuse me?" She's slipping into southern belle, but I don't spoil her game. "She said something about me?"

"As if you didn't know." I shove the bottom corner of Lizzie's page in her face, the one that mentions Shelby by name.

An eyebrow raises. A hint of the real Shelby slipping out before poise is recovered, quickly, and it disappears. "And what, pray tell, is the relevance of my participation in the Sisterhood?"

I don't have an answer for that. So I say, "It's been a very influential institution."

*Shelby, baby, I know of your penchant for flattery.*

She touches her cheek, feigning a blush. "We did convince the Players to put on *A Raisin in the Sun*."

"I loved your hair in that."

She touches her perfectly arranged coif—quite a departure from the Afro she sported in that play. "*Noir est belle*," she agrees.

"Indeed."

Shelby frowns, and the façade slips away. "You sounded just like her then." After a moment, she adds, "Lizzie."

"I knew what you meant."

"Indeed."

A shiver, slow starting, shimmies up my spine. Lizzie loved to talk high society, but only as a means of playing pretend.

I shake the icicles off my back. "So . . ."

"So," Shelby mimics, a perfect imitation of me. She could play any one of us if she tried.

I gesture to the page. "What did you do?"

"Who says I did anything?" She snatches the page from my hand. My blood boils as she eyeballs Lizzie's secrets, but I wait for her to finish before taking the entry back. "She mentions *my name* and my political prowess. Two months before prom night, when her troubles began. So I don't see the connection—"

"Don't you?" I fold the page in half. "Opening night was a lot closer to prom. And Lizzie pinned a lot of hope on that performance . . ."

I don't have to say the rest. We both know how this story plays out. Lizzie is giddy. Lizzie is getting respect. Then, come opening night, *Shelby* emerges from the recesses of the stage to play the role of Titania.

And I'm supposed to blame coincidence?

*Please.*

"'Tonight, the role of Titania will be played by Shelby McQueen,'" I recite, quoting the programs. "But it wasn't just opening night, was it?"

She sucks in a breath.

"So here's the thing." I slide the page into my pocket. "Whoever's passing these around thinks you're important. And until I know why, I have no choice but to imagine the worst of you. Trust me when I say my imagination is an ugly place these days."

Shelby holds my gaze for several long seconds. Finally she sighs, dropping the act. "Fine. But I have to show you." She pushes off the piano, leading me past an utterly distracted Madame Swarsky. "We're going to the costume room," she calls as our teacher flings scarves about, dressing a fellow actor for a role as a gypsy.

The Drama annex is separate from the main part of the school, so we have to cut across campus to get to the costume room. The closest door is only a few yards away but Shelby takes the long way to avoid passing under the clock tower. I raise my eyebrows at her decision but secretly I'm thankful.

Anytime I pass it, I feel like it's going to fall on me.

When we reach the costume room Shelby sweeps inside, banging the door against a gangly creature measuring the hem of some sparkly pants.

"Damn, Shel," says Jesse Martinez, enigmatic transfer student and professional chameleon—the only boy in our class who can pull off a rock 'n' roll tee and ripped jeans on Monday and a wasp-waist dress on Friday. In our production of *Midsummer* he played Puck. He might even be a better actor than Shelby, but he never gets cast as the romantic lead. As with-it as Madame Swarsky may be, she knows boys who wear skirts make the upper crust nervous. Last thing she wants is to piss off the straight-laced alums who keep the Drama program alive.

"Ladies changing," Shelby sings.

"Scary," Jesse shrieks, pulling his knit hat over his eyes. His black hair pokes out beneath it, curling on the ends.

Shelby and I laugh as he skitters to the door. "Boy wears more dresses than either of us," she says when he's gone.

"Business, business," I remind. "Show me."

Shelby blushes and turns away.

"Why, Miss Shelby McQueen. Is that embarrassment I see?"

She screws up her face, pushing past rows of dresses to get to the back. I just hang out, touching satin and lace, leather and velvet, feeling like I'm traveling backward through history. And I don't mean the America-was-ripe-for-the-picking shit we get in History class. I mean elaborate medieval and Renaissance gowns hanging from the ceiling, brushing our heads, stacks of bell-bottoms and peasant tops filling the built-in shelves, and row upon row of retro dresses crowding the floor racks. Swarsky is a purist when it comes to costumes—"Anything that can be authentic should be authentic"—so while the damsel-in-distress–type gowns are obviously fakes, most of the stuff from the last century is true vintage.

Shelby emerges from the abyss clutching some long, mangled thing. A gown, I think, once adorned with beads and leaves. Now ripped all the way down the back, dangling loose threads.

Yeah, I recognize it.

"Isn't that—"

"Not exactly," she says.

I step closer, and Shelby unfolds the green and purple mass of strings. A disconnected sleeve slips to the ground. Beads follow in its wake, too tiny and too many to count.

"Are you sure?" I ask.

"Positive." Shelby's face is a mask, and I can tell she's hiding something beneath it.

"It looks like the dress you wore in *Midsummer*. The one Lizzie was supposed to wear."

"It *is* the one she was supposed to wear," Shelby says. "I should know. I chose it."

Not surprising. Shelby's been advising Madame Swarsky since she was fourteen.

Still, something about her story rings false. "Why did you pick out a costume for a part you didn't get?"

Shelby's dark eyes flash. "I picked it out before the cast list was posted. I picked it out for *me*."

"Ah. There it is."

She runs her fingers over the gown, caressing a torn leaf. "When Lizzie got cast, I was . . ."

"Spiteful?" I suggest, unable to stop myself. "Enraged?"

"Disappointed. I've stood by Madame Swarsky's side for years. I've consulted on the costumes, the music, everything. Under my leadership, I've transformed our pathetic Drama Department into a thriving success. We're actually making money on our productions—do you know how many years it's been since that's happened?"

"Twenty-three?" I guess.

Shelby doesn't laugh. "I took a program that was failing miserably and I gave it new life. And Swarsky repays me by ripping away my rightful part and giving it to a, a . . ."

"Slut?" I bait.

"A *nobody*."

"Lizzie had talent."

"Lizzie could sing," she says flippantly. "But she couldn't act as well as me and you know that. I'm not saying it to be rude, Angie. It's the truth."

"Maybe they wanted some fresh blood."

"They had plenty of parts for new talent!"

"She does look like a fairy."

*Did*, I remind myself.

"But not a Fairy Queen," Shelby says.

I have to stop myself from glaring. "Why didn't you just ask Swarsky what her reasons were?"

"And appear undiplomatic?"

The laughter falls from my mouth. Her words are too ridiculous. "You destroyed her dress!" I yank the gown from her hands. It rips further in my carelessness. "It's kind of sad, really. This was the best you could come up with?"

Her face is devoid of amusement. "That dress was handmade by Swarsky's great-grandmother. Worn in an actual Broadway performance of *Midsummer*. It was worth a fortune." She touches the dress. "Four thousand hand-sewn beads. You can still find them rolling around on the floor if you look."

"Okay, this is getting less funny." I hand the dress back to her. It's making my hands feel dirty. "Does Swarsky know?"

"Do I look expelled to you? I convinced her it was probably some ill-tempered freshman. I said I'd look into it."

"How philanthropic."

"Look." She hangs the dress back on a hanger. Robbed of its structural integrity, it keeps trying to slip to the ground. "I made a mistake and I paid for it. Literally." Reaching to a nearby rack, she pulls out another dress—a modern-day version of the vintage original. "When Lizzie heard what happened to the dress she was devastated. Not for herself." She huffs. "For Swarsky. She agreed to sew a new dress."

"For money? That doesn't sound like Lizzie."

"For free. I paid for the fabric."

"Poor baby."

"It was expensive!"

"I'm sure it was."

"So Lizzie got her dress and the glory of re-creating it. And the play didn't suffer for it."

"And Swarsky lost a priceless heirloom," I point out.

"She'd already donated it to the school."

"And Lizzie never even got to wear it."

Shelby crosses her arms over her chest. "She got to wear it during dress rehearsal."

"I'm utterly disgusted. Are we done here?"

"That's up to you, Detective."

"If I'm the detective, then you're my suspect, and you're not making a very good case for yourself."

"I'm not trying to make a case for myself!" She gestures to the dress. "You think I'd be showing this to you if I were guilty?"

*I think it's the* only *time you'd be showing it to me.*

But to Shelby I say, "So you *didn't* force Lizzie out of the play?"

She waves a hand dismissively. "The girl got cold feet. I'm sorry it's not more scandalous than that."

*Oh, sure, I'm the drama junkie here.*

"And you're not floating the diary entries?"

She cocks her head. "Why the hell would I do that?"

"Guilty conscience?" I suggest. "An overwhelming desire to get caught? You already confessed to something pretty massive—you're the actress, you tell me the motivation."

Shelby doesn't flinch. She's so well versed in authority, she doesn't have to push me around to show me who's boss. "I have no reason to feel guilty. I righted my wrong. Now, if you'll excuse me . . ." She brushes past me, heading for the door.

But I've got one more question to ask. "Did you write SUICIDE SLUT on the senior lockers?"

Shelby freezes. For one, brief moment, I think I've ruffled her feathers. But when she turns, she doesn't look affronted. She looks perplexed. "I saw it in the auditorium."

"Wonderful."

"And no," she adds before I can launch into a tirade about the lacking moral integrity of Kids Today. "I did not write SUICIDE SLUT on the lockers. Hell, I didn't even write regular-ass SLUT." She laughs. "Nice world we live in where SLUT acquires categories of its own."

"It *is* a category of its own."

"It's a tool," she says simply. "To dehumanize people—like the N-word or any other derogatory name. If a girl is a slut, you don't have to treat her like a human being. But you already know this."

I nod, though I'm not sure if she's implying I've been a victim of the S-word myself, or if I should understand because of what happened to Lizzie. Shelby's a smart cookie. Too smart for the high school crowd. Couple of decades ago, she'd have become a playwright whose views on race and sex would've changed the world. This day and age, she'll probably rise to fame as a social media starlet and end up on some second-rate cable network.

Then again, what do I know? I'm not exactly living the dream. Once upon a time, I had plans to become a world-renowned psychologist, to help dictators work through their anger issues. You know, save the world? Then Lizzie left and I realized I couldn't save anybody.

I catch Shelby's eye. "You swear you didn't call Lizzie any names? Not even during the play? I know you were angry . . ."

"Cross my heart and hope to—" She stops, inhaling sharply. "Listen to me. I've been called names since the moment I was born. Mostly by people who don't even know me. I would *not use that word.*"

Suddenly I can't look her in the eye. Shelby's pretty well respected at Verity, but it hasn't always been this way. When she launched the Sisterhood her freshman year, the backlash was pretty bad. People said she was being exclusionary for only inviting girls of color to join. But our school is, like, ninety percent white, and the kids who didn't call her nasty names pretty much ignored her. *They* were the ones being exclusionary, while Shelby was trying to find somewhere to belong.

I meet her gaze. "Okay," I say, nodding slowly. "I believe you."

And maybe I do. She's very convincing. Of course, as an actor, she's supposed to be. Plus, there are too many things left unsaid. I have a hard time believing Shelby replaced the dress out of the goodness of her heart. Guilty conscience or not, she must have at least suspected she'd get to wear it.

And she was right. Shelby got her costume, and her coveted role of the Fairy Queen, just in time for opening night. Drake and I sat in the front row, waiting for Lizzie to sing her lines. But she never did, did she?

She dropped out and never told us why.

I called her that night, but she didn't answer her phone. I asked her why a dozen times at school, but she wouldn't give me a real answer. She kept saying unsatisfying things, like "It was getting in the way of my schoolwork" or "I wanted to spend more time with my friends." At the time, I thought she was embarrassed about getting cold feet.

Now I wonder . . .

According to the diary, Lizzie pinned all of her romantic hopes on that performance. Drake was going to hear her sing. Drake was going to fall in love with her. They were going to ride off into the sunset.

Why give all that up for one seedy romp in a hotel room?

No, someone pushed her out of the play. It's the only thing that makes sense. And with that single, selfish act everything was set in motion: Lizzie's desperate, last-ditch attempt to gain Drake's affections; the vicious bullying that followed; and my beautiful best friend's tragic leap to her death.

Would any of it have happened if that role hadn't been stolen?

# five

I'M HALFWAY DOWN the hall when I notice the crowd. Four guys are huddled near the stairwell, passing something back and forth like a basketball. But it isn't an object. It's a person.

*Jesse.*

I hurry toward them.

The guys are laughing, shoving Jesse around. To his credit, he's spewing all kinds of shit I wouldn't repeat to a truck driver. He's feisty. He pushes back. And honestly, he's not much smaller than these guys (they aren't the mammoth jocks you see in movies), but there are four of them, so it's not like it's going to be easy to break free.

"Hey, boys," I call, pushing my way into the circle. I recognize two of the guys immediately: Zeke Bentley and Troy McGibbins. Pretty-boy Zeke went out with Kennedy for an entire month last summer, breaking her all-time dating record. Red-haired Troy went out with Cara sophomore year. Sometimes, it seems like we only recognize people based on who they're doing.

The other two guys could be anyone.

"What's going on?" My voice is light, but it darkens when I realize Jesse's clutching something. Pages. "What are those?"

"Nothing." Maneuvering like a master magician, he slides the pages into his waistband, where they're protected by black taffeta and raspberry lace. His skirt is Parisian froufrou, like something out of a movie about diamond dancers. Lizzie would've gone gaga for it.

Guess who isn't impressed?

That's right: Zeke and Company. They take turns reaching for the pages, bumping Jesse in the process. On TV, gay guys are always scheming to get into the pants of their straight guy friends, but in real life it's almost the opposite of that. These guys take liberties, backing Jesse into a corner, reaching down his skirt while he shrinks into himself.

"Give it a rest," I say casually, like I'm asking which celebrity they're most itching to bang. Deep down I'm seething, utterly shaken by the sight of such blatant violence so close to Lizzie's death. Do they honestly think what they're doing is different?

Zeke makes a grab for Jesse's waist. "Relax, Angie," he says, like I'm going to join in on the merriment. He looks clownish, with that bleached-blond hair and overtanned skin. "We're keeping this pervert in line."

"It's a tough job," Troy adds, tugging at his own waistband. His jeans keep trying to slip down below his boxers. A glance around the circle shows more of the same: low jeans, name-brand T-shirts in primary colors. It's like they're in uniform.

Except for Jesse.

"You really should get to class," I say, channeling the innocence that came naturally to Lizzie. In interactions like these, it's best to play the ingénue. "That'll be a nice change of pace for you, won't it, Troy? Being late?"

He narrows his eyes. "What's that supposed to mean?"

"Well, Cara said you were always early," I explain. "So I never understood why you still got shitty grades. Unless . . ." I knot up my brow, like I'm utterly bewildered. "Do you think she wasn't talking about class?"

"Oh, *shit!*" Zeke howls, slapping Troy on the back. A slow blush is creeping up Troy's neck. He's got that milk-pale skin that shows every emotion. The other guys are laughing, nudging each other in the ribs.

But I'm not finished yet. "You forget, girls tell each other everything." I shift my attention to Zeke. "Every. Little"—I bring my forefinger close to my thumb—"Thing."

"You're a stupid bitch," Zeke snarls, slamming his fist into a locker. The message is clear: another word, and it'll be me. I keep my mouth shut, smart enough to know when I've already won, and after a minute of angry staring the guys amble away.

They can't look each other in the eye.

I turn to Jesse. "You okay?"

The question seems to catch him off guard. He's staring at the locker Zeke attacked. "Yeah." He nods, glancing at me. "You?"

"I'm fine. I . . ." The words die on my lips. I realize I've never looked at him. I mean, *really* looked. He has this way of avoiding detection, moving behind the scenes like some sort of spirit. But face-to-face he's not what I expected. His fathomless black eyes are framed in eyebrows worth killing for. I could tan for months and never get that brown-sugar skin.

Up close, he's downright pretty, and it's not just the eyeliner.

"Listen, Jesse . . ." My gaze trails to his waistband. It's awkward, looking at him this way, but what choice do I have? "Were those pages in your locker?"

He shakes his head. Taking one step to the left, he reveals the words SUICIDE SLUT on the locker behind his back. Locker 105.

"Marvin's," I murmur. My head is down, so I don't think Jesse can see my lips.

But he catches the movement. "Marvin? Like Marvin Higgins?" He steps closer, eyes narrowed. "How do you know that?"

"I . . ." I stumble backward, trying to think of an explanation. He can't know I stole the locker list. "He and Lizzie were friends. Or neighbors. I don't know, exactly." I shrug, like it's no big deal. "But I've seen them talking here."

*That's true*, I think, exhaling slowly. *The best lies are born out of truths.* And even though I never knew the exact location of Marvin's locker before today, it's a logical enough explanation that Jesse seems to believe it.

Still, he's got questions. "Why would those show up in Marvin's locker?" he asks, tilting his head to the side. His dark hair catches the light, and I find my gaze traveling to where it curls over his ears. Avoiding his eyes.

"Maybe she wrote something about him," I suggest. "If you let me look—"

"Are you *kidding*? What kind of sick fuck invades the thoughts of the dead?"

*Me. Everyone. Right?*

"You asked me a question," I stammer. "I gave you one possible explanation. God, Jesse, get off your high fucking horse. You act like it's so terrible to want to understand."

"It isn't." His voice is softening. "But there are lines you don't cross. She didn't write this for you to read."

"You're right," I say, but already I'm devising ways to get my hands on those pages. If I just reach out quickly . . .

"If you're thinking of reaching down my skirt, I'd advise against it."

"I wasn't—"

"Yeah, right."

"I just want the pages, Jesse. It's not like I'm Zeke Bentley!"

"What's the difference?"

I freeze. "I'm not like those guys. I'm *nothing* like them." I shake my head, trying to convince him. Trying to convince myself.

But here I am, backing him into a corner.

*Maybe I'm* exactly *like them.*

I take a step back. "Look." I hold up my hands, like I'm surrendering. "Lizzie was my best friend, so unless *you're* putting those in people's lockers, I don't understand—"

Now he's angry. Pretty mouth contorted, he leans in. "First of all, you can't prove shit. Second of all, Elizabeth Hart had no friends after prom night, least of all you."

My face flushes. "How would you know that?"

"Everyone knew it. Lizzie became Frankenstein's monster and you were the one leading the pitch-forked mob against her."

"I didn't lead anyone!"

"You didn't *stop* anyone."

"I was . . ."

*What were you, Angie? Furious? Heartbroken? Or were you afraid they'd turn on you too?*

"I loved Lizzie," I say as the end-of-class bell rings. Students sweep into the hallway, moving around us effortlessly. "That's why I couldn't believe what she did."

"But you did believe it. You believed it without batting an eye."

My heart seizes. I'm leaning into the locker for support. "What are you saying?"

He shrugs, taking a step back.

*He can't just say something like that . . .*

"What did she tell you?" I ask, trying to define Lizzie's relationship with Jesse based on the smattering of memories I have.

Sure, they hung out a lot during the play, but I didn't think they were close.

"What would she tell me?" Jesse asks casually as people brush past him. Someone almost knocks him over completely. It's like they don't even see him. "What would anyone tell me?"

"I'm right here. I'm talking to you."

"Only because you want something." He doesn't look angry anymore. Just disappointed.

"I want your *help*," I say softly. Tears are filling my eyes with no warning. I cover my face, furious at myself for behaving this way in public. I'm in the middle of the hallway. Anyone can see me, judge me, hate me.

*And all of them will.*

The tears recede. My eyes trail to the writing on Marvin's locker. To the scribbling of SUICIDE SLUT, taunting everybody. "You see this?" I struggle to keep the sadness from my voice. "This is the reason I need the diary. I have to figure out who's doing this."

Jesse looks at me suspiciously. "You don't know?"

"Know what?"

"Lizzie's doing it."

"Get bent."

He leans against the locker, running his fingers over the writing. "You don't think so?"

"Why would she?"

"To remind them of what they did."

I shake my head, but my pulse is racing. "You don't honestly believe that."

He shrugs. "Why would someone living do it? They don't get the thrill of hurting her anymore."

"They're just words," I say, though I don't believe it. But I want his reaction to my dismissal. I need it.

"Right. Totally," he says.

"So you agree?"

"Of course I do." He flashes a grin, but his eyes remain distant. "I'm Mexican and I'm wearing a skirt. The kids that *don't* want to beat the queer out of me want me deported."

"That sucks, Jesse. But I don't—"

"Let me break it down for you." He speaks slowly, his voice laced with false enthusiasm. "You should hear the fun names they come up with for me. Or hey, you can ask Gordy."

"Jesse."

"Oh, right, he killed himself too. Only nobody gives a shit about *him*."

"I do. I give a shit."

"You do a good job of hiding it."

I pause. "Were you two . . . ?"

"Fucking?"

"Close?"

"He was a friend."

I nod slowly. "So how do you feel about the people who made his life hell?"

"You know how I feel."

"Yeah." I hold out my hand. "Exactly."

He frowns, teeth tugging at his lip. "I still wouldn't read his personal thoughts."

"Well, I guess that makes you better than me." There's no bitterness in my voice. Just defeat.

"Please, Jesse? I really need your help with this."

Those must be the magic words. Jesse pulls Lizzie's pages out of his waistband. I take them before he can change his mind.

"You show these to anybody, I *will* make your life miserable," he says.

I want to thank him but his threat pisses me off. "What could you possibly take from me that I haven't already lost?"

He shrugs, walking backward into the crowd. "I'll find something. There's always something."

I shake my head. The boy is clearly delusional, but I don't have time to worry about it. Drake Alexander is weaving through the crowd, making a beeline for yours truly. Tall, pouting, break-your-heart-gorgeous Drake. His eyes are a lighter shade of blue, but our hair was identical before I dyed mine. We used to sit face-to-face, my fingers in his hair, his fingers in mine.

Then his fingers went all over Lizzie and I didn't feel like cradling his head in my hands anymore.

He calls my name: "Angie," lilting sweet.

His voice, more than anything, is what gets to me.

But my legs take me away from Drake, away from the heartache I feel when he's near, and my body has no choice but to follow.

I'll come back for him later.


I MET DRAKE around the time I met Lizzie, but in elementary school he was just another boy carrying cooties and destroying rosebushes with a stick. I didn't really think of him in that way until the summer after seventh grade. He returned from vacation looking like a different person. He was taller, his olive skin was tanner, and his mother had allowed him to grow out his hair. It curved on the ends, falling into his pale blue eyes and calling to me.

*Touch me, Angie,* that hair said. *Run your hands through my luscious locks and find heaven there.*

(Warning: Trips Down Memory Lane May Lead to Over-dramatizations.)

But still, the guy was hot. I was hot for him, and I wanted to talk to Lizzie about it. Too bad I didn't know what to say. Sure, I could wax philosophical for hours, but love? Lust? Where would I even begin?

Thus began my relationship with Tennessee Whiskey.

I know what you're thinking. Kids? Liquor? No way! Relax. I'm not saying I was an adolescent boozehound. I didn't start sleeping around or driving drunk. The alcohol didn't even lead to harsher drugs. In a curious twist of irony, it did exactly what I wanted it to do. It helped me talk about my feelings.

(Results may vary.)

So there I was, thirteen and on the way to Drunk Town, sitting cross-legged on the floor of my bedroom and chatting Lizzie's ear off. And, okay, I hadn't gotten around to mentioning my undying passions for Drake, but I was rambling about my parents' divorce for the first time.

"It's just so sucky. Like, ridiculously sucky. I have to live here at Dad's and, like, see my mom twice a month? That's some high bullshit." Okay, I'll admit it: the alcohol was affecting my vocabulary skills. At least Lizzie didn't seem to mind. She just sat there, rocking a little, and pouring another shot when I got too embarrassed to speak.

"Okay, on three," she said, holding up her glass. "One. Two."

"Three!" I swallowed the liquor too quickly. It burned all the way to my stomach. "God, that's foul."

"I kind of like it." She poured herself another. "It burns, but it's good, like cleansing." She tilted the glass against her lips, tossing back her head. She looked like a professional, hair flying behind her, all blond and shiny. Just looking at it made me want to hack off my messy brown waves.

"Show-off," I said as she slammed down the glass.

"Keep up." She poured another drink. "And keep talking."

"About what?"

"Whatever. I like it when you talk to me." She smiled, all sweetness. She was practically swimming in a pair of my jeans and an old black tee. Since her dad still insisted on dressing her like a little girl, she'd taken to wearing my clothes whenever possible. Eventually it became routine for her to stop by every day before class. No one wants to show up to middle school in her Sunday best.

Of course, there were all kinds of middle school sins to avoid. Showing up ugly. Showing up fat. Showing up the wrong skin color or the wrong sexuality or from the wrong part of town. The wrongness Lizzie felt in a pink frilly dress was the same wrongness felt by girls in skirts "too short" or clothes "too baggy." It was the wrongness I felt when I looked in the mirror and found a hundred flaws without even trying.

Sitting in that bedroom, looking at Lizzie, I was all too aware of my wrongness. "I've talked enough," I said. "It's your turn. Tell me something secret. Who do you like?"

"Who do I like?" Lizzie sputtered, and she wasn't even taking this shot. "I don't—I don't have a crush."

"I totally believe you," I said in this obviously insincere voice. "Hey, we should start a liars' club."

"Shut up." She punched me in the arm, blushing hard. "Why would you even ask me that?"

"Because you're so painfully transparent. Come on, Lizzie. Tell me."

"No." She held a pillow over her face, hiding.

"Tell me."

"There's nobody!"

"Liar." I grabbed a pillow of my own, smacking her with it. "Tell me and I'll tell you."

She peeked out from her fluffy sanctuary. "You like somebody?"

"I might."

"I . . ." She shook her head, mussing her hair on the pillow. "No, I can't."

"Oh my God." I rolled my eyes. "Okay, give me a hint. What color hair does he have?"

She was silent. Finally, voice muffled, she said, "Brown."

My heart did a flip but I tried not to dwell on it. Lots of guys had brown hair. In fact, most of the guys at our school had hair that was brown or brownish black.

"What color eyes?" I asked, my voice so casual you'd never know I was freaking out. "If you even know."

"Blue," she said without hesitation. I guess now that she'd opened up she wanted to see things through.

But I was starting to feel hot, uncomfortably so. The open window just wasn't doing its job. Even worse, my brain wasn't doing its job, which was to calm me down when I started to feel too much. Maybe it was the booze. Maybe a part of me already knew she'd set her sights on the boy of my dreams. The boy who, if given the choice, would choose Lizzie in a heartbeat, because her wrongness could be erased with a simple costume change and my wrongness went as deep as my bones.

And I'd be crushed.

"Okay, your turn," Lizzie said, surprising me. "What color hair does your crush have?" And she kept looking at me with that sweet face and I knew I couldn't say it.

"Blond," I lied.

# six

BEFORE I LEAVE campus, I stop off at the office to tell Ms. Carlisle that Freshman Forgetful remembered her locker combination. And, since I'm there, I use the student computer to look up the local listings for Higgins. There are three, but only one with an address next to Lizzie's.

As I dial the number to the Higginses' landline, I wonder how many people looked up Lizzie's number in a similar way, calling her house in the middle of the night. Whispering taunts they wouldn't say to her face. I mean sure, it wasn't nice of her to sleep with my boyfriend, but I was the only one with the right to be mad. Did they think they were helping me somehow? Who did these people think they were, the morality police?

Talk about hypocritical.

And then there's Marvin. Marvin thought Lizzie was his soul mate, and now he's acting all secretive. Methinks there's a story there.

Nobody answers at his house. I leave a quick message asking

him to meet me tomorrow for lunch. Hopefully, the possibility of a lunch date will trump his fear of my kicking his ass.

I can't imagine a girl has asked him out in the past four years.

After that I've just got time to kill, hours and hours until the blue light of morning. Late afternoon used to be my favorite time of day. Now I can't get enough distraction to pass the time. I just end up thinking of Lizzie, and crying, and then hating myself for it.

This time I've got my key in the ignition and my phone in my lap when the tears start to blind me. I'm telling myself to *calm down* and *get it together already* and digging my nails into my thighs because sometimes that centers me. But today it's not helping. Nothing's helping, and I feel myself spinning out in every direction. I feel the car moving and it's not. I'm just sliding backward into this murky swamp and my limbs are too heavy to move and there's *nothing* that can help me.

I feel like Lizzie's emotions are slipping into me. I feel her despair, her inescapable desire to feel nothing. To be nothing.

*Maybe she really is haunting me.*

I shake my head, run my hands through my hair, wipe the mascara out from under my eyes—any stupid thing I can possibly do to keep myself busy. If I can sidetrack myself long enough, this feeling will subside.

I'm getting very good at this.

And with these shaky movements I push my Lizzie-the-ghost thoughts away. The pages Jesse gave me are on the seat next to me. Material. Tangible. Someone living brought them to school with a purpose.

The ghost thoughts are just there to distract me.

To make me feel like she's still around.

And she's not.

I'm alone.

I drive home with nothing in my head. I watch the movement of the streets. I manage not to hit or be hit. Though it's wholly unnecessary, I remember to breathe. I perform the tasks required of me to keep my heart beating.

That's all anybody can really ask of me.

Mom's out when I get home. She has me all week. For five days I'll curl up in the lap of luxury. Then it's off to broken fences and a leaky roof across town with Dad. I'm rich. Then I'm poor. Then I have money again. It took the longest time for the kids at school to make up their minds about me. I suppose it's hard to treat someone appropriately if you don't know what her classification is.

This wasn't a problem for Lizzie, of course. She liked me for my personality.

*I thought she did.*

The house is dark, and I keep it that way; Mom's golden walls look too bright with the lights on. Between the vaulted ceilings and the green-and-gold stained glass windows, you'd think the woman lived in a cathedral.

I don't belong in this pristine place.

I flip on the TV before I even take off my shoes. God bless America's number one drug of choice. From there it's two hours of mind-numbing reality TV followed by game shows not commonly watched by anyone under eighty. At seven I order takeout from Huang's Formal Palace. At Mom's house, dinner falls under my short list of responsibilities. By the time the week's over I'll have takeout coming out of my ears, but it's better than ramen or macaroni with powdered cheese.

Mom doesn't get home until after nine thirty. I've eaten and am half passed out on the green velvet sofa by then. In my head, I've kept a running tally of the number of times I've thought of Lizzie in her open casket since I got home. Right now I'm at eleven and a half; if I can change the subject in my brain before an image fully forms, I only count it as a half.

The day of her funeral I had the tally up to three hundred and twelve, so I figure eleven and a half is pretty damn good. And I'm able to eat again, at least in small portions, so that's good too.

Mom looks mildly annoyed to find me on the couch. After a ten-hour day at the office (corporate law, business suit, killer heels) she's all about the couch and a bottle of wine. Red, of course. "White is for people who don't know what they're drinking."

I scoot over so she can plop down.

Mom frowns. "If I can't stretch out my legs I might as well get into bed." She runs her hand over my head mechanically. Anytime Mom makes contact it feels like I'm being soothed by a cyborg. Damn it if the cyborg isn't doing its best to mimic human affection. But there's something missing.

"Huang's," I say, pointing to the kitchen.

"Honey." She's shaking her head. Her hair doesn't move, it's got so much hairspray in it. "You know I can't do carbs."

"I got you meat. All meat!"

She purses her lips. "We did Huang's twice last week."

I cross my arms. "You get here first, you order," I say because she has no possible retort. Dad got greater custody in the divorce because she didn't want it. She's only taken over because a work accident messed up his knee. She's even paying him alimony. People at school find that hilarious, for some reason.

Of course, I'm the idiot who trusted Kennedy with that information.

Mom's frown lines deepen. "Fair enough," she says, looking at her hands.

*Hmm. Capable of feeling guilt. Therefore, not a cyborg.*

"You didn't overtip?" she says as I roll off the couch. Mom slides into my place, smiling for the first time since she arrived.

"Of course I did," I say. Rich people stay rich for a reason, but my soul dies a little if I tip below twenty percent.

I pull a bottle from the wine rack and hold it out for her. She takes it with this movement that is, like, pure instinct.

"Thank you, dear," she says, cradling the wine to her chest.

"Mmm-hmm. 'Night." I kiss Mom on the forehead like she's my teenage daughter and carry my bag to my fake-furnished room. When Dad had his accident, she filled it with posters of boy-bands and these creepy collector's dolls. And I have to pretend to like it because, you know, Mom's trying. But Jesus, Mom. Even at twelve I had better taste.

So now, before I go to sleep, I have to choose between staring at a fourteen-year-old one-hit wonder or a doll that could come to life at any time. You'd think this would help distract from the Lizzie-casket thing, but it just gives me more to worry about. Maybe if she'd gotten me one of those gigantic teddy bears, I could sleep with it on top of me, like some sort of furry guardian.

These are the things I think about at night.

I try to focus on the bumps in the ceiling, the way I focused on the road driving home. But my mind has been numb for as long as it can handle and now the thoughts are spinning. The faces of people I interrogated today dance through my mind. I like to think of it this way, as interrogation. Like this is some kind of official investigation. Like I'm not just wasting my time. I cling to the idea that justice might bring me some kind of reprieve.

Didn't work for Batman. But it might work for me.

Sigh.

Now come the bedsheets, the comforter, the fancy pillows. I burrow under the covers to hide from whatever lives on the outside. Lizzie's pages are beckoning to be read, over and over again, until I've got them memorized.

Every time I read them, I feel worse.

I hate this so much. Lying here doing nothing. So many hours wasted. I should be preparing for my meeting with Marvin.

Scratch that.

I should be kneeling at Lizzie's grave, begging forgiveness for the way I treated her. So I didn't write SLUT on her belongings. I still didn't come to her defense when the school tore her apart.

*Face it, Angie. You abandoned her.*

I've started having the most terrifying dream.
I'm standing at the edge of my yard, and in the
distance, I see a tangled forest. I feel I would do
anything to keep from going into that wooded
darkness. Inside that forest lies the root of all
evil.

Then the creature comes up behind me.

I can never make out his face. His claws are
sharp, curling and curling like a dead person's nails.
Eyes red. Gaping maw.

And he likes the taste of humans.

I start running. Into that forest I go, leaping
over fallen logs, pushing my way through brambles.
My skin is cut and bleeding. There's so much blood
I can't see my hands. I look up and he's above me,
falling as if from the sky. Come to swallow me
whole.

Come to crush me.

I understand, in that moment, that I deserve to
be caught. I understand that entering the forest
invited the evil into me.

Just as his claws sink into my skin, I look up at

the sky and ask forgiveness. But it's too late. The
evil swallows me.

It eats me alive.


Tonight, I awake covered in sweat. My blankets
are soaked through. My nightgown is plastered to me
like I've crawled out of a swamp and my lips bleed
from where I bit them.

I kick the covers away, tearing off the
nightgown like a skin. I know that I'm awake now,
that I'm safe, alive, but I still feel his eyes on
me. I still feel his claws sinking in. I stand up in
the dimness and walk to the window. The blinds are
open, to keep my room illuminated. There's a
movement in the house next door as I approach. A
sudden closing of blinds.

I know that I'm awake. But this time, the eyes
I felt on me were real.

# seven

I MEET MARVIN AT the cafeteria door but grab his arm before he walks through it. "Not so fast," I whisper in his ear, unleashing hot breath. "I'm taking you somewhere a little less crowded."

His eyes pop like I've said the magic words. (Here's where I play him like a fiddle.)

"What makes you think I want to go anywhere with you?" he asks. He's wearing this shirt and vest combo you generally see in retirement homes. Plaid pants, like he's planning to golf.

Wish I could say he's dressing ironically.

"Oh, come on, Marvin. I know you." I set a hand on his shoulder. "You don't want to choke down mystery meat beside your lowliest contemporaries. You want to be inducted into the crooked world of Verity's elite."

*Maybe . . . wet your whistle where Kennedy McLaughlin leaves lipstick stains on rum-spiked coffee mugs?*

After all, everyone knows he's into blondes. And Kennedy's

Queen of the Summer Court as far as this school is concerned. My guess is he planned to practice his moves on Lizzie before pitching for the big leagues.

*Classy.*

"Am I right?"

Marvin just bobs his head.

*Game. Set. Match.*

So that's how we end up at the Cheer Queen's café hideaway. Marvin stops at the doorway and peers inside the building that's too cool to be named. No doubt he's hoping there's a whorehouse hidden within. Maybe I'm even one of the working girls.

*Sure, Marvin. It's your lucky day.*

We sit at a corner table, draped in shadows. The occasional cobweb waves from above. The place is eternally decorated for Halloween, just not on purpose. Marvin orders coffee, black. He probably saw someone order it in a movie that way. This boy is much more electric-green soda than black coffee.

Is everyone at Verity playing pretend?

"Kennedy and I found this place sophomore year," I say, sipping my latte in a way that leaves foam on my lip. I let it sit for a second before licking it off. It's so over-the-top I almost lose it. "It's kind of been our little secret."

"Why me, then?" he asks, his coffee already forgotten.

"I wanted a quiet place to talk. When I thought of us sitting in some cheesy cafeteria, well . . . I just couldn't picture it."

Marvin raises his eyebrows. "What a surprise. A cheerleader with a mind."

I almost gouge out his eyes right then. Patience gets me through it. Recently acquired patience.

"No offense," he adds.

"Of course not," I reply.

"I just always thought Lizzie was the smart one, and you were her . . ." He struggles to find the words.

"Popular—"

"Traditionally attractive friend."

If I take this as a compliment, he'll go back to assuming I'm the dumb bimbo. If I take offense, I'm the oversensitive chick. "If Lizzie was smart," I say, "she must've liked me for a reason."

"That's true," he agrees, as if it honestly never occurred to him. He leans back, eyeing me coolly. "What can I do for you, Angie?"

*Angelina*, I want to correct, but that would be counterproductive. So instead, I tell him, "I'm getting a C in Mrs. Linn's." In addition to Math, Marvin and I share an English class.

He dips a finger into his coffee. "I'm sorry—did you ask me here to tutor you?"

I ignore him. "I had a really stupid thing happen with my term paper last semester. Remember that week we got to spend in the library? To do research on our topics?"

"Vaguely." He sounds bored, oh so bored.

Hey, I bet he wants me to entertain him!

"I remember it very clearly," I say, leaning in. My arms are crossed, but he doesn't know I'm doing it protectively.

"Oh yeah?" He peers down my shirt like the crease between my breasts belongs to him. It's all I can do not to kick him under the table.

"Yeah," I say. "So I've hit my stride. I've written seven pages in the span of an hour, and I'm, like, five hundred words from finishing my paper when something really weird happens. I hear this heavy breathing coming from the other end of that long computer desk."

Marvin sits up straight in an instant. "Was there a dog in the library?"

"You'd have known if there was. You were there too, remember? You were writing that paper on sex in Shakespearean lit?"

"Love," he corrects.

"Totally." I nod like I believe him. "So I get up to look, but I can't see anything. That shelf of reference books is sitting in the middle of the desk. And I'm like, when did that get there?"

Of course, I know when the shelf was moved. Right about the time Marvin volunteered to be the librarian's aide.

His blush confirms my theory. "Miss Marilyn thought it would remind us that you can look things up in books too," he explains.

"I bet someone suggested it to her."

"Maybe I did." He wrinkles his brow. He's got this zit trapped between two wrinkles that looks like it's going to burst. "That proves nothing."

"No, I suppose it doesn't." I lean away, readjusting my top. "Anyway, I hear this panting, and it's totally breaking my concentration, so I creep down the row of computers, all stealthy like." I wink. "Even dumb cheerleaders know how to spy. And I peer through the reference books and out the other side."

"Oh God." He's shrinking in on himself.

But my story's just getting interesting. "And what to my wandering eyes should appear but a little scum bucket perving on the *nastiest* websites I could ever imagine."

"Please stop."

"I mean, this was not normal stuff. This wasn't even normal hard-core. This was, like . . ." I open my hands, as if searching for the words. "I don't even want to say. It was definitely the worst—"

"*Okay*. I get it. Just—"

"I'm not finished yet," I say in singsong. "So after a minute this perv-master realizes the typing on the other end of the desk has stopped. And he starts to figure out what the typist is doing, and he totally freaks. He starts closing web windows like you wouldn't believe but they just keep popping up. And he's sweating and wheezing and I honestly think he's going to cry so I start to slink away, figuring I don't want to be the cause of an eighteen-year-old's heart attack. And just as I disappear into a row of autobiographies, I hear the sound. That zap."

"Crap."

"Exactly," I agree, nodding vigorously. "In his panic, this cretin drops to the ground and turns off the power strip that's connected to all the computers. I lose seven pages of my fifteen-page paper. I miss the deadline. I get an F on the assignment."

"Why didn't you just work at home like a normal person?" He narrows his eyes, but the movement looks forced, like he's trying to appear disdainful. Really he's scared, anyone can see it. His fingers tap out rapid rhythms on the table, and he can't stop watching them. "Well?"

*Because my dad pawned his computer, like, months ago . . . because Mom protects her laptop more than she ever protected me*—but I don't say those things, because Marvin wouldn't understand. He probably has separate laptops for homework, porn, and video games.

"My computer crashed," I lie. "And I had to take it in."

His smirk says that would never happen to him. It makes me so mad. He has all this high-tech equipment, but still he chooses to look up dirty things at school. What would compel him to do something like that?

"Wait—why didn't *you* work at home?" I demand.

He shrugs like it's the stupidest question in the world. Like I'm the stupidest girl, and he's so goddamn smart it pains him to be in my presence. But his answer is less than satisfying. "I wasn't working."

"Oh, you were working, all right. Working out a problem.

Rubbing one—well, never mind. The point is, I told Mrs. Linn someone turned off the computers."

"You did?" His hands are curling and curling, but there's nothing to hold on to.

"I did. But she wouldn't change the grade on my paper unless I told her who did it."

"And you didn't?"

"No. I didn't."

"Why?" He catches my gaze.

*Because Lizzie begged me not to. Because she was such a good person, it made me want to be a better person too.*

"Because it would have ruined you," I say, and that's true as well. I do have compassion, or at least I used to. "The stuff you were looking at was bad, Marvin. Like, lock-you-up-and-study-you bad. I felt sorry for you."

"Well, don't."

"Trust me, the feeling is passing." I hold up my hands. "But as far as I can tell, I did you a big, fat favor, so you owe me one."

He takes a moment to answer. His shoulders are sagging, like his body's too heavy to hold up. "What do you want?" he asks finally.

"Just the name of the person who's writing on the lockers. And bringing Lizzie's diary to school. It has to be the same person, don't you think?"

"It seems likely," Marvin agrees. "But I don't know who's doing those things." He clears his throat when I go to speak. "I only know who was doing it before."

"Before? Before, when she . . . Oh my God. Tell me." I touch his clenched hands, like we're famed superheroes coming together to save the planet. Like we're actually friends. "Please?"

And then, just as Marvin opens his mouth, Kennedy McLaughlin slides into the seat next to mine. She's got on these dark, low-rise jeans and a man's white collared shirt. The loose fit of the shirt only enhances the possibility of what hides beneath. I expect Marvin to be drooling.

But the look he gives Kennedy is pure hatred. "Speak of the devil," he says.

# eight

"WERE YOU TWO talking about me?" Kennedy slides a roll of papers over to me. I hardly have time to catch my breath. Marvin *saw* Kennedy doing something to Lizzie. He witnessed it.

He reaches for the pages.

I slap his hand. "I don't think so, computer boy."

He scowls as I put them in my bag. Yes, I glance at them. Yes, it's Lizzie's handwriting.

"I found them in a locker," Kennedy explains, just glancing at Marvin. "I figured you'd want them."

I don't thank her. I can barely stop myself from glaring. Why did she lie to me?

*Why did I believe her?*

All I want, in that moment, is for her to disappear so that Marvin can explain, but I know that's not going to happen. Kennedy sticks like glue when she wants to.

"What was said?" She turns her golden gaze on Marvin. Already she's picked up on his feelings about her. Smart lady.

*Smarter than me, apparently.*

"Huh?" I come back to the world slowly. Sitting here with the two of them, it's like two universes are colliding. I don't like it.

"What were you saying about me?" she asks, batting dark lashes. Those lashes betray the fakeness of her hair color, but some things about her are real. Her wicked mind. Her razor-sharp wit. The ability to destroy a reputation in ten seconds flat.

"Oh that." I smile easily. At least, it looks easy. "We were arguing about who the hottest girl in school is."

Marvin jumps in. "Angie here said it was you, but I said—"

"You were far too beautiful to be grouped in with the rest of us," I finish for him.

Kennedy gives me a grin. She knows better than to show her claws in mixed company. "Well, I think you're both wrong. Jesse Martinez is the fairest in the land."

It takes me a minute to realize she's not kidding. "He's nice looking," I say. "Kind of stuck-up, though. Or something."

Marvin takes a sip just so he can sputter at me. I think that's why, at least. "Are you two joking? He's a *freak*."

"Oh, right," I reply. "Says the boy who's into all sorts of things."

"What's that, now?" Kennedy perks up.

"Nothing," Marvin says with me.

*Smooth. We should go on stakeouts together.*

He looks at his watch pointedly. "Well, I got to get to class. Ladies." He tips his head at me. "Kennedy," he snarls.

"Wait." I reach for his hand.

But he's too fast for me. "So nice chatting with you," he says, rising from his seat. He's gone before I can think of a way to keep him. I feel Kennedy's gaze locked on me. "What?"

"Are you two dating?" she asks.

I don't give her the satisfaction of a disgusted reply. "We're talking," I say, which could mean a lot of things. "Why'd you follow me?"

She pouts. "I thought this was our secret place."

"Not anymore," I say. I can't help it. If she did something to Lizzie, I don't want her on my side.

"Fine." She slides out of the chair, all grace. "You're welcome for the copies."


MARVIN PLAYS INVISIBLE for the rest of the day. Maybe he's afraid of invoking Cheer Wrath. Or maybe he's just full of it. I don't know. Something about his tone rang true, and not because I want to blame Kennedy for Lizzie's harassment. He seemed to genuinely hate her. I'm not sure he'd be able to fake that.

Still, I can't confront Kennedy yet. I have no evidence. Just Marvin's implication that she's guilty. If I'm going to go head-to-head with the most powerful girl in school, I'll need more than that.

Besides, we saw what a rumor did to Lizzie. I want facts.

When the last bell rings, I do a quick survey of the rooms accessible to students. Lizzie's epithet has been scrubbed clean from the lockers, but that hasn't stopped it from showing up in other places. The upstairs girls' room is its new favorite. The black scribbling mars a nearby stall. I slide my finger over the inscription.

No smudges.

That means the inscription's been sitting a while, at least half an hour. But I know it wasn't here yesterday. It doesn't take a genius to decipher my next course of action. If the writing only shows up in the girls' room, the clues point to the culprit being a girl. But if it shows up in both rooms . . .

I know, I know. Sneaking into the boys' bathroom is not every girl's fantasy. But it's not like I can trust a guy to do it for me. So that's how I find myself leaning against the door to the boys' bathroom, fingers pinching my nose, using my elbow to ease open the door, when Jesse passes by.

"Hey." I try to keep my voice casual.

Jesse stops, slowly, and pivots to face me. I can't help but notice his outfit, which is funny because I could barely tell you what I'm wearing without looking down to remind myself. My fashionista days have fallen by the wayside.

Not so for Jesse. Today his clothes could have come from the girls' or guys' department. He's got on pinstriped black pants and a crisp white shirt, not unlike the one Kennedy was wearing. Add to that suspenders and a pinstriped black fedora, and he's ready to take on Hollywood in the Golden Age. Naturally, the hat's pulled down.

All hail the king of covert existence.

Everyone can see the flashy clothes. No one can see the eyes.

He makes an exception for me. "Oh, you remember me?" His voice is not hopeful. It's full of disdain.

"I need your help," I say conspiratorially.

He does a fluttery bow. "How can I be of service, Princess?"

Ah, so I'm the Princess of Verity High. And apparently I treat my subjects like shit. Nice of him to inform me.

I beckon for him to come closer. He glides over effortlessly. "Somebody's written something in the girls' bathroom," I say.

"Scandal!"

"In Lizzie's handwriting."

"Oh."

"As you know, I'm trying to catch the culprit."

"And send him to the guillotine, no doubt." He makes a dramatic gesture, pointing off into the distance.

"Try to stay with me." I snap my fingers.

He shows a hint of a smile. Maybe he likes sassy?

I smile back, and it's actually genuine. "So I'm trying to figure out if it's just in the girls' bathroom, or if it's in the boys' too. You dig?"

"I follow you. You want me to check out the little boys' room for you."

"No. I want you to give me the all-clear so I can check myself."

"Trust issues," he sings. Still, in one fluid movement, he slips into the boys' room. He's back in less than a minute.

"All clear?" I ask.

"Clear as can be. But I didn't see any of that writing in there." He leans against the wall, crossing one leg over the other. His shirt looks bright against his golden-brown skin.

I dip my head toward him. "How do I know you're not lying to me?"

"I guess you don't." He taps my nose with a finger. It startles me, how warm he is. "You'll have to take my word for it."

"No offense," I say, surveying the empty hall, "but I'm not in the mood lately."

And then I'm gone, into the abyss of toilet-papered tiles and rust-stained urinals. The only possible explanation for a smell this bad is a fountain of urine and a pile of old socks.

I'm in and out as fast as can be.

Jesse's standing guard when I come out. Unfortunately, Drake is with him. My heart starts to race. I want to bolt, but I can't leave without thanking Jesse. Plus, my legs have gone all wobbly. "Listen, Jesse—"

"This is why you're guarding the door?" Drake interrupts, brushing Jesse aside like a shopping cart. "What the hell, Angie?"

"You were right," I say to Jesse, taking small pleasure in sharing a secret with him in front of Drake.

"Told you it was clean." Jesse winks for added effect.

"You and I have a very different definition of that." We share a smile.

Next to us, Drake is fuming. "You want to tell me what the hell is going on?"

"Relax." I almost touch his chest, the way I used to when his jealousy would surface. "We were out of TP in the ladies'."

If he knows I'm lying, he won't call me on it. He's got a vested interest in staying on my good side. He still thinks he might find a way back into my pants.

*What a waste.*

"Thanks for your help," I say to Jesse, touching his shoulder lightly.

He jumps at the touch. I think it surprised him more than it surprised Drake. "No problem," he says.

I turn to leave but something stops me. I'm wary of leaving the two of them alone together. "Don't you have something to do?" I ask Drake. I motion to the bathroom.

"It went away."

"Right."

"It did."

I wish I knew what he was thinking. Most people I can read, but Drake is locked tight with a padlock and chains. It's hard to find a way in.

"Fine," I say, thinking on my feet. "Jesse, can you help me with one more thing?" The longer I look at the pair of them, the more I'm certain it's a bad idea to leave them unsupervised. I'm pretty sure Drake would sucker punch Jesse in a heartbeat.

Jesse looks at me funny, like he knows what I'm up to. "Sorry, I can't."

I wonder if I've insulted him. "It'll just take a minute."

"Sorry," he says again. He begins to walk backward, lowering the bill of his hat. I let him go.

"I need to talk to you," Drake says when he's, like, three feet away.

"Not today, Drake." I make a move to leave.

He catches my arm. "It's really important."

I slide out of his grasp, trying to pretend I hate the feel of him. "I have somewhere to be."

"I'll come with you," he says.

"I don't think you want to."

He comes up beside me, tucking a hair behind my ear. He leans in so only I can hear. "I want to."

Oh no. Not the voice. Gruff and tough Drake gets sweet faster than you would believe. That voice has melted me on many occasions. Soft in my ear. Lips tickling me. But it's not going to get to me today. I don't love him.

I hate him.

"Baby, please," he murmurs, and my legs go wobbly again.

God, do I hate him. I try to think of the bad things. *Did he use those eyes on Lizzie? Did he use that voice?* But I can't. I'm falling.

I crash right into the truth.

You don't fall out of love with someone just because he betrays you. That love stays inside you, battling against the hate. Right now my love is battling my hate so hard I can barely breathe, and all I want to do is get away from him.

Or fall into him.

There is only one way out of this. I have to scare him away.

"I'm going over to Lizzie's," I say. "I promised her dad I'd go through her older belongings. He's running that charity thing for underprivileged kids." I look up and meet his eyes. "He can't even go into her room."

"Okay." Drake nods, but his voice has the shakes. "Well, I'd go, but he doesn't exactly—"

"He's not going to be there."

"Oh. Well, okay. I can . . ." He's looking around, as if searching for signs of escape. I wonder what about this makes him so nervous. Is it simply the thought of being in a dead girl's bedroom? Or is it the fear of facing the reality of Elizabeth Hart, the fear of seeing her as a human being? I think after they slept together he kept her as a fantasy, someone who drifted into his life for one night and then disappeared. I think it was a lot easier that way.

"I wasn't inviting you," I say, backing away.

He chases after me. "Do you really want to go there alone?" he asks, and it's the worst thing he can say. I don't want to go there alone. Not without Lizzie's dad. Not with just myself and all that emptiness. I might sit down on the floor of her bedroom and never get up again.

"I'll be fine," I lie.

"Come on, Angie." He's close, but he's not touching me now. And I'm just lost enough to believe it's out of respect. "Let me help you. You always do everything alone."

"There was a time when I didn't." A time, like two months ago. "But I've learned my lesson."

"Don't punish yourself for my mistake," he says, hand sliding up my neck.

"I'll keep my distance," he says.

"I just want to help," he says.

I'm shuddering now, and it's not because I'm disgusted. "Fine. Let's go," I manage. I don't really want to be around him. I don't want to talk to him in any capacity. But he's going to keep following me, and calling me, and looking at me until I agree to talk to him. And since doing this alone is suddenly terrifying, I opt to give him one final chance to speak. Whether or not I listen is up to me.

Drake holds out his arm for me. I ignore it and pass him by.

It isn't until I see Jesse posed against a nearby locker that I realize he was listening the whole time.

# nine

Lizzie's house looms over us, specter white and ominous. Gaping windows stare down at us like eyes. Drake's body is pressed against me, too close, as I struggle to find my spare key. Maybe he's scared to be here too.

Or maybe he just wants something.

My key turns in the lock. Part of me was hoping it wouldn't. Part of me keeps thinking this whole goddamn thing is a nightmare, the house, the charity drive, Lizzie's untimely death.

I push open the doors and think, *Untimely? That's a laugh.* When are we ever prepared for something like this? How can we ever rectify the absence of an entire fucking person? She was here, and she was there, and now she's gone.

And my heart knows it. My eyes know it, as they flutter to the places where Lizzie lived.

There's the faded blue couch where she'd curl up under blankets and watch TV. Lizzie was always cold; I used to press myself against her to lend her my heat. Through the entryway to the kitchen, I see the counter where forever ago we made cupcakes and topped them with My Little Ponies. We were too young to know what heat does to plastic. We actually cooked the ponies in the oven. When Lizzie cried at the loss of her babies, I told her we were making art.

The frosting matched the melted plastic perfectly.

"I can't stay in this room," I mumble, leading Drake up the stairs. His footfalls sound heavy on the angel-white carpet. The portraits of Jesus are judging me, like: *Why are you here when you treated her so badly?*

But I can't go back now.

A stack of boxes sits outside Lizzie's door. I grab one, forcing myself to cross the threshold into her room. I've only been here once since she died; I came back with Mr. Hart the day of her funeral. Absolutely nothing has changed since then. Crosses decorate the walls, proclaiming a faith Lizzie was born into. Stuffed animals cover her bed. Lizzie's room is creepier than mine—another example of parental influence on decorating— except she doesn't even get the jailbait boy-band posters. Mr. Hart's religious sensibilities wouldn't stand for it.

I wonder what it was like growing up in this house, unable to talk about crushes or feelings. Lizzie's mom died when she was a baby. She was an only child, though we used to joke about being sisters. And, as it turns out, she couldn't even confide in me.

"Where to begin?" I ask, avoiding Drake's gaze. This is the first time we've been alone since prom night. I mean, if standing speechless in a hotel room counts as "being alone."

Drake sits on the edge of Lizzie's pink-and-white-flowered comforter. "No idea. This room is, uh . . ."

"She liked it," I snap, which is a total lie. Lizzie was artistic and free spirited. A wild child. This room is a page out of *Cultist Child Bride*. "You're welcome to leave."

"No." He's at my side in an instant. His eyes keep flicking to the window, like he's checking for something. "It's just weird being here."

"It's a pretty picnic for me."

"I'm sorry, baby," he murmurs, and it makes me cringe.

"Do not call me that." I turn away from his pretty eyes. "Do *not*."

"All right," he says to my back.

I start going through Lizzie's books. *The Golden Compass. A Wrinkle in Time.* Classics blending fantasy with science. Lizzie was a skeptical Christian.

"It just seems like there are so many better worlds out there," she used to say. "I can't believe this is the only one."

Somewhere, in another dimension, maybe Lizzie is alive and I'm the one who's dead. Maybe it's better that way.

My eyes start to sting. I turn away from Drake. When the tears stain my cheeks I wipe them away like I have an itch. It takes him a minute to realize what I'm doing.

"Hey." Coming up behind me, he puts his arms around my waist. Tentative, like it might hurt me. He's being gentle to make me forget his carelessness. I know this. I've seen this before. But it feels so nice to be held that I melt into him.

"Hey," he says again, wiping tears from my face. Taking good care of me, damn him. "It's okay."

"I can't do this," I manage in stilted breaths. "I can't do this with you here and I *can't do this*."

"You mean us?"

His arrogance infuriates me.

"No, not us, Drake." I squirm out of his embrace. "I cannot be here sorting through her things like she's . . . like she's . . ."

Dead.

*She is dead, Angie. She's never coming back to this room. And if you don't gather together her things to help some orphan, her father's going to have a complete meltdown.*

*You have to do this.*

"Okay," I say more to myself than to Drake. "Okay. I can do this." I wipe my face with the sleeve of my black sweater. That's right, that's what I threw on this morning. With a pair of dark-rinse jeans. I've been wearing more and more black lately.

"I'm sorry," I say, detangling myself from his clinging hands. "It was a mistake to bring you here. We can talk later."

"No, *I'm* sorry," he says. "I didn't really need to talk." His gaze shifts to the window again. Ever vigilant. "I just wanted to spend time together. I miss you."

"Well, I don't miss you." I force myself to be cold, to feel nothing. "Please leave."

He stares at me like I've twisted a knife in his heart. It's so damn ironic, I almost laugh. But after a minute of painful silence, he turns and leaves. He does that Charlie Brown head-hang thing all the way out of the room but I don't care. It made me feel gross to see him touch Lizzie's things.

Now I'm alone. I start to sort through Lizzie's closet, pulling out stuff that's been hanging there for years. I can't just paw through her belongings for my own benefit. That would make me feel gross too. But I can gather things for charity and keep my eyes open for clues.

I'm not exactly sure what I'm expecting.

Half of these dresses have a story behind them. The dress she wore to Sunday Service. White, frilly, and ridiculous. The *Alice in Wonderland*–type number she wore the first day of high school. No sign of the dress she wore to prom, but I remember it. Pale blue and flowing. She looked like she'd sprout wings and ascend to heaven in that dress.

It looked different after Drake was through with it. He tore the thin strap right off. He was never passionate like that with me. Brisk maybe. But not rip-off-your-corset passionate.

I lean against the closet door and close my eyes. It doesn't help to blur the images in my mind. I've imagined this scene so many times I should be used to it by now.

. . . Drake crawling over her on the bed . . .

. . . Lizzie cradling his head . . .

. . . His hand trailing down, between her . . .

I find myself falling, my legs suddenly incapable of holding my weight. Grasping at her clothes to keep from hitting the ground too hard, my hands dig into heavy, beaded fabric. Lizzie's golden cocktail dress.

All the bad images disappear.

I look up at the golden creation as if in worship. That dress meant the world to her. She saved for it for months, doing little jobs around the church for her dad. Cleaning the windows. Scrubbing on hands and knees like Cinderella. I teased her about that, a bit. I would have bought the dress for her if she'd let me. But Lizzie wouldn't even take me to the shop where she found it. She was too proud to let me help.

In the end, it was all for nothing. Lizzie fell for the dress without ever trying it on. On her lithe frame the dress was a smock. But she'd worked so hard to get it, I refused to take it off her hands.

*No matter how many times she offered it to me.*

So it hung, lifeless, in her closet. At least she didn't wear it to prom. Sure, she'd have looked like an angel, with that long, sun-spun hair. But Drake would have ruined it, like he ruined the other one. Lizzie would have been heartbroken.

*She was heartbroken anyway. We all broke her heart.*

I lay the dress on her bed. I can't imagine giving it away. Really,

I can't imagine giving any of her belongings away, even the kid stuff. It just makes everything feel so final.

But what choice do I have?

When I'm finally finished packing her clothes, I hold the cocktail dress up to myself in the mirror. Lizzie was right about it complementing my dark hair. But I never wear glamorous things. My prom gown was as no-nonsense as she'd let me get away with. We bought ours together, of course.

I hear a sound at my back. I turn, dress still in hand.

Outside the window, two men are arguing. I recognize their voices before I make it to the glass. They sound like they're about to kill each other.

*Maybe Drake wasn't being paranoid.*

I press my face closer to the glass. Down below, I can just make out their outlines in the fading light. Drake pushes Mr. Hart. Mr. Hart pushes back. This is bad, but it can only get worse, and there isn't much time to stop it.

I race out of the room.

I'm halfway down the stairs when I hear the car door slam. Drake peels out of the driveway and down the street. After that, it's a matter of seconds before Mr. Hart starts unlocking the front door.

I hurry back up the stairs. If I can make it to Lizzie's room before he gets inside, maybe I can pretend I didn't hear them yelling. I'm not eager to discuss Drake Alexander with Lizzie's dad. I'm certainly not eager to discuss Drake and Lizzie's sex life. My battered heart couldn't handle it.

I make it just in time. Now I'm panting, and I have to sit down on the bed to slow my beating heart. Lizzie's golden dress is still clutched in my arms. I hear the footsteps on the staircase, but I'm not prepared for how loudly Mr. Hart bursts into the room.

"*Did you invite that boy?*" he demands, slamming the door against the wall.

I curl in on myself.

"Did you?" he yells, advancing. I close my eyes. Nothing about this makes sense. He's wearing this sad, old-man sweater. In the span of a week, his gray hair has gone completely white. He should be docile, maybe desolate.

Instead, he's enraged.

"Answer me!"

"He must've followed me," I lie.

"Are you telling the truth?" He steps closer to the bed. His slacks are wrinkled; I think Lizzie used to iron them. He's falling apart right in front of me.

"Of course," I insist. "When have I ever lied?"

*That's a good one, Angie. Teenagers don't lie about anything.*

But his glare softens, just a bit. I think he's still trying to figure out what kind of girl I am: the bad girl who invites boys into her bedroom, or the good girl who holds up crosses at the sight of them.

Finally, he steps back. His gaze has shifted to the dress. "You found it," he says. "I always thought it would look nice on you."

I hug the dress, as if it has the power to protect me. And maybe it does. He just keeps staring at it. "So did Lizzie. She says she bought it for herself, but . . ." I stop, second-guessing. "I don't know. I just thought maybe she knew she couldn't wear it."

He frowns, cheeks drooping toward his chin. "She's so darned skinny."

*Was.*

But I don't say that. I say, "She could eat, like, three pizzas and not gain an ounce."

"She didn't, though, did she?"

"No." I force a laugh. "Of course not."

"She was a good girl. She was my angel." His voice is cracking. I lower my head. I'm hoping this passes for a nod.

"Why don't you call it a night?" he says, swallowing thickly until the moment passes. As if it ever will. "The dress is yours, if you want it."

"Sure, thanks." I don't have the heart to tell him it'll just hang in my closet. "Give me a minute?"

He nods, shuffling backward.

I wait for him to reach the stairs before returning to my task. Clearly, I'm not going to find much for clues here. Lizzie's life was so squeaky clean. That's why her rendezvous with Drake was so hard to process. Still, just when I've tucked her last childhood storybook into the charity box, I get the strangest feeling. I think of Shelby destroying Titania's dress when no one was watching. I think of Marvin trolling for porn on the school computers. I think of the secrets we all keep.

Crawling on my hands and knees, I lift up the dust ruffle at the bottom of Lizzie's bed. Nothing there. I can't bring myself to go through her drawers—that seems too invasive, somehow. But if Lizzie had something to hide, she wouldn't put it in her drawers anyway. She'd put it somewhere her father wouldn't think to look. Somewhere innocent looking. As quiet as can be, I look behind the crosses on the wall. Nothing.

Lizzie's pristine row of teddy bears stare back at me from the bed. Honestly, I should've packed them already, but they always freaked me out. Now I walk toward them, mesmerized with possibility. One by one I pull the bears forward, looking behind their backs. Nothing. Nothing. No, wait.

Something.

The little book is turned on its side, tucked into a teddy bear tuxedo. I lift it from its furry hiding spot. Shame and excitement bubble up from my stomach, warming me. What could it be?

Oh. *From the Depth of Her Breast.* Looks like a book of cheesy love poems. Lizzie's secret would be that cutesy. I flip open the book. Hmmm, nope. A book of cheesy *sex* poems. Still not the clue I was looking for.

I go to tuck the book into my pocket. If Lizzie didn't want Daddy to see it, I'm not going to leave it behind. The book won't fit, not entirely. It's too bulky for this stupid jean pocket. I pull it out, trying to smash the pages together. That's when I see it. This little white corner peeking out of the yellowed pages. A note.

My heart races as I open it.

The note consists of one line, next to a winking smiley face:

*The only thing worth reading in the library, for the only one worth anything in this town.*

Um. Wow. It's not Drake's handwriting. I know that for a fact. Anyway, poetry (even of the sexual persuasion) is so far beyond Drake's gift-giving scope it's not even funny. Once, we had to write an original poem for English class. It could've been about anything, in any form we wanted.

Drake stole his from the Internet. It was called "Ode to a Broke Down Truck." Mrs. Linn thought it was a great allegory for the human condition.

He got an A.

I refold the note and stick it in my purse. Now the book slides into my pocket, barely. I want to keep it close to me. Hanging the dress over my arm, I close up the box for charity and set it outside the room.


I'M HALFWAY TO my car when I finally look at my phone. After all these years, a part of me still hopes Mom will check in. No such luck. Instead, I've got two texts waiting for me. One from Drake, saying "I'm sorry, baby," and one from a number I don't recognize, asking "Are you okay?"

What the hell? Is Drake using another number to get to me?

I hit the callback button as I walk to the curb.

"Hello?" The voice is male but different from Drake's. More energetic.

"Who is this?" I ask, unlocking my car.

"What, you mean you can't tell?"

I slide into my seat, closing the door. "*Jesse?*"

"Good voice recognition."

"I don't know anyone else who sounds like you."

He laughs. "Naw, you just don't *talk* to anyone who sounds like me. We got other Mexicans at this school."

"You honestly think anyone else at Verity has your voice? It's kind of . . ."

"Unique," he supplies. "Yeah, I'm just messing with you. I like to see how much teasing you'll take."

"What a sweet guy."

"I'm an enigma, baby."

"How did you get my number?" I ask, staring through the window. Outside, the world is darkening to black. It's kind of soothing, the way it blots out everything.

Well, almost everything.

"Kennedy gave it to me."

*That*, I wasn't expecting. "You know each other?"

"Depends on who you ask." He pauses, chuckling. "She's got the hots for me. Thinks her tits can turn a guy straight."

"If anyone can do it . . ."

"Sure, that's how it works."

"If anything, it was a compliment to—" I stop. "You're messing with me again."

"Maybe." I can hear his smile. "You seem to respond to it."

What is this guy's deal? "You want to tell me why you texted me?"

"If I get to it."

"Jesse Martinez."

Another pause.

"I was worried," he says softly.

"Worried I was traumatized by seeing the guys' bathroom?"

"I'm being serious."

"For once. You always surprise me."

He's silent, suddenly.

"Why were you worried?" I press.

His voice is a whisper now. "I don't know . . ."

Ho-ly shit. Is Jesse Martinez getting shy with me?

"Spill it," I say. "You swiped my phone number!"

"I was worried when I saw him talking to you."

"Who, Drake? He's harmless."

"You sure? He did a number on Lizzie."

"We all did," I say, getting that sinking feeling in my gut. That inescapable guilt. "And you're right, he's a jerk. But he's not dangerous."

"If you're sure."

"Positive. I've known him since we were kids."

"All right then." He sounds anxious to get off the phone. Like he's said too much and wants to take it back.

"Okay, well . . . thanks," I say.

"No problem. I just figured, you know, earlier . . . You were looking out for me."

So he did know I was hovering at the bathroom to protect him from Drake. Wait, why am I insisting Drake is harmless?

"What did you think he was going to do?" I ask after a minute.

Jesse keeps me waiting. "I didn't know that he was," he says finally. "Just a feeling I had."

Hmmm.

"Well, I appreciate it. But you don't have to worry." I slide my key into the ignition. Not that I have anywhere to go, not really. "I can take care of myself."

"So can I," he says. "But you keep looking out for me, don't ya? 'Night, Angie."

"Good night," I say, but the phone's already dead. Jesse's gone and all that's left is silence.

My transformation is complete. Once a caterpillar creeping along the halls unseen. Now a butterfly torn to bits. Bleeding red. This school becomes the glass cage from which I cannot escape.

The taunt is tiny. A baby's scrawl. There, on the corner of my locker door.

SLUT

To go from virgin to harlot in the span of a day . . . this must be some kind of record.

I doubt I'll be given a prize.

Even worse, if my father learns of this, I'll be the girl locked in the tower. Home school. No contact with the outside world. Part of me wonders if it would be for the best.

A small part of me.

Instead I hold my head high, walking the halls as if this title were my birthright.

My scarlet letter.

Tonight I etched the word into me with a blade from my father's razor. Small, red letters above my hip. I romanticize the idea of being branded. It's the only choice I can make. There is no coming back from where I have been.

Still, throughout the night I keep opening my eyes, hoping this dream has passed, praying harder than I've prayed since I was a child that this is just a dream, just a dream, just a dream.

Wake up, Lizzie. None of this really happened.

Why would it happen to me? What did I ever do to anyone? I spent my life caring for those around me, putting my feelings last, remaining silent so as not to upset them with what I really want. So as not to bother them, I've bottled it up. I've done everything I could to make things easier for them.

Surely they would do the same for me.

But they don't. Clearly, I am not worthy of such things. No one will step up beside me, hold out a hand, listen to my voice, except when I sing the songs they've chosen for me. How many girls feel this way, ignored until we speak the words they have given us to speak? How many boys learn to converse through violence so as not to invoke the earthquakes their voices might bring? How many years have we sat, silent, waiting?

But I must have missed my turn. That elusive moment between speaking too soon and remaining silent too long. That night, in the hotel room, when it was just you and me. The moment passed, my voice was taken, and now they'll all speak for me.

They are speaking for me.

SLUT

Couldn't they, at least, pick a word that means something?

Ask a hundred people the meaning of that word and you'll hear a hundred answers. It means absolutely nothing. But the moment it is unleashed, it changes me. They look at me differently, all of them. As if I am no longer human. As if I am somehow a monster to be destroyed.

These things I have feared about myself. Now they are telling me.

And still, I sit up in the night, willing the world to rearrange so that this will have all been a dream. A nightmare from which I can escape. But sitting up only serves to rustle my nightdress, tugging at the blood that dries on my skin. The scabs rip away, awakening fresh wounds.

The shock of it knocks the breath from me. It takes my breath away.

I remember his voice then. Too real to have been a dream.

There in the room, he whispered to me, "You take my breath away. I want to do that for you."

I didn't say anything, not then. I admit to wondering what he meant. But I'm sorry now.

I was wrong for wondering, and they won't let

me forget that. I'll be sorry forever, until the day
I die.

When someone says "Take my breath away" they
don't literally mean take away my breath; tear
from me that intangible thing that makes me
human, that makes me alive. They mean, surprise me
with the urgency with which we kiss. Surprise me
with your lips' desire.

Surprise me.

Don't destroy me.

# ten

THURSDAY MORNING BEFORE first period I trap Marvin against his locker. Don't worry, I'm not actually employing violence here. I just kind of corner him until he has nowhere to go.

"It's now or never, Marv. You spill the dirt on Kennedy or I march right into the principal's office and tell them why your right arm's so much stronger than your left."

"Shows what you know." He turns his back to me, opening his locker. "I'm left-handed." He's trying to appear casual, but he keeps dropping his books and this little deck of cards leaps off his top shelf, spilling on the floor.

"What's it going to be?" I crouch to pick up the cards. They're from that game, Alchemy, the one where you get to be wizards and elf-knights and princesses.

*Every teenage boy's dream, right?*

Something about the cards looks familiar. The artistry is really unique, but Marvin steals each one before I get a good look.

"I told you." He shoves the deck in his pocket, just like I did with the book of poems. "I'm not talking about it here."

"What are you so afraid of?"

"Use your brain, Angie."

*Oh, right, because I'm a cheerleader.*

"My brain?" I puff up my lips. "Let me see if I can find it."

He snorts derisively. He's such a sweetie. "I don't know if you noticed, but I'm not exactly at the top of the food chain here. Getting my ass kicked by a bunch of cheerleaders? Not going to help."

"I'm offering you Cheer Immunity."

His lips curl, but he doesn't speak.

"Come on, Marvin." I play-punch him like we're buddies. "You've pretty much told me it was Kennedy. I just need the itty-bitty details."

He pauses as the first bell rings. Underclassmen scurry to their classes, but we seniors take our time. What do they expect? We're almost out of this place.

Marvin ducks his head closer to mine. "If I tell you this, we're square," he says, all low-voiced and authoritative. "You forget what you saw in the library. Promise?"

"Scout's honor." I make up a hand signal on the spot.

"Okay." He inhales like he's about to implicate the president in a sex scandal. Looks like Shelby has competition as Drama Queen. "The day SLUT showed up on Lizzie's car, I got excused from first period to work on a library project."

"I bet you did."

"I did," he almost-squeals. "Miss Marilyn asked me to put parental controls on the library computers. She caught one of the underclassmen looking at naked celebrities."

"I'm going to fall over from the irony."

"At least I cleaned up after myself."

"Ew."

He sneers. "I don't mean literally. Don't be such a prude."

"Considering the alternative, prude's looking mighty decent these days."

He's quiet for a second. "Guess it's different for guys."

"Ya think? Tell me what you saw."

"Kennedy on her hands and knees in front of Lizzie's car."

I take a minute to collect my thoughts. Nope. They're not collectible. "Did you actually see her writing anything?"

"The car was covered when I got there. But it wasn't just writing. She *scratched* that word into the paint. Used a key or something."

"*A hundred times,*" I whisper, remembering that morning. I never saw the car, but everyone had a story about it. *The words were written in blood. They wrapped around the car in a spiral.* People talked about it like some kind of spell had taken place; like writing that word, over and over, had the power to transform Lizzie.

*But if she needed to be transformed, what was she before?*

"What'd you do?" I ask Marvin.

"I yelled at Kennedy to stop."

"And?"

"She bolted."

"And you bolted too, didn't you?"

"No." He's shaking his head. "I mean yes. But I went to find Lizzie."

This catches me by surprise. "You did?" I take a step back, as if to see him more clearly. It doesn't help. "Did you find her?"

"Right after first period." He smiles. "We left, just the two of us. We were like Bonnie and Clyde, two lovers on the lam."

Except for the lovers part. And the lam. Pretty much all of it.

But to loverboy I say, "Did you go back to her house?"

That dreamy smile slips. "It was a mistake. Her father was supposed to be at church, setting up for some event. We should've had plenty of time to paint over the words." He squeezes his eyes shut, but they open almost immediately. I wonder if he's sick of seeing the same dark images behind his lids.

God knows I am.

"He came back?" I ask softly.

"He was already home," Marvin says. "He must've forgotten something. He dragged me out of Lizzie's car, like *I* was the one who defiled her."

*Defiled*, huh? Ironically, he sounds like Lizzie's dad. But I don't point out the comparison. I'm too disturbed by what he's saying. "He dragged you? Mr. Hart? Did he touch Lizzie?"

He starts to shake his head, but something stops him. "He locked her in the house. I heard screaming; Lizzie could yell when she was angry. They both could . . . I didn't think he was going to let her come back to school."

"Apparently they reached a compromise," I mutter, trying to push the memories away. But there they are, flooding my head with ugliness. Lizzie was out of school for three days. When she came back, her father was driving her to and from class.

He'd sold her car.

I exhale slowly. My chest feels tight, and the last thing I want is to cry in front of Marvin. But that sadness creeps up on me, lacing my veins with cold. "She hated being treated like a kid," I say, half to myself. Across the hall, one of my classmates skitters around a corner, and I'm happy for the distraction. The boy's wearing blue jeans under a black lace slip.

I'd recognize those long legs anywhere.

"Listen, Marvin," I say, making a move to chase them. "I appreciate—"

But my gratitude never makes it past my lips. Marvin grabs me, spinning me around to face him. "Not so fast," he says.

"Ho-ly shit." I try to take back my arm, but he's got me in a death grip. He's gone from superhero to villain in an instant. I match his tone. "You just made the biggest mistake of your life, little boy."

To my surprise, he laughs. "You want to talk about mistakes? Let's talk about Lizzie trusting that freak and getting pushed out of the play. Let's talk about me going into the bathroom this morning, to find SUICIDE SLUT written there."

"The *guys'* bathroom?" My heart races. "Oh no."

"Oh yes." Marvin grins. "Right after Jesse Freakshow Martinez used it. So don't say I didn't warn you, little girl."

He drops my arm and stalks away.


FOR THE FIRST half of first period, I focus solely on Kennedy's guilt. I'm not ready to make Jesse a suspect yet. Honestly, I'm not ready to admit he's capable of evil whatsoever—it's easier to imagine him dancing alongside unicorns in a forest of candy canes.

After a half hour of this, I'm feeling more grounded.

Fact is, I need an accomplice to clinch Kennedy's confession, and Jesse's the only person in this entire school who might help me. So why not kill two birds with one stone, so to speak, and spend a little more time with him? With any luck, I'll be able to lure Kennedy into confessing *and* prove Marvin's evidence against Jesse is circumstantial.

Oh yeah. That's definitely the way to go.

And I'm *definitely* not blinded by my desire to prove Jesse's innocence.

I shoot him a text near the end of the period. He doesn't respond until after the bell rings. *Such a studious boy.* For all the transparency at this school, I can't quite figure him out.

*But I will.*

I try to get him to come to my locker. We've got, like, seven minutes until second period starts. For some reason, he refuses. We have a mini text war that lasts until the bell rings. That's when I know I've lost. As a consolation prize, he agrees to meet up at lunch.

I walk to my next class begrudgingly.

Time drags. I want it to be lunchtime so badly and the clock just *refuses* to cooperate. I try to trick myself into enjoying French, you know, so time will fly? But the clock outsmarts me. It knows how I feel about conjugating verbs.

We spend the hour learning about je ne sais quoi. Then in Art we paint pictures we could've created in kindergarten. I'll graduate high school with a major in Cynicism and a minor in Irritation.

I am seriously depressed by the time my meeting with Jesse arrives.

He keeps a safe distance as he approaches my locker, like he's afraid I'll be branded his new hag. As if polishing my rep is at the top of my concerns.

I pull him closer. I can feel the curve of his bicep beneath his tailored suit jacket. He's wearing this pink, see-through petticoat over flared jeans that could've come from my closet. Ballet flats.

"You don't have to do that," I say as he slinks out of my grasp.

"Do what?" His smile is casual, but his eyes keep straying to the arm I grabbed, like he's not used to being touched. I wonder if I shouldn't have done that.

"Are people actually weird about standing next to you?"

He looks up through his lashes. For a second, I think he's going to bat them. But he remains guarded. "Most people don't see me."

I try to push away the guilt, at least until I can turn it into something useful.

"I see you." I look directly into his eyes. For a second I'm just swimming in them. They're so dark they're almost black. But they're also warm, if that makes sense. It's comforting and intriguing at the same time.

I wonder what he sees when he looks at me.

"So what's up?" he asks, leaning against the locker to my right. On our other side, Lizzie's locker stands empty, stripped of its belongings. Sometimes, I think of slipping a note in there just to battle that emptiness.

"I was hoping you'd do me a favor," I say.

Jesse smirks, but he's followed my gaze to Lizzie's locker. "I bet."

"How close are you with Kennedy?" I force myself to look at his face. To look away from another place where Lizzie *was*, and isn't anymore. "Tell me the truth."

"She flirts with me," he says. "I'm safe for her, you know? She can say whatever she wants and I won't expect anything."

I nod, leaning in. This part is important. I need to give him enough information to pique his interest without turning him off to my plans. Even without Marvin's warning, I'm not convinced I can trust him. I think he's closer to Kennedy than he says.

"I heard a rumor she did something to Lizzie."

"A rumor?" His tone is sharp. He's either genuinely pissed or the world's greatest actor.

"That's right."

"I want to know specifics. I want names."

"You'll have that, if you help me."

Maybe a good actor can spot a bad one. He narrows his eyes. "I don't believe you."

"That's your choice. Look . . ." I pause as several Cheer Bears stroll by. Kennedy's heading up the pack, with Cara and Elliot swaggering behind. The "twins" are holding hands, but their eyes are trained on Kennedy.

*Please don't see me. Please don't see me. Please don't— Damn.*

Kennedy turns, catching my eye. The minute she sees Jesse she pivots, like a puppet on strings, and leads her girls over to our private meeting. "Hello, darlings." Her smile is spun from sugar but her eyes could cut glass.

Jesse lifts her hand and kisses it, like a knight. "Hey, sweetie."

Elliot scowls. Cara looks perplexed. I'm guessing this flirtation between Kennedy and Jesse often takes place in unknown places. Her friends on the squad just wouldn't understand.

I don't understand either.

*What does she want from him?*

"Hello, ladies," I say cheerfully. Between Kennedy's blond hair, Cara's black, and Elliot's red, they look like a modern version of Hecate. Like they're three parts of the same being.

They're even wearing red, white, and black.

"Having a nice day?" Jesse asks Kennedy, eyeing her white dress, and now I'm wondering: *What does* he *want from* her? Does being seen with the Queen of the school offer him some protection? Right now, it doesn't seem to be causing anything but confusion.

"Better now," Kennedy says, and her little Cheer Bear followers scrunch up their faces. It's like they're embarrassed to be seen next to Jesse, let alone talking with him. They tug on Kennedy, not so subtly.

She turns on them. "What, do you guys need to pee? You're acting like babies."

Cara frowns. Elliot fiddles with a string on her crimson top. As charming as they are, they have no power over their leader.

Queen Bee returns her attention to me. "What's going on?" she asks.

"Drama project," I say quickly, and Jesse tenses. I feel bad for lying, but I can't tell the truth: *We're plotting against you, you two-faced Bee. That's not a problem, is it?*

"Too bad. I'd hoped it was interesting," Kennedy says. "Hey, I left you something in your locker," she tells Jesse.

"Did you, now?" He sounds genuinely intrigued. But part of me wonders if he's forcing it, if he hears what she's saying between the lines. Sure, she'll stop by for a minichat in the hallway, but anything more personal has to be done in secret.

And yeah, I wish I knew what her note said. But it's not like I'm going to break into Jesse's locker. I do have a line.

"Can we go?" Cara asks, laying her head on Kennedy's shoulder. Elliot chimes in, saying, "I actually do have to pee."

Kennedy rolls her eyes. "I don't remember signing up to be a mother," she deadpans. But she backs away, leading the girls as much as they're leading her, and soon they're all three swallowed by the crowd.

"Well," Jesse says, so loudly it startles me. "They're gone now. You can stop pretending we're working on a Drama project. Whatever that is."

"I didn't mean—"

"It's fine," he says, but his eyes are shining like I actually took an arrow to his heart. He laughs, a bitter sound. "Not like we're friends."

I watch him walk away in slow motion. I don't know why I can't move. My limbs have suddenly forgotten how. Or maybe they've decided they don't deserve to move.

*Honestly, Angelina, are you so obsessed with catching Lizzie's tormentors that you'll step on everyone to get there?*

No. Maybe. I don't know.

For a moment the paralysis is complete. Even my brain is frozen. Then, just as quickly, the spell breaks, and my body shifts into fast-forward mode to make up for it. I sprint through the halls after Jesse. Losing him in the crowd is not an option.

Lucky for me, he doesn't try too hard to get away. I catch him at his locker. He's pulling out a bouquet of daisies.

"Got a date?" I say, coming up behind him.

He slams his locker shut. "At this school? No thank you."

"Come on, Jesse, you said you'd talk to me."

He starts to walk. Even with my long legs, I practically have to jog to keep up with him. "That was before I realized how humiliating it was for you," he says.

"Give me a break. I didn't want Kennedy to know I was talking about her. Well, trying to. You're not making this easy."

"Sorry." He pushes through the doors and out onto the grounds. The grass is slippery, and I take great pains not to fall on my ass. Out in the park, trees shake their branches at the sky, loosing leaves into the air.

"It's cold," I murmur, hardly warmed at all by the effort to keep pace with Jesse.

"Give it a month," he says.

"Yeah, and then another month until it's freezing again. I hate this town."

"You eighteen?" he asks as we enter the parking lot.

"Just about."

"Then you've got nothing keeping you here."

Wrong. There are a lot of things keeping me here. People, actually. If he would just slow down, I would tell him about it.

He does me one better. He stops completely in front of this brown, beat-up clunker that looks like the opposite of what he would drive. "Well then." He bows, waving his arm regally. "This is where I bid you adieu, Your Majesty."

"You are royally starting to piss me off," I say as he slides into the driver's seat. "Ten minutes ago you were all set to have lunch with me. Now you're—"

"Oh, honey, no." He scoffs. "I agreed to chat with you. Besides, isn't it against the rules for you to convene with me? Won't I give you some kind of disease?" He goes to close his door.

I put my hand on top of it. He'll either have to slam my fingers or let me speak. I pray he's in a giving mood. "You're totally misunderstanding me," I say. "But if it helps, I apologize for upsetting you. I wasn't trying to—"

"Apology accepted." He turns the key in the ignition. "Now, would you mind taking your paws off my Corvette?"

Yeah, right. This car is so old I can't even remember the name. But I smile anyway and lift my hand. "Your chariot," I say obligingly. It's obvious I'm not going to win this one.

*Unless* . . .

Let's see what happens if I change my tack.

"Hey, Jesse?" I say as the door closes in my face.

*Damn. Too late.*

No, wait, he's rolling down the window. "Yes, Princess?"

"Do you want to come over after school today?" I feel like I'm in kindergarten, talking to him this way, but what else can I do? I really do need his help.

"Let me guess, you'll have the cops waiting?"

"Yeah. I totally have connections with the police." I roll my eyes. "Because this is a movie. Come on, Jesse. You've got to take a chance on something."

He raises his brows. "You think I don't?"

"You eat alone almost every day."

"You watching me?"

"Lovingly."

"That's not surprising." He blows me a kiss. Then, for a moment, he's silent. I'm just about to call it quits when he whispers, "Lizzie sat with me."

My eyes trail to the ground. "Yeah, she did," I say softly. "You guys spent a lot of time together when you were rehearsing, didn't you?"

He nods slowly. My downcast eyes catch the movement. "Gordy sat with me too."

I nod back, though I don't remember seeing them together. Gordy was even better at playing the invisibility game than Jesse. Except in the guys' locker room. He always came out with bruises.

And nobody ever said anything.

"Sure you want to risk being seen with me?" Jesse asks.

Big sigh. "Yes, I will 'risk' it. I'd be honored if you'd come over after school today. As long as you agree to hear me out."

"Aw. I thought it was because you liked me."

"You drive me fucking crazy. Take that however you want."

"Sure thing." Putting the car in gear, he backs out of the parking lot before I can think of a witty remark.

I'm certain he's going to blow me off. But after the last bell rings I see him waiting outside of Drama class, all set to escort me to the parking lot. We drive separate cars to my mother's place. That way if he needs to storm off, he can do it real dramatic-like. Yeah, I'm starting to understand this boy.

I think.

# eleven

I BURST THROUGH MOM'S front door, flinging my backpack onto the couch. Sure, I'm usually a neat freak, but something about Mom's museum-quality decor makes the house feel unlived in. And since I already feel like an intruder in her house, I do what I can to make things seem more comfortable.

I know, I'm a textbook case of Neglected Child. I try not to think too hard about it. Any good psychologist knows better than to analyze herself.

Of course, any human psychologist will do it anyway.

It doesn't help that Jesse's looking at me like I'm an alien. "You live here?"

"No, we're breaking in." I kick my shoes in two different directions.

He slides his off in a neat little row by the door.

"You don't have to," I say, nodding to his feet. He's got pale pink polish on his bare toes. "I mean you can. But it's not a rule."

He looks at the snowy-white carpet. "You sure?"

"Pretty much. Where do you want to talk?"

"I'll take a cosmopolitan in the arboretum." He tilts his head to take in the vaulted ceiling. I start to feel warm. Is this what they mean when they say an embarrassment of riches?

"Sorry." I perch on the arm of the couch. "It's not viewable to first-time visitors."

"Naturally." He fidgets a little, looking like he wants to lean against the door, or bolt through it. "Where would you go if you hadn't invited me over?"

I look up at him, not sure why he's asking.

"You did invite me over, didn't you?" he says when I don't answer right away. "I didn't just imagine that."

That's when it hits me. He feels like he's intruding.

Interesting.

"You didn't imagine it."

"Okay." He catches my gaze. For some reason it makes me blush. When he looks at me like that, I feel like he can read my every thought. "Something up?"

"No." I look away. "Nothing."

"Oh, I get it." He steps toward me. "You were planning to do something private. A little *alone* time, eh?"

"No— No, I wasn't!" Now I'm blushing badly. I don't understand my reaction. I'm not usually so easy to rile. But Jesse says things to me that other boys won't. I honestly think he would say anything without regret. Like he's not afraid of anything.

I miss that feeling.

Now he's smiling. It's less of a leer and more of a challenge, like he wants me to fight back. To play along.

I don't give him the satisfaction. Smoothing out my feathers— er, hair—I lead him through the room. "Actually, I was going to make chocolate chip cookies."

He touches his heart dramatically. "You bake?"

"I dabble. But I'll just do it later."

In the kitchen, I flip a switch and light spills over everything. The countertop island. The little nook with the bay windows. For the millionth time, I wish my parents could've just worked through their differences. My dad would've appreciated living in this kind of comfort. Me, I just feel out of place.

I have no way to impart this to Jesse without sounding ungrateful.

"Thirsty?" I ask.

"Hungry," he says, touching the surface of the island. "For chocolate chip cookies."

I look at him. "Seriously?"

"You know the last time I had homemade cookies? My mom doesn't have time for that shit."

"Neither does mine." I open my hands, as if to say *Duh*.

"I'll help." He clicks on the oven.

"You know how to cook?" I ask, gathering ingredients, though I'm not sure this is a great idea. Convincing him to pull a fast one on Kennedy doesn't really mix with sugar and chocolate chips.

Or does it? Maybe I can use the treats to butter him up, pardon the pun.

He smiles like he knows I'm scheming. "Me? Cook?"

"I bet you do," I say, and it's not just because he's pulling milk and eggs out of the fridge. "I bet you cook for all your siblings."

All right, I admit it. I'm fishing for information. He's standing in my kitchen, about to make cookies with me, and I know next to nothing about him. And yeah, I know baking isn't the same as hopping into bed together. But there's something intimate about this. We're sharing a moment.

"You got me," says Jesse, studying a bag of chocolate chips. "I'm usually the oldest kid in my house."

*Usually? What the hell does that mean?*

I snatch the chips from his hands.

"I was looking for a recipe," he says.

"Recipe? Please. All you need is in here." I tap my head.

"Wow," he says as I reach for the flour. "I didn't see you as a little Sally Homemaker."

"Hey, maybe we have a label maker somewhere. You could stick the label right on my forehead." I tear the flour bag too quickly, roughing it up in my hands. White dust explodes into the air. "You know, so everyone will know exactly who I am."

"Okay, okay." He wipes the powder from my forehead. I jump a little at the feel of him. "I was just teasing. So, what's the occasion?"

"My mom's on this diet," I say, pulling myself onto one of the high stools. "She's always on a diet, those really bad ones where you just eat bacon or lettuce or something. And it's freaking ridiculous because she's stick skinny and she's destroying her body."

Jesse laughs. "Sounds like a high-class problem."

"No shit," I agree, though I'm not sure what he means. I pick up a knife and start hacking up a stick of butter. I'm halfway through the stick when it hits me: dieting is for people who have the money to buy too much to eat.

Jesse sticks his finger in his mouth, and I study the litheness of his arms. He's not scrawny, but he's certainly not carrying excess fat. I wonder if he's ever had too much to eat in his life.

I return the chocolate chips to his hand.

"So you're making dessert because your mom's on a diet?" he says, popping a few chips in his mouth.

*That, and getting yelled at is better than being ignored.* But since this isn't an After School Special, I say, "She shouldn't be on a diet."

"But she is." He reaches for the eggs.

"That's the thing. She's got a sweet tooth like you wouldn't believe. Probably because she's always depriving herself. And once she breaks her diet she's off, at least for that week. So she'll eat normal."

"Sneaky." He cracks the eggs expertly into a separate bowl for me. That's when I notice his hands. Those hands could make a rusty piano sing.

He moves them like instruments.

"I do what I have to." I shift my gaze to my own hands. I must look like a flour-covered mess. At least he won't make me feel ugly. Not the way Drake used to. I'd tear my room apart trying to find the right outfit and he wouldn't even compliment me. I guess some guys just don't.

Jesse notices me looking at my hands. He gives me that mind reader look again. It should freak me out but it doesn't because his words are so sweet. "You look like a snow princess."

"Thanks." I laugh into my hand to hide my smile.

*Oh no.*

I've heard this laugh before. I know what this laugh means.

For a second, I let myself analyze him, just to prove I'm not feeling what I think I'm feeling.

He looks up at me. His eyes are glittering in the light and his lips are curling. There's sugar on his cheek. I want to touch it.

Oh crap. I am feeling what I think I'm feeling. This boy is starting to grow on me. Quickly. He's cute. He's sweet. He definitely makes me laugh.

*Yeah, and he's gay, Angie. You can't jump him.* God forbid I become like Kennedy, convincing myself I can "turn" him with my womanly charms.

Wow. Kennedy. I haven't thought about her in the past half hour. I haven't even thought of my investigation. That's got to be the first time all week.

I should be happy, but all I feel is guilt.

"Hey. Space traveler?" Jesse says.

"What?"

"Earth to Angie."

"Oh. Right." I shake myself, trying to remember Marvin's warning. Trying to remember anything that will provide me some distance.

But when Jesse holds up his bowl, miming "Can I?" I say, "Sure," without even asking what he means.

He dumps his bowl into mine. We both reach for the spoon. I want to fight him for it. No, I want to spoon-duel until we're both laughing so hard we can't breathe. Instead, I grease a pan and let him stir alone. After we add the chocolate chips, we drop the balls of dough onto the pan.

"Now what?" he asks as I slide the pan into the oven.

Now we deal with the task at hand.

I need to get him out of the kitchen, away from cheery yellow walls and the smell of sugar. I need to get him somewhere as depressing as the situation.

"Let's go to my room."

Jesse doesn't argue.


UPSTAIRS THE WORLD is dark, with no light shining through my ugly olive curtains. If Jesse's expecting a princess canopy over my bed, he doesn't say anything to reveal his surprise. Instead he perches on the edge of the bed, tentatively, like a bird on a branch.

"How long?" His eyes are glued to the door.

"Until my mom gets home?" I wave my hand. "Don't worry, she won't care that you're up here."

He raises his eyebrows. "Until the cookies are ready."

"Oh." I hover by the bed. "Ten to twelve minutes."

"Then that's how long you have."

"Until what?"

"Until my mouth will be too full of cookie goodness to talk about serious stuff."

I sit on the other side of the bed. I'm keeping my distance. "Come on."

"I'm serious. You don't know how much I'm looking forward to this." He leans back on his elbows. "You need a new decorator, Princess."

Just like that, he's up to his old tricks. I can't help but feel relieved. I'll have a hard time romanticizing him while he's infuriating me.

"So . . . Cara's having a party tomorrow," I say, playing with my hands.

"Ooh. Fancy."

"You know where she lives?"

"I got a general idea." He lies back on the bed, hair splaying out around him. It's dark and wavy, only curling on the ends. I wish my hair were like that instead of a tangled mess. It takes me an hour every morning to straighten it.

"Can you do better than that?" I ask.

He closes his eyes. "Gated community. Fifty or so servants."

"She lives close to Kennedy."

"I know where that is."

I wonder if he meant to give me that piece of information. His indifferent expression doesn't change a bit.

"I need you to come to the party with me."

"Like a date-date?" He wiggles his eyebrows suggestively. And I like it. I like it too much.

"I need you to question Kennedy about something," I say, shifting my gaze from his face. But it trails back.

"And then I come running to you with her answers?" he says.

"No. I'll be listening."

"In the closet?"

"Sounds better than under the bed."

"Wait, are you serious?" He stands. In one instant, all that playfulness has left his face. "This is psycho shit."

"No, it's not." My cheeks are red. I can feel it. All the blood in my body is rushing to my face.

"We're not spies, Angie."

"I'm not trying to be."

"No." He's heading to the door. "No way."

I push off the bed. "Wait."

"No."

"I'm serious. Wait. Please?" My voice is rising. Panic fills my throat like bile. If he leaves, that's it. I'm screwed. "Kennedy will never confess to me."

"Maybe there's a reason for that." His hand's on the knob and it's turning, turning. This is slow-motion torture but I can't stop him. I feel like I'm trapped in a dream.

"Just listen to me!" The strength of my voice surprises both of us. I slump onto the bed, head in my hands. "Fuck."

"Angie," he says, whisper-soft and sweet.

Tears seep through my fingers. I'm utterly humiliated. "Just go."

"Come on." He sits next to me. "Angelina."

"Go." I squeeze my eyes shut so that nothing can escape. "You wanted to go so badly. Get out of here."

"What about the cookies?"

I seriously cannot believe it. I lift my gaze to find him grinning.

"Goddamn it," I say.

"They're probably done by now, don't you think?"

"Don't make me laugh," I say, but a chuckle breaks through my hand.

"I mean, I don't want to be a dick, but if those suckers burn, I'm going to be *pissed*."

"Stop it." I'm laughing more than I'm crying now.

He scoots in close. "Can I hug you?"

"Yeah. Yes." I can't even explain how good that sounds.

His arms go around me, slow like wings. I bury my head in his neck. He's so warm, and I feel frozen from the inside.

"The last person who hugged me was Drake," I say into his skin. "And it's just, really . . . It's not the same."

"I bet." He cradles my head with his hand.

I close my eyes. I'm not crying anymore. Enough time has passed that I can almost pretend I never did. My mother isn't the easiest person to cry in front of. I sort of have this guilt associated with it.

*Stop analyzing*.

I take in a shaky breath. "Sorry."

"Stop it."

"I feel stupid."

"Well, don't. You got to let this go, baby," he murmurs in my ear. Slowly, he untangles himself from me. I realize I was sort of clinging.

*Baby*.

The word hovers in my brain. It's probably something he says to everyone. To Kennedy. To Shelby. But it makes me feel like I'm still in his arms.

"I can't let go," I tell him.

"You have to."

Heat rises. I want to cry again. But I won't. "I just keep thinking of Lizzie," I say before my throat can close.

"I know."

"I don't just mean her. I mean what they did."

He just looks at me.

"I think of Gordy too, and all the people whose lives are just shit. I think of how we destroy them."

"Bullies suck."

I shake my head. "That sounds like some big kid kicking a little kid on a playground. It sounds like a cartoon."

"Easier for people to ignore."

"But it's more than that. It's ripping someone to shreds for our own fucking amusement." *Or to distract from our own insecurities*, I think. "Until they have nothing left."

"Angie . . ."

"Until the only possible relief comes from dying. You know how messed up that is?"

"You're preaching to the choir here."

"Then you understand why we have to do something."

"We can't do what they did," he says. "We'd become them."

My heart skips. Feeling reckless, I reach up and brush the sugar from his cheek. His eyes follow the movement. "What else can we do?"

"Live above it. Be better than that."

"I'm sorry. I can't."

"Angie."

*Call me baby again.*

God, that thought just fucks with me.

"I mean I *can't*," I tell him. "I'm angry all the time. I just want to hurt everyone who hurt her."

He sighs. "You know I can't help you do that."

"I know, but . . ." My sigh puts his to shame. "I need your help. I need it."

"I will not willingly help you attack people. I'm sorry."

"I won't ask you to do that. I just . . ." I pause, glancing at my alarm clock for effect. "Let's go check the cookies."

"No."

"Excuse me?" I wait for him to grin.

He doesn't. "You honestly think you can ply me with delicious baked goods?"

*No. Unless you let me.*

I laugh but it's forced. "Yeah, right, come on. You really think I would do that?"

"I think you're doing it."

"I— Oh God." I drop my head into my hands. "I'm sorry. I'm so sorry. You're right. I don't know what's wrong with me."

"You lost your best friend. It's making you crazy." He lifts my chin with his hand. "And it *is* making you crazy. I'm not afraid to tell you, girl."

I smile, a little. "I'm not trying to manipulate you."

*Yes, I am.*

"I mean, I'm not trying to hurt you." I hold his gaze so he can see that I'm being sincere. Those dark eyes stare back at me. "I just need to understand."

"Can you promise me you won't use the information against her?"

A pause. "Is that the only way you'll help me?"

"Yes." He answers without hesitation. It must be nice to have that kind of integrity.

But I'm the one who's going to get things done. "You have my word. I just need to know if she's guilty."

"Guilty of what, exactly?"

"Writing SLUT all over Lizzie's car."

He takes in a breath. "Really?"

"She was spotted at the scene of the crime. On her hands and knees, no less. The whole shebang."

"Who told you this?"

"I can't reveal my sources. I have it on good authority, though."

Well, I have it on *an* authority. "But what I really want to know is why. Did she really hate Lizzie that badly?"

He squirms. "I'll be lucky to get her alone for two minutes."

"She likes you. You told me that."

"To fess up to this, she'd better love me."

"Who wouldn't?"

I'm teasing. I totally am.

"I meant what I said before." He touches my hand. "You have to let this go."

"You have to let this go, *Princess*," I correct, though it's not the word I'm wanting. Too many games I'm playing. My head starts to spin.

"As you wish," he says, bowing his head.

"Get up." I stand to hide my burning cheeks. "Your cookies are going to be black."

"They better not be!" He skips past me to the stairs. "Cookies, cookies, cookies," he sings.

I'm laughing as I follow him down.

And I'm thinking of how I never felt this comfortable with my ex.

# twelve

BY THE TIME we were in high school, Lizzie and Drake were both gorgeous in their own way. Superficially speaking, they were made for each other. But there were other factors to consider. Like, for example, Drake's parents were separating just as mine were finalizing their divorce. Who, in all of Verity, could comfort him better than me?

I just needed to get his attention. I needed, at least, to keep these beautiful people from leaving me behind.

So I decided to give myself a new look. I spent a decent chunk of my savings on tools to straighten my hair. Then came the contacts, the form-fitting clothes. I even practiced my walk. And when I swaggered into Verity High, with a carefully perfected look of disinterest, I pretty much expected someone to hurl fruit at me.

But you know what? They kind of bought it. The girls didn't sneer at me, at least not to my face. And the guys actually noticed I existed. Sure, I lived in fear of someone discovering my inner freak, but I'd felt that way for years.

This way, I got to have a little fun.

So there I was, the first week of school, lounging by my locker with my BFF, when who should appear but Boy Crush No. 1, dark-haired, blue-eyed Drake. He'd grown even taller over the past few years, and his wavy hair crept past his ears. He looked like a god. No, he looked like a model, and I was willing to buy whatever he was selling.

Too bad he wasn't selling to me.

"Hey, Lizzie." He smiled sweetly at my beautiful best friend.

"Hi, Drake," said our resident flower child. She was wearing brown boots and a white lace dress. Homemade. Suddenly I felt incredibly generic in my low-rise jeans and department store T-shirt. Like a copy of a copy. "You know Angie?" she asked, nodding at me. Bless her, she remembered me. I wasn't invisible.

"Of course I know Angie." Drake's hypnotic eyes shifted to me. He actually smiled.

"Hey," I said, all ease and grace. Of course, any minute I'd forget how to use my legs. Never mind that I was propped up against the lockers.

*I'd like to prop* him *up against the lockers.*

Now my face was burning. My entire being was burning, filled with embarrassment and yearning at the same time. With Drake's eyes on me, I felt mature, powerful, and wild. I didn't want the moment to end.

Of course, it did.

"Hey, can I talk to you a minute?" he said.

The "yes" was already out of my mouth when I realized he'd returned his attention to Lizzie. "I mean, you guys talk," I said quickly. "I'll see you in class." Really, it was a miracle those words made it past my lips. I could feel the tears forming in my eyes, stinging and reminding me of my place.

"Hold on," Lizzie called after me. "Drake, we were talking."

"This'll just take a second," he promised.

"That's not the point." It was amazing how cool she was being, when she should've been basking in the joy of Drake's affections. She was so nice. Too nice.

She deserved him.

I twisted my grimace into a grin. "We'll talk later. We have all day to talk."

I hurried to the bathroom. I thought I was going to erupt but the tears never came. I just stood there staring in the mirror, wondering how I ever thought Drake could love me.

Just then, a stall opened and the first of two crazy things happened. This tall, leggy blonde with boobs out to there stopped dead in her tracks, eyeing me up and down.

"You're hot. Are you a freshman?"

"Um. Yeah."

"You should try out for the squad."

*The Geek Squad? Ha-ha, very funny.*

I just looked at her, afraid to open my mouth.

"Trust me, it's not as dumb as it sounds," she said, adjusting her sweater to accentuate her chest. Her nails were painted to match. Everything red. "The cheering is just a cover for the real fun."

"Meaning?"

"You know, the parties, the pranks." She rolled her eyes dramatically. "The prestige."

"You want me?"

"Oh, please. Insecurity is so boring." She smirked at my reflection, fluffing up her hair. "So your hips are a little wide. Wear skirts."

I gasped. "Are you my fairy godmother?"

"Good, you've got a sense of humor. You'll need that, cheering for guys who can't play."

"And my gigantic hips won't be a problem?" Sure, I knew they were big. But hearing it still sucked.

"Oh, don't twist your panties." She pinched my cheek, but it wasn't motherly. It was a warning. Those sharp nails could draw blood at any time. "I already said you were hot."

I smiled. I couldn't help it.

"Besides," she said, turning back to her reflection, "if big hips were a deal-breaker, I wouldn't have invited my little sissy to try out. Maybe you know her? Name's Kennedy."

"I've heard of her," I said casually. Of course, who hadn't? Kennedy McLaughlin was the girl who got a real live pony on her seventh birthday. What kind of person would forget that?

"You'll hear more," Big Sissy said. "Three o'clock, okay?"

She didn't wait for my reply. She sashayed out of the room just as the bell rang. But I was frozen in place. A part of me suspected this bathroom was a portal to another dimension, a dimension where dorks were sexy and popular. I wasn't sure I wanted to leave yet.

Good thing too. Just seconds after Cheer Girl's exit, Lizzie swept into the room, looking frazzled and a bit out of breath. And then the second totally crazy thing happened:

"He's going to ask you out," she said.

"What?"

*Alternate dimension, remember? Just go with it.*

"Drake is going to ask you out." She started reglossing her lips.

"Are you okay?" I teased. "You look pale. Do you have a fever?" I held my hand to her forehead.

"I'm not hallucinating!" She jerked away from me. Her reply was a bit snappish. Was she mad? Or disappointed? I reminded myself that she liked Drake too.

"I'll just tell him no," I said. It was the last thing in the world I wanted to say. But Lizzie was clearly upset.

Smoothing down her hair, she turned to look at me. "Why would you do that?"

Any other time, in any other bathroom, I would have just lied. But there, that day, I couldn't.

"Because I know you like him."

"I *what?*" She scoffed way too loudly. "I do *not* like him."

And she started listing off her reasons. He was ordinary. He was boring. Too tall. Kind of clumsy. At first, I thought she was trying to convince herself. But by the end of the list I started to believe her. After all, it was possible that I'd misread her all this time. Lizzie was so protective of her feelings. She could've liked any number of brown-haired, blue-eyed boys.

"Are you serious?" I asked.

"Why would I lie?"

I looked at her then, really looked at her. I think I was trying to see into the depths of her soul. It struck me, in that moment, that I had blabbed so many of my secrets, yet I knew so few of hers. Who *did* she like? What did she *really* think of me?

She hadn't said a word about my transformation.

"You have to tell me," I said. "You have to tell me who you like. It's the only way I'll believe you."

"Do you want to go out with him?"

"Yes." Again, I couldn't lie.

*Stupid bathroom.*

"Do you?" I asked gingerly.

Lizzie lowered her head. Why was it so hard for her to open up to me? What was she afraid of?

"I don't," she said.

"I don't believe you."

"I'm not lying."

"You're not telling me the whole truth."

"I will."

"You promise?"

"Yes." She lifted her head. Her voice was shaking, and her green eyes glittered in the fluorescent light. "Just not today."

Any other time, in any other bathroom, I wouldn't have chosen to believe her. But there, that day, I did.

# thirteen

P ARTY TIME!"

Okay, that's what I would be saying if I could go back in time. If I could just return to the beginning of spring I would be fun-loving Angie, joined with Drake at the hip and up for a grand old time. Preparing for a bash after Lizzie's death is a bit like returning to the Alternate Dimension Bathroom.

The motions are all the same, but they feel different.

"You look different," my mother says as I examine my reflection in the glass of the front door. It's eight thirty-five. Jesse is late.

I shiver before I realize Mom's talking about my outfit. She's not so good at the whole mind-reading thing. "I look sexy," I say. "Don't you think?" I'm wearing this skintight suit over a satin corset that pushes my boobs up to my chin. Everything black. I look dangerous and feminine and masculine at the same time.

Jesse better love it.

Mother doesn't. "I think you need some color," says the collector of the cement-gray pantsuit.

"I want to complement my date."

"No shit," she says.

I follow her gaze through the glass. There's Jesse skipping up the walkway, wearing his raspberry froufrou skirt over dark pants.

"He's going to outdress me at every turn," I say. "This could be a problem."

Mom can't read sarcasm. "Do we need to have a talk?"

"About how happy you are that I've made a friend?"

"Angelina."

"Yes, he's gay, Mother. So you don't have to worry about me sleeping with him."

She frowns into her Syrah. "Your father did talk to you about sex. He did," she insists to herself.

Oh my God. This is not happening.

"Um. I'm seventeen years old," I say.

"Answer the question."

"Yes, he did. Totally."

*Is she kidding?*

"Honey?" she says.

"Pills. Bitchiness. Bloating. No baby." I can see Jesse poised to ring the bell. "We done here?"

She kisses my forehead rigidly. "Have fun, sweetie."

I'm out the door faster than she can say "condom." Jesse waves to her as I close it in her face. "Wow-y, mama," he croons, looking me over. "You look like sex on wheels."

"On *heels*." I lift my foot. My shoes are chunky with a strap. None of that stiletto crap for me.

"Retro."

"You look great," I say. His hair is slicked back, kind of. Some of the strands are trying to rebel. He's got on this black collared shirt. I can't tell if it's a women's top or one of those really tight tailored ones for men. And then I wonder why that should matter.

"You ready for this?" I take his arm.

He hesitates. "I've never been invited to a fancy-people party. You think they'll throw things at me?"

"Only if they want to invoke my wrath."

He lays his head on my shoulder. "You scare me, honey."

"You love it."

The drive to Cara's is short. The "fancy-people" houses are all within a five-mile radius of each other. Elevated on a hill, looking down on the town.

*Looking down.*

The night is dark, but Cara's house blazes from within. She's got these red lights on in the living room like it's a brothel. Maybe it is, in a way. I don't think very highly of these people.

Could you tell?

There are so many cars out front I have to park two blocks away. Jesse bolts around the side of the car to open my door. He takes my arm again as we reach the walkway. We're almost to the house when he stops.

"This is wrong. We've made a mistake."

"No, it's fine," I say. A few stocky boneheads are standing on the porch. "They'll let us in, no problem."

"That's not what I mean." He pulls me over to the shadows. "If Kennedy sees us here together, she'll know we're in cahoots."

"'Cahoots?' I thought you said we weren't spies."

"I'm being serious."

"Kennedy's not here yet."

He frowns at the street. "You didn't see her car?"

"I didn't look for it."

"So?"

I start to walk forward again. I'm practically dragging him along. "So. Beauty Queen? Most popular girl in school? If you think she's not fashionably late to everything, you haven't been paying attention."

I can see his cheeks growing round in the darkness. He's smiling. "All right, fine," he says begrudgingly. "But once we get inside you better not stick to me."

He has a point. But I'm not leaving him alone with these freaks. "I'll stick to you like glue, baby." The word is out of my mouth before I can stop it.

INSIDE OF CARA'S minimansion, the crimson-walled living room swells with the push of bodies, the pulse of the music. Furniture has been pushed aside, and red lights flicker, inviting us into the inferno. Though it's entirely unnecessary, the fireplace is lit.

People are already taking off their clothes.

I don't mean everybody. The party's not that orgiastic. But a few key players hint at a world of possibilities: a redhead in the corner flashes a polka-dotted bra to her girlfriends, while two shirtless guys flex muscles no high school boy should have. These are the boys who'll spend their lives trying to look like the Photoshopped actors in *Details* magazine. They'll kill themselves for their bodies, just like the girls do.

Still, these flashes of skin can't compare to the girl standing on the wet bar, reciting a scene in iambic pentameter. A very saucy scene, if her lewd gestures are any indication. Miss Shelby McQueen gives the people what they want, and tonight the people want sex. Her black flapper dress swishes as she thrusts her hips.

I step back.

"You okay?" Jesse asks, lips close to my ear. He's pressed against me, due to the lack of room in this crowded space.

"I'm fine," I lie.

In reality I'm shaken. This amped-up sexuality reminds me of other things, of people who'll whisper *I love you* when they're inside of you, only to turn around and do the same with your best friend. When Jesse whispers "Let's go out back," I let him lead me toward the back porch. There's a bowl on the wet bar marked Mystery Juice and we stop there, because, you know, when in Rome.

After that we slip into the darkness.

Except it's not dark. Not entirely. Out here they've strung up dangling icicle lights and people are pressed together by choice. Farther out, there's this beautiful stretch of grass just calling to us, and that's where we go.

"Let's hang out here for a while," Jesse says, sitting on a bench that's clearly made for lovers. Little flower beds surround the entire yard, in shades of purple, pink, and red.

It's Valentine's Day every day at the Belle estate.

"Good plan." I sit beside him. There's not much room on the bench, and I'm close enough to Jesse to feel him shaking. But when I go to give him my jacket, I find no goose bumps on his arms.

He's not shivering.

He's scared.

"I brought you into the belly of the beast, didn't I?" Sure, no one's shoved him or called him a name yet. But no one's smiled at him or welcomed him into a hug either.

They'll ignore him, just like they did with Lizzie.

*Until they get him alone.*

"I'm okay," he says, looking up at the sky. Those icicle lights are nothing compared to the stars, and I follow his gaze, soothed by the vastness of space.

"Are you sure?" I ask softly. "Because I can find another way—"

"No, it's fine." He turns to look at me, and the lights are reflected in his eyes. "I was curious."

"Well, curiosity quenched, then."

He laughs. "Besides, it's nice out here with you . . ." He trails off, hands curling over the front of the bench. When he leans back, taking in all the stars, I can't help but notice the muscles in his arms. They're sort of . . . delicate, compared to the ones on the show-offs inside. The kind you get from working in the yard or picking up little kids.

The kind you get from life.

Jesse closes his eyes, and my gaze trails to his face. I'm watching his mouth to see if he really wants to stay. Everyone looks at the eyes, but the lips are so telling.

I watch them carefully as I say, "Can I ask you something?"

His lips twitch. I can tell he's fighting a smile. "Aw, hell," he says, "tell me you're not serious. Tell me you didn't bring me here to interrogate me."

"No, of course not." I bring my cup to my lips. It tastes like rum, light and dark, with juice for coloring. The second it hits my stomach I start to relax. This isn't healthy, but I don't know how to stop it.

"I'm waiting," says Jesse, opening one eye.

"I just, I sort of wondered . . ." I take another sip. They call it liquid courage for a reason. But it's also liquid stupidity, and it goes from one to the other really fast. You have to be careful. "I saw Shelby in there." I gesture to the house. "And I know she's your friend—"

"No," he says, but doesn't elaborate.

"Well, you worked together on plays and stuff."

"Yes."

"And you get along."

He shrugs, as much as he can from his position. "I get along with everybody. If it's up to me."

I have nothing to say to that. And since I can't bear the thought of him pushing Lizzie out of the play, I do something stupid. I give him an out: "Then you know what Shelby did when Lizzie got cast."

He doesn't say anything, but now both eyes are open.

"Jesse?" I exhale slowly. "Do you know—"

He sits up fast. One blink of the eye, and he's right there next to me. As if taking my lead on irresponsible coping mechanisms, he takes a gulp of his punch.

His face scrunches. It's so adorable, I'm almost laughing, and it softens the blow when he says, "I don't know what happened, exactly. But I think it had something to do with her dad."

"Shelby's dad?"

"Lizzie's dad. The preacher, right?"

My pulse quickens. I should be relieved that he's asserting his innocence, but I'm not. I'm afraid. "Yeah. You go to his church?"

"Hell no." He snorts. "I tend not to worship in places where people hate me."

I tilt my head in close, because he's clearly got something to get off his chest. "What makes you think he hates you?"

"He pretty much told her," he says, taking another sip. "I came over the week before opening night, to work on costumes. Lizzie's a hard-core seamstress, you know? Two sewing machines, all this fabric. We had a good time, but the next day at rehearsal, she's like, 'Let's go to your house,' being all shady. I had to bug her and bug her until she admitted I wasn't allowed over again."

"What? Why?"

He gestures to his skirt. "Think about it."

"Oh. Really?"

"I mean, I get it," he says. "Adults get uncomfortable. But I never got *banned* before."

"He banned you?" I laugh, though it's really not funny.

"Something like that," Jesse says. "Guess he pulled her real close and was like, 'You know how I warned you about premarital sex? Well, what *those people* do is a thousand times worse.'"

"Ho-ly shit."

"Pretty bad, right?" He shrugs, shaking it off. But I can tell it sticks. "I mean, I know that shit is out there, but it still sucks to hear about it."

"I'm sorry." I touch his hand, and I swear I'm just comforting him.

He doesn't seem to mind. He turns his hand over, lacing his fingers through mine. "I'm a big boy. Didn't I tell you?" He grins. "But I felt bad for her, you know, living with that guy?" He pauses, looks around. "I felt worse when I heard people gossiping about it."

I wait a beat, trying to piece together what he's saying. But I can't figure it out. "People found out Lizzie's dad's a bigot? So what? Why would they care?"

"I don't think it was that. I think it was the premarital sex stuff." He leans in. He smells like punch. I can smell the fruit on him more than I can taste it. Maybe everything tastes sweeter on him.

Maybe I shouldn't be having thoughts like that.

I take back my hand. He follows the movement with his eyes, saying, "You know how Shakespeare is: he sounds all fancy, but mostly he's just talking about sex?"

"Oh, yeah. Oh shit." My brain is reeling. I'm too embarrassed to admit I didn't know Shakespeare wrote so much about sex. But I think of Shelby, standing on the wet bar, reciting something fancy.

Something fancy about sex.

"But what could they have done with that information?" Now I'm leaning in. Our lips are close, our upper bodies almost touching. This is the good and bad thing about playing detective. When you hate the person, it makes your skin crawl to be this close. But when you don't hate them at all . . .

"I don't know." Jesse shakes his head. His hair tickles me, and I want to tuck it behind his ear. "But Lizzie was weird about me coming over that day. Weird, like, 'Don't tell my dad we're doing this for a play. It's just a school project.' Shit like that. I didn't think anyone was listening, but we were talking in the auditorium, and anybody could've been hiding in the wings. We talked *a lot* in there, Angie—"

"Oh God." My hand goes to my lips. "I never even thought about it. But Lizzie wouldn't invite him, would she? Not if there was as much sex as you say. He would've forbidden her . . ."

And there, ladies and gentlemen, is the piece I've been missing. Only one person could keep Lizzie from performing in the play. The same person who kept her from riding to school in the car she loved.

Daddy dearest.

# fourteen

KENNEDY DOESN'T SHOW until well after Shelby leaves, and by then Jesse's already drunk. I don't think he usually drinks. We're back in the living room, and he's bopping around to *the dumbest* song in the world while I'm trying to calculate the likelihood of Captain Morgan blowing our cover. Drunk people aren't exactly known for their discretion. They act first and think later. Then again, if Kennedy thinks he's wasted, she might open up more easily. There's no harm in blabbing your secrets to a confidant who won't remember it in the morning.

Of course, she won't plan on my listening in. But what she doesn't know won't hurt her. Jesse made sure of that.

*Damn him.*

Right now, Kennedy's on the other side of the room, watching some guy do a beer bong. She hasn't even looked in our direction. Then, out of nowhere, Jesse goes all gentleman on me and offers to get me another drink. My "no thanks" is halfway out of my lips when I realize he's giving me a sign. I swallow my words and nod, not trusting my voice. I'm nervous, okay? I can admit it.

Kennedy squeals when she sees him and they do that Parisian air-kiss thing. Then she gives him this hug like she's never been happier to see anybody in her life. She holds on way longer than necessary, which means she's either really lonely or really drunk. And since she never goes anywhere without a slew of copycat cheerleaders and a bunch of drooling douche bags, I'm guessing it's the booze.

She probably took shots on the drive over.

For the first time I wonder if she has some kind of death wish. Not all attempts at suicide are as obvious as Lizzie's.

Jesse steers Kennedy to a painting above the mantel: a satyr surrounded by nymphs. She has to turn her back on me to look at it. He winks in my direction, whispering something that makes her bray like a donkey.

*That's my cue.*

I turn and push my way through the crowd. It's not as easy as you'd think. These bulky guys are gathered in clusters, and their drunkenness has apparently rendered them oblivious to their surroundings. I push. I try to slide through. I say nice little "excuse me" type things. No dice.

*Time to improvise.*

"Oh God," I moan, slapping my hand over my mouth. I practically fall into the guy standing closest to me. He leaps back like he's perfectly content to watch me crash to the floor. Better I crack my head open than get vomit on his superawesome Sports Shack T-shirt.

Still, my act does the trick. The crowd parts to let through the sick girl. I bolt up the stairs like I'm going to spew Mystery Juice all over the place and open the first door I see. I'm hoping for Cara's bedroom.

*Wrong! Try again!*

The master bedroom sprawls out before me, all pomp and

frills. These people actually have black satin sheets. I'm turning around to leave when the absolute last person I want to see steps into the room. He checks the lock on the door before he sees me.

"Got big plans?" I ask.

Drake practically jumps out of his skin. God, what I'd pay to see that. I'm actually envisioning it as he closes the door and leans against it: that pretty exterior sloughing off to reveal his true form.

"Angie." He wipes his forehead like it's sweaty. "Hey. I didn't know you were here."

"I imagine it's difficult with me standing right in front of you."

*Why are you being so hard on him? He's human, like Lizzie's human. They made a mistake.*

Still, it bugs me when he doesn't look wounded.

Actually, he kind of laughs. "Hey, can I talk to you somewhere?"

"Somewhere . . . else?"

He glances at the door. "Yeah. Don't you think?"

"What?"

"I mean, Cara'll probably be pissed that we're in here."

"Look at you, growing a conscience. You surprise me every day."

*Get him out of here. You have no time.*

"Give me a break," he says, looking at the door again. I want to ask what he's checking for but there's *no time.*

"You're right," I say. "I want to talk to you too. But this place is so crowded. Meet me at my car in two minutes?"

"Your car? We can just go down—"

"Please?" I place my hand on his chest, over his heart. "I really want to be alone with you."

"Okay." He opens the door a crack and peers down the hall. "Okay, good. Let's do that."

"Cool." I push past him. "I just have to pee."

He grabs my arm. I can see Jesse at the bottom of the stairs, trying to pull Kennedy away from these brothers who've been fighting over her all year. I wave to him but he doesn't see me.

"That one's full." Drake nods to the bathroom. "I think someone's sick in there."

"I'll wait," I say. I'm giving him a nudge toward the stairs when the bathroom door opens. Out comes Cara herself, wiping vomit from her mouth.

"Hey, baby." She slumps against Drake. Her dark hair spills over his shoulder. "I got the—Angie!" she shrieks, just noticing me. "I'm so glad you came!" Pushing off Drake's chest, she hurls herself at me. Her arms drape sloppily around my neck.

Kennedy and Jesse are climbing the stairs, Drake's standing, stunned, between us, and I'm stumbling under the weight of a drunken hug-attack. Could things possibly get worse?

*Come on, Universe, I dare you.*

My head is spinning. I'm frozen in a vortex of possibilities: Stall Jesse. Throw Drake over the banister. Question Kennedy. Get Cara *off me*.

"Look." Drake's voice penetrates the vortex. "This is not what it looks like."

"Oh my God, the best line ever." I shift Cara to my left shoulder. My other arm is free now, for punching. Or whatever.

"Wait," Cara slurs, doing this sad fairy jig to keep from falling. "Are you mad?"

"I'm great, sweetie," I tell her. There's no point in lecturing a drunk person. Living with Mom has taught me that. "You listen to me," I hiss at Drake. "If you ever want to speak to me again, you'd better do exactly as I say."

"Angie." He gestures at Cara. "I wasn't—"

"I hope not." I lead Cara into her parents' room. Drake follows. "She's completely wasted. That's disgusting."

"*I'm* wasted . . ." he says pathetically. And the thing is, he's *totally not.* I've seen him wasted. This is buzzed at best.

"Please hold while I contact Future Rapists of America." I lay Cara on the bed. She curls up happily. "Now go stall Kennedy. I don't want her seeing her friend like this."

Yeah, I know, how thoughtful of me. Apparently I'll lie about anything to get my way. On the other hand, I only have sex with fully conscious people, so I don't feel too bad about tricking Drake.

I cover Cara with a blanket and turn off the light. A quick look through the door shows Drake blocking the stairs. Still, Kennedy and Jesse are almost to the top, and both will see me if I step into the hallway. Drake's midway through some animated story, pulling back his arm and letting it fly like he's throwing a football. Or giving them an archery lesson.

Could be either with him.

I say a quick prayer that the story is interesting. Then I drop to my hands and knees. Down low to the ground, Kennedy won't be able to see me, so I worm-wiggle across the carpet toward the other bedroom. This type of thing is always supersexy in the movies. In real life it's sad and ridiculous. I have to laugh to keep from crying.

Still, the moment I'm safely hidden behind Cara's bedroom door I start laughing giddily. I can't believe I actually did it. I waste no time in slipping into the closet. It's got those double doors with slats you can see through, if you stick your nose up to them. I won't be able to see Kennedy that well but I'll be able to hear everything.

Yeah, I'm feeling pretty smug. Except when Jesse flips on the bedroom light and I realize I've left Drake a door away from Cara.

Okay, he's sleazy, but he's not that sleazy.

*He can't be.*

I send him a quick text reminding him to meet me at my car, and threatening his manhood if he so much as touches Cara with a stick. He doesn't reply, but I'm sure he got the message. One time he stopped in the middle of sex to answer a text.

Jesse sits down next to Kennedy, complimenting her bright pink party dress. I lean in, listening.

"I look like crap," she counters. She's a little calmer now that she's away from the craziness. Maybe she's not as drunk as she seemed. That's okay, I decide. Getting answers from her when she's wasted feels a little too much like Drake scamming on Cara. Not the same thing, sure, but still dirty.

*Says the girl crouched in the closet.*

Jesse touches Kennedy's hair. "You're full of shit."

She giggles, laying her head on his shoulder. "I'm glad you came tonight."

"I wanted to talk to you."

"You did?"

Jesse looks at her, frowning. I can just make out the curve of his lips through the slats in the door. "I heard something bad."

"Good-bad?" she suggests.

He shakes his head.

"What is it?" Her voice is a gushing whisper, like her life depends on his answer. I guess when reputation is all you have, well . . . it's *all you have.*

"Something about Lizzie," he says.

"You know how I feel about—"

"Something about Lizzie's car."

"Oh. Shit."

He scoots away from her. I can hear it better than I can see it. "It's true then."

"Look, they didn't mean it," she says, gesticulating wildly. "They were just being stupid."

"They? Who are they?" He holds up a hand. "The rumor is about you."

"Me? *No, no, no.* That's bullshit. You heard wrong."

"You sure about that?"

"You know me, Jesse. You know how I feel about her. *That family.*"

What about Lizzie's family? There's venom in her voice I've never heard.

"You don't have to tell me." He glances nervously at the closet. At me?

"I would never do that," Kennedy says. Her voice is pleading. "I would never even draw attention to— What exactly did you hear?"

"Pretty much you, on your hands and knees, in front of Lizzie's car."

"I was on my hands and knees, yes, but not in front of—" She stops. "Sorry. Not the time for joking?"

"I don't mind." He sounds amicable enough. I can tell he believes her. Or he wants to believe her. Sometimes there's not much of a difference.

"Look," she says, leaning into him again, "if I tell you, will you promise to be discreet? If people find out who wrote on that car, things could get really ugly."

*Good. That's the idea.*

Jesse hesitates. I know he's thinking the same thing I am. I only promised Kennedy immunity because I had to. I said nothing about her accomplices.

Still, he can't stop her now without raising suspicion. "I won't tell anybody," he says in a low voice.

"The girls did it. Cara and Elliot. They did it for me."

"What?"

"No, not *for* me. I didn't tell them to. They did it because they know how I feel about her. How I felt. They thought they were doing a good thing, like I was going to give them a cookie or something."

"So you didn't have anything to do with it? You didn't even go near the car?"

"I went to clean up after them," she snaps. Clearly she doesn't respond well to accusations. "I didn't want people seeing that. It's beneath us."

"Apparently not."

"Hey, I tried my best."

"Her car was covered when people got to school. Your best seems kind of—"

"I got caught!"

"By who?"

"Some dork with a sketchpad."

"Who was it?"

"I don't know." She shakes her head. That blond hair flies out around her, like dandelion spores before they've taken to the wind. "He was too far away."

"So you bolted?"

"Yes, I bolted! The guy was a creeper! I think he pulled out his phone." She lowers her voice. "Think of what he could do with a picture of me next to that car. Print out copies and pass it around?"

Oh God. What are the chances the guy peeping on Kennedy with a sketchpad *isn't* the guy who sketched the imitation playing card of Lizzie?

*Or imitation Alchemy card*, I think, remembering Marvin's hurry to hide those cards from me.

For a moment, I imagine my heart is covered with scars. Here, a crack for Shelby. There, a slash for Marvin. A little *X* for Elliot and Cara. A gaping wound for Lizzie.

Jesse's words bring me back. "At least you tried," he tells Kennedy.

"I had to try." She inhales slowly. "When they told me what

they did, it made me realize how messed up it was to blame her for what happened."

"It's okay," Jesse says, and I can feel his gaze on me. I wish I could move this damn shirt that's dangling in my face. Slowly, carefully, I reach up and slide it to the left.

The hanger gives a screech.

I freeze, holding my breath. We've come too far to mess up everything with this nightmare of a paisley shirt. I curse Cara for buying something so ugly. I curse myself for getting into this situation.

But Kennedy doesn't even look my way. She's too busy blinking furiously. Her teeth are attacking her lip. "It's not okay," she says, swallowing. "You should've heard the way I chewed them out." She lowers her head to her hands. "I've been so mad for so long. I hated him."

*Him?*

"It's okay," Jesse says again. His hands are fidgeting. He doesn't want her to talk about this here.

But I do. I really do.

"I guess I hated her too," says Kennedy. "I just wanted . . . I didn't want to hurt them. But—"

"I know." He keeps trying to cut her off, but short of covering her mouth, he's helpless.

The words are spilling out of her. "I didn't want to know they existed. I just wanted them to disappear. And then she died, and I felt like—"

"You didn't cause it."

"I didn't help!" She lifts her head. Her mascara is smeared. I have never, ever seen Kennedy cry.

It's horrifying.

Jesse's looking in my direction more and more and I want to yell at him to stop it. Of course, that would be counterproductive.

This time she notices. "What are you doing?"

"I don't think we should talk about this here. Anybody could come in—"

"From the closet? Are you worried about monsters?"

"N-no." He gestures to the bedroom door. "I just think—I feel like—"

Oh no. He's losing it. Mayday! Mayday! Someone please intercept . . .

"I am sick to death of keeping quiet," says Kennedy. "The one time I want to talk about it—"

"I know, sweetie. I know." He reaches over and touches her face. She's mesmerized, temporarily. Then he leans in and kisses her cheek, close to her lips.

Now my heart is pounding like I'm being chased. Or like I'm missing something. Or like I know too much to process.

Jesse pulls away, tucking her hair behind her ear. "I just don't trust people here," he says. "You can talk to me anytime."

"I know." She nods, watching him. "I'm sorry I lost it."

"You didn't. It's fine."

"I think I need to get out of here."

"I'll call you a cab."

"I'm fine," she says, standing. But it takes her two tries, and that doesn't help her case.

"*Fine* is putting it mildly," Jesse jokes. "That's why I don't want you messing up your pretty face."

"Okay." She laughs, despite herself. "Fine. You take good care of me."

He slides an arm around her waist. "It's easy."

They're halfway across the room when Drake decides to text me back.

And, yes, I did forget to put my phone on silent.

# fifteen

KENNEDY FLINGS OPEN the closet doors. Cara's room unfolds like a purple explosion. Her walls are lilac, her comforter's so dark it's almost black, and a dozen violet and plum pillows cover her bed. Cara's a modern-day princess.

And Kennedy's a queen who wants my head. "What the hell do you think you're doing?" she demands.

*I'm screwed. I'm screwed. I'm royally screwed.*

Even worse, I've screwed Jesse. I have to find a way out of this.

"Did you plan this?" Kennedy's eyes are all fire, flicking from me to him. Her mouth is so big it could swallow us both.

I rise to my feet. "How *dare you*," I snarl at Jesse, widening my eyes for half a second to warn him.

"Wh-what?" he says. I can tell part of him is terrified. But the other part wants to see where I'm going with this.

*Bless his curiosity.*

I stomp out of the closet, lightly pushing his chest. "You told me you wanted to come here with me."

"What?" Kennedy says.

I ignore her. "You said you wanted to dance with me. And then you disappear and I track you down with this . . . this . . ."

"Go on," she challenges.

"She's so typical," I shriek. "So obvious. Is that what you want?"

Jesse shakes his head. "I don't understand."

"You know he's gay, right?" Kennedy holds out an arm to separate us. "What happened to you, Angie?"

"I made a mistake," I say, slapping her arm away. Yeah, I'm risking getting punched here, but it's worth it. I've never played *complete psycho* before. It's kind of comforting to have no boundaries. "I actually believed you liked me."

Jesse opens his mouth but I cut him off.

"And now I find you kissing *her* when you're supposed to be here with me?"

"That was a friend kiss," Jesse insists. "Kennedy and I are friends. Like you and me . . ."

"Oh sure, that's why you made cookies with me. At *my house*."

"You went to her house?" Now Kennedy's staring at him.

"That's why you called me baby." Okay, I'm drawing on real experiences now but only to make it sound genuine. It's *not* because I actually felt close to him in certain moments. That would be ridiculous.

Kennedy's hands go to her hips. "You called her baby?" She huffs. "You never said that to me."

"Please," Jesse drawls, all flair and sass: something he does, I've noticed, not when he's comfortable but when he's cornered. "I call you that all the time, honey. You need to open your ears." He turns to face me and, because Kennedy can't see it, winks. "You're a psycho."

I hold a hand to my lips. "Don't say that."

"You hid in here to listen to me?"

"Of course not." I shake my head like he's being dramatic. "Cara said I could borrow a sweater, so I came up here to get one. Then I heard you coming in the door, and I closed the closet to see if you were cheating on me. I had every right, because look at what you're doing! So you can't say—"

"Cheating? Honey, are you delusional? I just—I can't—" He flings his hands in the air. "I need to get out of here."

"Oh, sure, run away from our problems," I shout after him. He's taken hold of Kennedy's arm and is leading her out of the room. "This won't just go away!"

I tromp after them. Already they're halfway down the stairs. "Call me?" I yell as they disappear into the crowd.

My heart is racing.

Another text comes in. I pause to check my phone. Drake's first message says, "What the hell?" His second says, "I wasn't going to do anything."

That reminds me. I check on Cara before heading downstairs. She's sleeping soundly on her parents' bed. The blanket is just as I left it. I take that as a good sign. Still, when I see Elliot dancing in the living room, I tell her Cara's passed out in the master bedroom. She seems sober enough to keep an eye on things.

Outside, the cold air is a pleasant relief for my too-hot skin. I feel itchy, like you do after rolling in grass. From the porch, I can see Jesse getting into a cab with Kennedy. I guess there really wasn't any way for us to leave together after my little outburst.

*Little. Right. That performance should get me an Emmy.*

Drake is still waiting for me by my car. I can't believe it. He starts to stammer as I approach. He's shivering from the cold. I walk right by without saying a word and get into the driver's seat.

He has to jump back when I pull away from the curb.

The motion of the car is soothing to my nerves. The exhaustion hits me all at once. My body and brain are conspiring to make me fall asleep. I flip on the radio to keep me company. The drive isn't that long.

*I've made it through worse.*

Because I have the radio blaring, I almost miss it when the text comes in.

It's Jesse. He says, "You were amazing," just as I pull into my mom's driveway.

Suddenly I'm wide awake. I write back, "You were better."

My heart drops when he doesn't respond right away. I've been sitting in my car for several minutes when he texts, "I miss you, spy-buddy."

It takes two seconds for my brain to fill up with the words, *No, no, don't you dare*, but only one second to hit send.

"Come over," my message says.


"I TOTALLY JUST snuck out" is the first thing he says when he gets to my house. He's grinning from ear to ear. I bet it's the first time he's snuck out in his entire life.

"You won't have to sneak in," I reply, ushering him inside. Mom's lounging on the couch, half-awake. I haven't warned her that we're having company.

I'm such a naughty kid.

Jesse creeps in. He's changed into jeans and a jacket, with this long embroidered scarf wrapped around him, like, a hundred times. He looks contained.

"Come on," I tell him.

Mom opens her eyes. "Honey?"

"Don't get up," I say.

Her eyes drift to Jesse. She's sitting up in an instant. "Oh my God. Is that Vera Barbatelle?"

He touches his scarf. "Fake."

"Nice replica." She's eyeing it hungrily.

"Let's not rip the clothing off our guests," I say.

"Elizabeth made it for me," says Jesse.

*Lizzie?*

Mother nods. "She was an amazing seamstress."

"We're going upstairs," I say.

Jesse eyes me like, *The truth? Really?*

Mom smiles sleepily, sinking back into the couch. "'Night, honey."

"Nice meeting you," Jesse says.

"Mmm." She's already drifting.

We hurry up the stairs like little kids. By the time we reach my room we're both giggling. I'm not even sure why. I feel like we're getting away with something, like we keep getting away with things. I hope our good luck continues.

*That'd be a nice change.*

Jesse sits in my desk chair this time, draping his jacket over the back. Is he trying to keep his distance from me? If playing a crazy person has taught me anything, it's how uncool it would be to do anything to make him uncomfortable. I sit cross-legged on the middle of my bed, giving him more space.

"I had fun tonight," he says.

"Really?" I had fun too, but I feel like I need to hear him say it again. Like maybe he's just trying to be nice.

"Hell yeah. Don't get me wrong; your jealous-girlfriend bit is scary as hell. But after I cleaned the piss off my pants, I was—"

"Golden?" I suggest.

He grins. "Thanks for covering for me. You didn't have to do that."

"I so did."

"Naw. But it was cool of you."

"That's me. Super cool." I stare at him a long moment. "We sure got a lot of information."

He nods.

"Then you know what I want to ask."

He sighs. "You know I can't answer," he says, and he's not looking at me. I wonder if he's already regretting coming over.

"Hey." I reach out a hand. It's too far away for him to take, but the gesture's what matters. "I didn't invite you over so I could drill you."

"Okay." He smiles a little. Was it my phrasing?

"But you know I have to ask."

"So ask."

"What the hell was Kennedy talking about? Why does she hate Lizzie's family? And who did she mean by *him*?"

The minute the words are out of my mouth, I get it. Not all of it, but enough.

He looks at me like he knows what I'm thinking. "I'm sorry, babe," he says. "I can't tell you."

*Babe.* Close to *baby.* But totally different.

*Enough with the jealous-girlfriend bit.*

"Kennedy hates Lizzie's dad?" I'm watching the air in front of me like the words might be hovering there. Like, at any moment, I can open my mouth and take them back.

Jesse says nothing but his eyes don't leave my face. I think he wants to answer my question. Why can't he?

"I mean, I know he's a frigid old thing. Kind of preachy." I chuckle, because that's his *job.* "Did she go to his church or something? What did he do, ban her when she got breasts?"

Nothing. He's fidgeting, so I know I'm getting close. I keep going even though I shouldn't.

"What could possibly have happened? God, it's not like he's

one of those child-molesting preachers. He's harmless. So why would she . . . Jesse? Why would she . . . ?"

His eyes are still on me. But now they've got that glistening, deer-in-headlights look to them.

"No. Oh, come on. No way."

He doesn't say anything.

That's all right. I can talk to myself all night. "No fucking way. I spent hours at that house when I was little. *I* went to church with her. *I* stayed after."

"I can't talk about this," he says.

"Just tell me I'm wrong."

"I can't talk about this."

"Why?"

"Because I can't keep secrets around you!" His eyes are so wide. "I look at you and you just *know* and it makes me insane because it doesn't make any sense."

"I know what you mean," I say, and I do. I feel the same way.

But he doesn't respond. He's gripping his hair like his brain might fall out. Like all those secrets kept inside will spill out onto my floor. And part of me wants them to.

Part of me wants him to get out of here so I can shift into denial.

"Please talk to me," I say softly.

"Why?" His eyes are closed.

"I need you."

It's not fair to say. If he doesn't want to talk, he shouldn't have to. But I mean it about needing him. Hearing it out loud makes it impossible to deny.

"Kennedy will kill me if she hears about this." He opens his eyes. His lashes are wet, but he's not actually crying. "These aren't my secrets to tell."

I shrug. "You haven't told me anything."

He tilts his head to the side. "Come on."

"You haven't." I scoot closer, toward the edge of the bed. "I wish you would, actually. I wish you would, for once, just be straight-up with me."

He hunches over, elbows on his knees, looking up through his hands. "You can't push me on this."

*Then why are you still talking about it?* I want to ask.

"She was my best friend," I say instead.

"You keep saying that, but you're forgetting something."

"What?"

"She's gone, Angie." He scoots the chair over to the bed. "You're not helping her by doing this."

"I never said I was." I turn away.

"Listen to me." He touches my arm and I hate how good it feels. I know he's just touching me out of pity. "You're digging up shit that isn't going to help you."

"Fine." I comb my hair with my fingers. "I'm sorry I pushed you, then. Let's just watch a movie."

"Okay." He nods, exhaling slowly. I can tell he's relieved.

When I pop the DVD into the player, Jesse joins me on the bed, but the mood's gone to shit. Neither of us is laughing at the jokes on the screen. I keep reading into the lines, like one of them will give me an excuse to bring up Kennedy again, and I'm pretty sure Jesse knows it. His entire body looks tense.

The minute the movie's over, he jumps up like his ass is on fire. "I've got to get back," he says. "I swear my mom still peeks in my room to see if I'm breathing."

"I don't think my mom's ever done that."

"Maybe you were too young to remember." He slides on his jacket. It's a tight-fitted trench with a belt. Perfect for stakeouts. I kind of want to borrow it. "Anyway, it's probably different when you've known her your whole life."

He catches my eye and I realize, once again, how little I know about him. Maybe I would if I weren't so busy asking about other people. Maybe that's why he's looking at me like that.

Or maybe he's just trying to say good-bye.

"I'll walk you down." I crawl to the edge of the bed.

"No worries," he says, crossing the room in two steps. He's gone before I have the chance to stand.

# sixteen

SATURDAY MORNING I go to see my dad. Maybe I've reached my limit on investigating. Or maybe I just need to feel like I'm not alone. I haven't heard from Jesse since he bolted from my room last night, and I'm determined not to contact him first. I'm not trying to play some game. I just need to know he wants to talk to me.

Dad's screen door is hanging on, like, one hinge. I wonder what he's doing with the money Mom gives him. I know it's not a lot. It's not like superstar alimony. But it should be enough to keep things from completely falling apart.

He greets me at the door. He's walking like his leg is fine, but his grimace shows me he's faking. I want to tell him to hobble all he wants.

Of course, that would just insult him.

We walk across the threadbare carpet, past the orange 1970s couch and peeling walls, into the kitchen. Every room is the same color it was when he moved in: white, bleeding into yellow. He insists on making me lunch, which is silly because I've already snacked on leftover chow mein, but I agree and then I hover, cutting cheese slices, melting butter, anything he'll let me. I don't want to ask him about work and he doesn't want to ask about Lizzie. We do this dance, trying to think of things to say.

"Kind of cold for June," he says, tapping the frosted window.

*Weather, Dad, really? Way to dig deep.*

It takes me a minute to realize how quickly time is passing. Lizzie's funeral was one week ago today. So he's still talking about her, in a way.

*Give him a break.*

When he flips our sandwiches in the pan, he burns his finger. He sticks it in his mouth, trying to hide it from me.

"Damn it, Dad, you always do that."

He chuckles a little. "Watch your mouth."

"Yeah, yeah." I want to nudge him in the side like I did when I was a kid. Now it would probably hurt him. He's wearing his usual faded T-shirt and sweats, and he's got that too-lazy-to-shave beard coming in. Or maybe it's more like too depressed.

"You want soup?" I ask.

He busies himself with the pan, moving it an inch left, an inch back. Trying to get the sandwiches to cook evenly. "Nah," he says.

I realize that means he doesn't have any. Bread, butter, and cheese are probably the extent of what he's got left.

"How's your mother?" he asks after another quiet minute.

"She's fine." That's all I'm going to say about her. The whole Angie-in-the-middle game got old years ago. Still, the words slip out of my mouth just like old times: "She's on Atkins this week."

He chortles into his hand. Maybe there's a nice irony to her dieting; like, he's not the only one who's barely eating. "That woman's going to disappear."

"No shit."

"Jesus, Angie. You sounded just like her."

I grin, though it's the last thing I want to hear. "It's contagious."

"Hmmm" is all he says. He pulls two plates down from the cupboard. They've got painted blue roses and tiny cracks in them. His and Mom's wedding dishes.

I wait for the inevitable. He leaves me hanging maybe two minutes.

"Why don't you move back in?" he suggests, setting the plates on the counter.

"Maybe," I say, just as casually.

*You can't afford to keep yourself fed* is what I want to say. *I'd have to get a job and then you'd feel even more guilty.*

"I'll stay for the weekend," I offer, and I can tell he hears everything I haven't said.

"Oh," he says to the cupboards. "Okay."

"I'll pick up dinner at the store."

"Now, listen—"

"I have to go there anyway to get lady items." This is a lie but I know he won't argue with it. Guys are all about blood and gore except when it's realistic.

"Sure thing," he agrees.

I slide the sandwiches onto the plates. "Straight across or diagonal?"

"Do you really have to ask?"

I cut them diagonally. We munch at the counter like two kids eager for recess.


I'M STANDING IN front of the frozen meat section, considering going vegetarian, when I crack. My hand pulls up Jesse's number without the help of my eyes. It just recognizes the motions. Who am I to fight it?

He answers almost immediately. Like maybe he was waiting for me.

*You wish.*

"Are you mad?" I ask, feeling vulnerable under the fluorescent lights.

"Are you going to apologize if I am?"

"Yes." I pick up a flank steak. Dad would kill me if I bought this. He'd kill me and then he'd eat until his pants burst. I throw it in the basket.

"What if I'm not mad?" Jesse presses.

"Then it hardly seems necessary." I know he can hear me smile. It warms me from the inside when he laughs. "Look, I'm sorry I put you on the spot, okay? I just really, really wanted to get the facts."

"That seems to be a pattern with you," he says. "You want the truth so bad you bulldoze over people to get it."

It takes me a second to realize he's serious. When I do, I just stand there, forcing people to maneuver around me. Rooted to the spot.

He must realize how much his words hurt because he changes course before I can speak. "I talked to Kennedy."

"You did?" My voice squeaks. This crotchety old lady glares at me like cell phones are the downfall of civilization. I cover the mouthpiece and tell her, "My daughter just won her first beauty pageant!"

Her eyes go wide like she's very afraid. I walk down the closest aisle.

"What happened?" I ask when Jesse doesn't reply. "Did you tell her what you told me?"

"I told her I didn't tell you."

"Did you tell her I figured it out?"

"Some, yeah," he says.

I pause. I'm trying to choose between instant rice and takes-too-long rice. I'm leaning toward the latter. It tastes better. "Was she mad?"

"She got pissed. Then she got sad. Then she got pissed again. She agreed to meet with you."

I freeze, hand on the box. "Seriously?"

"Yeah. But she says you can't ask her about what happened."

"That doesn't make any sense." I toss the rice into my basket too loudly. Apparently, I need to get my anger under wraps.

"Yeah, it does," he says. "She doesn't want to talk about the personal shit. Would you?"

"I guess I'd have to be in her position," I say. The old lady is eyeing me from the other side of the aisle, like maybe she wants to give me a lecture on teenage abstinence. I hightail it to the veggies. "She really agreed to talk to me?"

"If you don't push her about certain things."

I don't reply. How can I? He's right about the bulldozer thing. Chances are, I'll push her without even trying.

"Angie?"

"I'll do my best."

He waits a beat. "Does this mean you believe her?"

"I don't know." I keep looking around, like people can tell what we're talking about. "I can't yet. I don't think she's lying. I just feel like . . ."

"Maybe there's another possibility?"

"Yeah."

"Like she dreamt it?"

"No."

"Alien abduction?"

"Jesse, stop it. This is really big. You're talking about . . ." I lower my voice, pretending to choose between zucchinis. "How can I accept this? Why wouldn't Lizzie have told me?"

He's a long time in answering. By the time he does, I've picked my veggies and am moving to the checkout line.

"Maybe it's not something you broadcast."


I'VE GOT SEVERAL hours to kill before dinnertime at Dad's. I drop the groceries off while he's taking his afternoon couch nap. The TV's playing old recordings of ESPN: Dad's way of coping with too-high cable bills. Now I've got about twenty seconds to get out of here before the mega-guilt kicks in. I follow the line of shoes leading to the door. This ratty old pair points me right to his crutches.

Then it's too late.

I start cleaning in the kitchen. I use the broom, then the mop, then do a massive refrigerator overhaul of expired condiments. I don't understand how one person can use so many dishes. Seriously, is this a month's supply in the sink?

While I'm scrubbing down the counters, I think about everything I've learned over the past few days. I still can't wrap my head around the Lizzie's dad thing; can't believe it could've happened; can't believe she would've kept it from me. And then there's the little fact that we grew up together. Sure, I didn't meet Lizzie until I was five, but still . . .

*Maybe I was too old for him.*

Okay, that's seriously disgusting. My arms start to ache from the scrubbing but I can't stop now. My brain needs this distraction. I keep searching for clues to prove the abuse did or didn't happen. But those things happen behind closed doors, and sometimes you never suspect. He was so frail the day of her funeral, I couldn't have imagined he'd do something so heinous.

Of course, losing Lizzie might have derailed his desire to hurt children.

Or maybe it just worsened whatever was broken inside of him.

One thing's for certain: if he did hurt Lizzie and Kennedy, I have to make sure he never hurts anybody again.

I'm heading toward the bathroom when I send Jesse a text asking if Kennedy can meet up in the next couple days. The last thing I want to do is tackle the toilet, but it beats thinking about child-molesting preachers.

Jesse answers almost immediately: "You don't waste time."

"We're not getting any younger," I reply, and pull back the shower curtain. The three-month layer of grime on the tub screams *Fill me with gasoline and light a match*, but since I'm no good with explosives I attack it with a rag.

Jesse doesn't text back for a while. I imagine that means he's getting ahold of Kennedy. Still, I wish he'd indulge me with a play-by-play. Anything to keep my mind from doing its own thing. It keeps dancing into darker places, shocking me every time I let it spin. I wish I could focus on Shelby's Drama Queen antics or even Marvin's artistic renderings. I'm pretty convinced he's the one who made the Lizzie Hart playing card. But maybe it's just easier to think there isn't another guilty party out there, someone I haven't even considered.

I really don't think I can handle any more surprises.

Dad comes into the bathroom at half past five and tells me to get out. He fake-wrestles the dirty rag from my hand. "A man can clean his own john."

"If he can, then he should." I wash my hands, like, fourteen times and then I start dinner.

Dad says a prayer before devouring the steak. It's a ritual he started when his leg failed to improve. Naturally, this just makes me think of Lizzie's father. What kind of God would allow a man to do such things?

Dad smiles at me across the table. If he only knew what I was thinking. I let him ramble on about some football game that, like, changed the history of sports. I smile and laugh when it's necessary. To be honest, it's nice to see him excited about something, even if that thing has no direct relevance to his life. If things are going to continue this way for him, it's probably good that he has some distraction. When people focus too long on the emptiness in their lives, bad things happen.

I focus on the buttery taste of the rice, the burn of my soda, the way the zucchini just melts in my mouth. I think about what I would say if I were into praying. I'd probably just ask God to check up on Lizzie.

Maybe Dad does that for me.

He shoos me away when I try to do the dishes. Still, I manage to carry most of them to the sink before he's able to get rid of me. Then I'm a lie about homework away from shutting myself up in my room; it's so quiet in here it makes drying the dishes sound tempting.

The sound of my phone ringing is like a chorus of the gods.

Yeah. I've got religion on the brain.

*God help me.*

"Are you religious?" I say into the phone.

Jesse laughs. "Kind of," he says after a minute. "Why, are you scared?"

"In what way are you religious?" For some reason, I feel like his answer will tell me a lot about him. As if people's beliefs have anything to do with how they behave.

"My mom's a hard-core Catholic," he says. "But I'm kind of, um . . . spiritual, you know? I think the rituals are more about comforting people than actual divinity. Why? Does that offend you?"

"No."

"Didn't imagine so. You okay?"

"I'm great. I'm at my dad's house," I say, as if he's supposed to know what that means. I've gone from the parent who doesn't want me to the one who can't support me. I'm sitting in a bedroom with one thin blanket and a bunch of half-full boxes I couldn't bear to take to Mom's.

"Where's that?" Jesse asks.

"East Second, between Ellis and Harvey. You know, the real fancy part of town." Yeah, right. We're practically in the lap of the industrial district.

He whistles. "My own mansion's not far from there."

"But do you have the only brown house on the block?"

"That, I can't claim," he says.

"And does your bedroom face the power plant?"

"No, it does not. She said yes, by the way."

"She?"

"Kennedy."

"Oh. Oh, great," I say, even though it's pretty much the opposite.

It's great that my investigation has extended to include childhood trauma. It's super great that I get to hear my best friend's deepest secret from someone who hated her.

Why did Kennedy hate Lizzie? Did she blame her for what happened?

Already I've dropped the "allegedly" from my thought process. Already I'm starting to believe. Without allowing myself to consciously work through it, some part of me has realized that Kennedy's story makes sense. Lizzie was always very protective of her body. Lizzie never touched anybody, before Drake.

Lizzie never wanted to.

Jesse says, "She'll meet you at your bar on Monday."

"Before school?"

"After. She's taken a sudden interest in academics."

"God bless finals week."

"Exactly. Where's 'your bar'?"

I laugh a little. "It's this hole-in-the-wall coffee place. She treats it like her own personal saloon." I wait a beat. "Are you coming?"

"Do you need me there?"

*Do you even have to ask?*

"If you want," I say casually.

He waits a second before answering. "I don't know."

"Oh, come on. You can keep me on track. You know, in case I start to bulldoze her."

"I didn't mean that."

"Sure you did," I say too flippantly. "You were right."

Another pause. "I guess I could come by. Give me the address."

"We can just meet up after school."

"I got some stuff to do," he says.

*Oh no. He's pulling away from me. He thinks I'm a psycho. He doesn't want to be friends.*

"That's cool," I say, like he needs my permission. I'm starting to feel like nothing I say will be right at this point. "It's really close to school. On Emberson and Ivy."

"Oh, that place? I heard Marvin Higgins bragging about you taking him there."

My grip tightens on the phone. "Are you kidding me?"

"He wouldn't shut up about it."

"That little piece of—"

"Wait, so it's not true?" He's trying to stay serious but I can hear the amusement in his voice. "You guys aren't dating?"

"I think he's the one who drew that picture of Lizzie."

Silence. Total, dead silence.

"You know, the one where she's . . . undressed. Jesse?"

Great. I've done it again. If I could put my foot any farther in my mouth, it'd be coming out of my ass.

His voice is soft, broken. "I'm here."

"Did you not know about that?"

"I knew about it." He swallows. I can hear it. "Some of the guys forwarded it around."

"Are you serious?" I can feel the rage building inside of me. "That's so—"

"I know. It was from an address I didn't recognize. I sent back a pretty nasty response."

I sigh. "God, this just keeps getting worse. Every time I think I have a handle on things—"

"I know, I'm sorry. I need to stop telling you things."

"No, I want to know." My hand is starting to hurt. I realize I'm still clutching the phone. But I can't loosen my grip. "If I know who's guilty, I know who to expose."

"Angie."

"I know, I should just leave it alone. But doesn't it make you angry? Doesn't it make you enraged?"

"It makes me sad. I don't like talking about it."

And I need to talk about it. They call that a stalemate.

"I appreciate what you're doing for me," I say. I want to make him feel like he's helping. But I think it only makes him feel responsible for the mess I'm making.

"It's no problem. Have a good night, okay? Try to get some sleep."

Yeah, right. The shit I see in my dreams is no better than what I hear during the day. But I don't tell him that. I don't want to alienate him any further. So I just say "You too," like a sad little kitten, and I stare at the phone when he hangs up.

*Why am I so attached to him?*

That's a mystery I can't seem to crack. Maybe I'm just too tired or maybe there's no good reason for the intensity of my feelings. I keep glancing at the phone like he's going to call me back.

It's pathetic.

I'm just drifting off to sleep when the thought comes to me, an explanation I'll have forgotten by morning: I've hardly had a moment to myself all week and still I'm lonelier than I've ever been in my life.

# seventeen

I SPEND ALL DAY Sunday cramming for finals. Most of mine fall at the beginning of the week. Wednesday's the last official day of school, and by then I'll only have two tests left: History and Drama. So I'll worry about those last.

Monday morning I stroll into English and churn out an essay about overarching themes in American literature. I'm pretty sure I nail it. I'm great at making stuff up. After that, there's my oral exam in French, followed by an "interpretive drawing" in Art class.

Seriously, they should just give me the As now.

After school, I get to the coffee shop just in time to find Kennedy dozing off. Maybe I'm not the only one who's afraid to sleep at night. Her eyes are red, like she's been crying. She looks like a child who has a monster under her bed.

She looks like she knows she's about to wake it up.

"First things first." She sets some pages on the table. She's wearing her Verity High sweatshirt and jeans. Nothing flashy. "Someone was passing them around in Cara's third period. I told the girls to give me any they can find."

"Thanks," I say without emotion. I already know the pages are from Lizzie's diary. And if I'm supposed to show gratitude toward the people who wrote SLUT on her car, well . . . maybe they *should* hold their breath.

"They are sorry, you know," she says.

"I'm sure they are." I sip my latte. It tastes like nothing. A lot of things do lately.

"If they'd had any idea—"

"I didn't come here to talk about this." The last thing I want is to hear about the innocence of her friends. Of course they knew their attack would hurt Lizzie.

That's why they did it.

"Okay," Kennedy says. "I guess that's fair." She dumps some fake sugar into her coffee. Her flask is nowhere to be seen. Maybe she's started thinking about the reason she drinks so much.

Maybe I need to stop reading *Psychology Today*.

"I have some ground rules," she says.

"I heard." My eyes stray to the empty space beside her. Jesse's late or else he's not coming. Not that it matters, I tell myself. It's better for everyone if I don't care.

Kennedy nods slowly. "You have to understand I've never told anyone about this. Not the details." She takes a sip. "But if you need to know about Lizzie . . ." She trails off.

"I do," I say. Then, not to appear greedy, I add, "I feel like I do."

"Okay." She nods again. Her hair has fallen into her coffee. I wait a minute, contemplating moving it, when she finally notices. She squeezes the excess liquid with her fingertips. "I was so mad at her for so long. Then she killed herself and I . . . I wanted to feel relieved, you know?"

"Why would you feel relieved?" I lean back. I'm trying to

distance myself from her confession. But I can't separate from it; those words wrap themselves around me. The idea that anyone could be relieved by Lizzie's death is suffocating, and I find myself gripping the edges of the table, struggling for breath.

"I didn't say I was," Kennedy snaps. "I said I wanted to be."

"Why?"

"Think about it, Angie." She catches my eye. "Lizzie was the only one who knew what he did. So when she died . . ."

*The secret died with her.*

She doesn't say it. Neither of us says it. Still, those words hover between us, staining the air. Making it hard to see.

"Is that why you hated her?" I ask, wiping my eyes. "You thought she might tell somebody?"

Kennedy shakes her head. "I knew she wouldn't, even though I feared it. I know when I'm being irrational."

"That makes one of us."

She smiles. It strikes me, in that moment, that I've always been able to say anything around her. I don't censor my craziness like I do with Jesse.

But does that say something about her, or him, or me?

"I blamed her," Kennedy says. "I know that wasn't fair of me. But she knew what he was and she still asked me to stay." Her voice is flat like she's working out a math problem. Or maybe she's just had this conversation a lot in her own head. "She asked me to sleep over knowing what would happen."

"Maybe she thought it wouldn't, if you were there."

"I've thought of that. More so lately."

"Okay."

"I can't explain it, Angie. I can't explain to you why my four-year-old mentality stayed with me all these years. But I hated her for it. Maybe because I couldn't hate him."

"*Why?*" My voice is angrier than I planned.

"Because then I'd have to do something. I'd have to tell someone about him."

"And you felt you couldn't?"

"I can't explain it," she says again. "I can't explain how it makes you feel." She puts her hands around her mug, warming them. "How embarrassed and ashamed. You take on a lot of blame."

"You were kids."

"It doesn't matter. That stuff happens to adults too. I mean, that kind of thing. It fucks with your head so badly, you feel like if anyone knew about it, you'd be going through it all over again. And the way they'd look at you, wondering if you were telling the truth. Wondering what you did to invite it . . . I couldn't. I won't, still."

I don't point out that she's telling me right now. In a way, I know I trapped her into it. And I do feel bad about that. I'll feel worse when I finish what I've started, and I have the time to feel all the things I haven't allowed myself to really process. Guilt. Sadness. Immeasurable loss.

*Where is Jesse?*

"There's something I don't understand," I say. "After you stopped hanging out with Lizzie, I was with her a lot. I was with her all the time."

She nods, like she already knows where this is going. "I think maybe I stopped him, for a while."

"What do you mean?"

"I threatened to tell. Not to him. I threatened Lizzie. I told her if she ever talked to me, I would tell people what he'd done and they'd take her away from him."

"Jesus."

"I know. It was an awful thing to say to a kid."

"In a way, yeah. But she would have been better off."

"I couldn't . . ." Kennedy says.

I realize she thinks I'm accusing her. "I didn't mean it like that. I just mean don't feel bad for what you said to her. She must have told him if he stopped . . . I mean, I stayed over there for years, you know? And nothing. Unless he just spared me."

She shakes her head. "I watched everyone really closely. I was afraid to say anything but I also felt like if I knew he was doing it, I would have to. So I just kept an eye on things. On everyone I knew. Except Lizzie."

"How would you have known?"

"You can tell," she says firmly, and then backs off a little. "You can usually tell if you're looking for it. Kids act different when they're hiding something big. They retreat or else they start acting out."

I guess that's true—at least, I've read enough articles about it. It'd be a whole different thing to live through it.

"I can't believe she never told me," I say.

"Why would she? She wanted you to love her." She takes a big drink of her coffee. It's almost like, even though the alcohol isn't there, the ritual is still soothing. "It makes you think no one will love you if they knew. Like it's too messed up for anyone to handle. Lizzie was so sensitive. I think you'd be the last person she'd want to find out."

That hurts but I know it's true: I was the last person Lizzie wanted to lose. Still, she could've told me. Of course she could have. I wonder if her dad ever started up again, after Kennedy threatened him.

I exhale big, trying to push the thought out with my breath. It stays with me.

"Is that all?" Kennedy asks. "I mean, do you have what you needed?"

I don't want to say what I'm thinking, but I have to. It would be wrong not to. "Now that you've told me—"

"No."

"You don't have to do anything you don't want."

"No. No way."

"He's going on that yearly camping trip this summer, you know? That trip where all the kids from Sunday school spend a weekend with him?"

Her head just falls into her hands. "Fuck." She can't look at me. She *won't* look at me. She's pressing her fingers into her eyelids, like she's pushing the truth away. Or maybe just the memories.

"I'm sorry," I say quickly. "I'm not trying to pressure you, I swear. I just want you to think about it."

She looks up, wiping her face with her sleeve. Her eyes are still red but at least she's not crying. It scares me to see someone so *together* come unhinged. It makes me think none of us are in control.

"Okay," she says. "Yeah. I'll think about it."

"Thank you." I nod, scooting back. Giving her space. "For what it's worth, I really appreciate you talking to me. You have no idea how much."

"Good." Half of me expects her to smile, to say it helped to get things off her chest.

But the other half knows better. "Now I need something from you," she says.

"Sure. What?"

"Leave the girls alone."

I shake my head. I don't want to fight with her, but I'm not going to lie. "I can't do that."

"You don't know how this has affected them. You don't see the things I see."

"Unless you've seen them begging for mercy, you haven't seen anything."

"Jesus, Angelina—you're not God."

I laugh, because I've never been more aware of that fact. Never been more aware of my powerlessness. "If I were God, I would never have allowed people to be so evil. If I were God, Lizzie's body wouldn't be lying under six feet of dirt."

*Then again, if I were God, I'd know when to shut the hell up.*

"I'm asking you as a friend," she says, holding my gaze. "I did you a big favor today. And you've already taken Jesse—"

"Taken him?" I look left, then right. "Where am I keeping him?"

She purses her lips. "He was supposed to be my new bestie," she says. "A boy who would respect me without trying to take advantage. You know how rare that is?"

"Do you know who you're talking to?"

"Fair enough." She pauses, leaning in. "I don't know who invited Drake to Cara's party."

"I've got a pretty good idea." I can feel my cheeks warming. "Sorry about that night, by the way."

She laughs for the first time since my arrival. "You kidding? Your outburst made my night. I haven't seen a show like that in ages."

"So you knew I was acting?"

"Not at first. But you're smart, Angie. You'd never flip like that in real life."

*You want to bet?*

"Of course," she goes on, "you're proving my point. Jesse's your right-hand boy."

I wave my hand. "I practically begged him to do it."

"Even so. He wouldn't have done it for me."

*Why wouldn't he?* I wonder. I feel like I should know, but I don't.

"Oh, I almost forgot." She pulls a folded note out of her pocket. I open it immediately.

*Dearest Princess,*

   *My sincerest apologies. I couldn't bear to sit through it. I'm growing thicker skin as we speak.*

*Yours in Cahoots,*
*Jesse M.*


Next to his sprawling signature is a winking smiley face. And yeah, I read too much into it.

"You should be flattered." Kennedy downs the remains of her coffee. "He doesn't like very many people."

*I think you've got that backward,* I muse as she slides out of her seat. But I say, "I'm still not certain he likes me."

"Mighty insecure, aren't we?" She taps my nose. I unfold Lizzie's pages the moment she's gone.

Tonight, the dream begins the same. I'm standing outside my house, staring at the forest of evil. Then the creature appears and I'm running before I can even think. I run through the darkness. I run until I'm bleeding.

Then, something different.

I see a break in the trees. I race for that light as if my life depends on it. Really, it's my soul. The very essence that makes me a living thing. If I can just make it to that light, I will surely be free. Free from the creature.

Free from my own evil that draws him to me.

The light of God will fill me up.

I pass through the forest and find myself in the schoolyard. The grounds are empty but I can hear the creature panting behind me. I'm racing past the clock tower when I stop, for an instant, and look up. The tower is framed by the sun.

No—it's haloed in holy light. This is my sanctuary.

I just have to climb up to meet it.

The fire escape is right where it's always been, but the rungs are slippery. My hands keep sliding down. The creature grabs the end of my dress but misses my leg. Then I'm pulling myself up to the top and looking down at the world below. I'm victorious!

The creature has disappeared.

There's a rustling at my back. I turn. There stands the entire student body, sharp objects in their hands. They are screaming at me. I look down to see my own sharp claws, curling and curling like a dead person's nails.

I have not escaped the monster. The monster has become me.

I turn my head. I need to take a step back but there's nowhere to go. I'm stuck here on this little ledge and people are advancing. I try to tell them that I'm not really a monster, but they don't listen. Why would they listen?

Just look at me.

I look down. The world sways before my eyes. Then, just as I go to turn back, a flash of light catches my eye. It is you, standing down below, dressed in gold like an angel.

I try to motion to you with my hands. You look up but you don't see me waving.

I call down, "It's me! Please help me!"

Still, you show no signs of recognition. I am screaming myself hoarse, but still you don't hear me. Why won't you listen to me? Why won't you help me?

"I need you!"

The crowd is close now. They want to tear me to pieces. I am evil embodied and they must destroy me to survive. They must destroy me or they will become like me. You will become like me too.

I know then what I have to do.

My heart breaks as I turn away from you, away from everyone, and look up at the sky. I know the angels won't swoop in to save me.

I don't so much jump as

Just

Fall

Off.

I'm halfway to the ground when your eyes finally meet mine in recognition.

You step out of the way just in time.

# eighteen

THE MORNING OF her death, Lizzie arrived at school bright and early for the first time since middle school. She even beat security to the punch, barely. According to the police report, she shimmied up the old fire escape and pulled herself onto the clock tower ledge. The wind was fierce that day. She must have held on to the bricks for dear life.

Until she didn't anymore.

No one saw her jump. She might have simply fallen, like in her dream. It's probably better we don't know. What we do know is that she was alone. We know she was wearing a white dress, no shoes. But none of that is surprising if you knew Lizzie at all.

The surprising thing is she cried out. One single cry, following a life of silence.

Charlie Bigsby was crossing the parking lot when he heard it. The birds on the grounds took flight. Charlie had worked security at Verity for the better part of his life, but the most he ever expected to see was a fistfight. Maybe a realistic replica of a gun.

Seeing Lizzie's body sprawled on the cement, he must have lost a little piece of his mind. He managed to call the police; rumor has it his recorded statement is half gibberish. And then he just tuned out. Quit on the spot.

Then the students started to arrive.

They didn't tell us who died until later. In retrospect, it's probably a good thing. I would have insisted on seeing some kind of proof, and then my nightmares would be plagued with realistic imagery.

Maybe I would have lost it completely, like Charlie. Walked away and never come back.

I CAN HARDLY see as I stumble through the coffee shop and out onto the street. I must be crying but my face feels numb. I keep putting one leg in front of the other but I can't feel myself do it. I tell myself I just have to make it to my car, like it's the light at the end of some tunnel. It takes forever to get there. And when I get inside, it's dark.

Then I do something really dumb. I try to drive home while I'm still crying. I feel like I can do it. I keep wiping my eyes like my fingers are windshield wipers. This thought almost makes me laugh, it's so stupid, but then again, it's stupid thoughts like these that keep me from driving into a ditch.

I have to pull over twice before making it to Dad's. Then I do a little damage control with the rearview mirror and my makeup bag. I put a dot of concealer on my nose to hide the redness. Blush distracts from puffy eyes. When I walk through the door I'm damn near bright-eyed and bushy-tailed.

Dad's glued to the couch. I plop down and he puts his arm around me like we're buddies. He's watching recorded college basketball. I know I should get up and try to piece things together, but my brain just won't allow it. I turn off my phone and sit there for the duration of two games. We order a pizza so I don't have to do the scrounge/cook thing.

It's dark when I finally try to stand up. My legs feel sewn into the couch. Dad laughs at me as I hobble to my room, but he doesn't try to stop me. Maybe he can tell how exhausted I am. I guess I've kind of been ignoring it. I don't exactly love falling asleep these days. All the thoughts I try to avoid while I'm awake come crashing down on me.

Tonight the thinking-avoidance dance is worse than usual. No thought is safe. I can't even think of Jesse without this intense guilt pressing into me. Kennedy said he liked me. She's usually right about these things.

Of course, she meant he liked me as a friend, and that's where the problem comes in. I've been trying and trying to pretend that's all I want: a friend. Someone to help thaw the numbness inside of me. But my feelings for Jesse go beyond that, and anyone with half a brain can see it. And that just means I'm going to lose.

I have to let him go. He deserves to be around people who accept him as he is. If I keep getting closer to him, I'll just try to make him into what I want him to be. And that's sick.

Other people don't belong to us. They never have and never will. If Lizzie's words have taught me anything, it's that. And just like that, her face is all I can see.

Tears are pooling in her eyes, the way they did on prom night when I found her in the room with Drake. She's looking at me like this little girl who skinned her knee for the first time. Like she can't believe there's blood coming out of her. Like she's just now aware of her mortality.

And I just walked away. Again and again, I walked away as

her world fell down around her. As they destroyed her. We destroyed her.

*I'm sorry.*

I fall asleep telling her I'm sorry over and over again. The word penetrates into my dreams.

# nineteen

LIZZIE CAME UP behind me in the mirror, wrapping her arms around me. The movement smashed my boobs together even more. "I can't believe you talked me into strapless," I said, tugging at the fabric beneath my arms.

"You look beautiful. Black really is your color."

"How macabre."

For a minute I looked at the two of us in the hotel room mirror, light and dark, day and night. My black satin number was quite the opposite of her pale blue empire waist gown. She'd braided the two front pieces of her hair and pulled them back with a flower barrette. She looked like she'd just returned from conversing with little animals in the forest. I probably looked like a poser, but I'd been faking confidence for so long I almost believed the act myself.

And nobody had seen through it yet.

She laid her head on my shoulder, still hugging me. "I miss you."

"I'm right here."

"That's not what I mean."

"I know, I'm sorry." I turned to look at her. She looked surprised, like she wasn't expecting me to be so close. "But summer's almost here, and Drake's going on that trip with his dad, so . . . God, I sound pathetic, don't I?" *My boyfriend's leaving, so we can hang out more.*

Yikes.

Lizzie brushed the hair from my eyes. I'd parted it far over on the side, in an attempt to look glamorous. Even my eyes were dark. Smoky. Sultry.

Yeah, right.

"You don't sound pathetic," she said. "You sound like someone who's in love." She popped her glossy pink lips. She never needed to wear much makeup, did she? "Are you in love?" she asked.

It was weird. Even with Drake in my life, Lizzie and I still spent the night together about once a week. But she'd never asked me that. And I'd never offered it up.

"I love him." Wrenching myself from the mirror, I sat down on one of the two beds. Normal kids got ready for prom in their bedrooms, but Lizzie and I didn't feel at home in our houses. We'd checked into our room early, wanting a space that was our own.

Lizzie continued to fuss with her hair, giving me the space she knew I needed. "That doesn't sound so convincing."

Her tone was playful, but I caught the underlying message: If he's not so great, why do I have to share my best friend with him?

"I didn't mean it like that," I said. "Drake's great. He's sweet, he's funny. I know for a fact he looks hot in a tux."

She grinned.

"But we've been together for four years. For all of high school. This is the time where people break up or, like, get married."

Her grin slipped, but she caught it quickly.

"And I don't want to break up," I said. "But marriage? Seriously? I don't even know if I want that."

"Pragmatist," she teased, an old joke.

"Hopeless romantic."

"You don't have to make a decision yet. Just because other people do doesn't mean you have to."

"I know, but . . . I have to register for school," I reminded her. "I've got, like, two weeks left. Two weeks to decide between CU—"

"Where Drake is going."

"Or Colorado State—"

"Where *I'm* going." Lizzie smiled sweetly, as if to say, *Pick me!*

Of course, I hadn't told either of them about the acceptance letter to UCLA I'd buried under a mountain of socks in my top dresser drawer. They wouldn't have understood. Drake lived a charmed life in Colorado, and Lizzie refused to leave her widowed dad.

As for me, well, my parents would be better off without me. And I hated this wintry place.

But could I leave Lizzie and Drake?

"Well, even if you do go to CU," Lizzie said, clearly taking my silence to mean I'd chosen my boyfriend, "it doesn't mean you have to marry him."

"I know."

"Do you?"

"No." I shook my head. "I'm full of shit. Tell me what to do!"

Lizzie laughed. "Tell me if you're in love with him, and I will."

*I can't.*

If I admitted to being in love with him, he became everything to me. Then, if I lost him, I lost everything. Better to keep myself safe.

I said, "I just don't want to be like Romeo and Juliet, you know? They died for each other and they were, like, fourteen."

"So you wouldn't die for me?" She gasped, flitting over to me like a butterfly.

"That's different." I could still see us in the mirror. Even though we looked like opposites, we complemented each other. For the first time in my life, I let myself believe I deserved her friendship.

"So you would?" She put her hand over her forehead, like a damsel. "You'd die for me?"

"Of course I would. You're my best friend."

She stared at me a minute, like she wanted to say something important. But when Drake entered the room, she only whispered, "Me too."

I KNOW WHAT you're thinking. I was thinking it too. I'd wanted Drake for so long and now I was afraid to let myself fall in love with him. After all, he was just a guy, I told myself as we moved to the dance floor, leaving Lizzie behind. He didn't get involved when I talked about psychology, or politics, or the hundred little things that bothered me about religion. And when we made love, I tried so hard to get him to connect with me, I swear I missed out on the experience half the time.

He was average.

No, he was better than average, because he genuinely cared about me, and he did make me laugh, doing goofy impressions or telling me funny stories about the stuff that happened during practice. Hell, he didn't even balk when I *insisted* we bring my best friend to the prom, because she didn't have anyone to go with and wasn't it our responsibility, as good people, to make sure she had a rockin' time?

Drake was a great guy. I was lucky. And right now, he was doing that dorky thing where he tried to slow dance with me to a really fast song, and it was making me laugh. I leaned into him, watching the dangling star-lights twinkle over our heads. Behind his back, van Gogh's celestial masterpiece spread out across the circular wall, re-created by the art students. Even our outfits matched the *Starry Night* theme: Lizzie in blue, me in black, and Drake in a black tux with blue accents. I slid my hands up his lapel, wrapping my arms around his neck. It didn't even bother me that people were knocking into us and it was totally our fault. I just wanted to be close to him.

*Maybe I really am in love.*

For the first time in a long time, I felt safe. Happy.

Unfortunately, I was so immersed in this newfound feeling of happiness that it took me far too long to realize Lizzie was missing. Okay, I probably noticed after two or three songs. But I felt like an asshole, standing there clinging to my boyfriend while my best friend had fled the premises.

And, in that moment, I started to think about some things.

If Lizzie was really my opposite, then she *needed* romance. She was Cinderella searching for her prince. And though it was far from midnight, the sight of me, and so many others, pairing off in this beautiful ballroom was probably too much for her slippered feet to handle.

So she bailed. And maybe I should've let her. But it seemed unfair that she should miss out on tonight when she was the one who actually cared about these things.

I detangled myself from Drake. "Lizzie left."

"What? She's right over . . ." He trailed off, pointing in some vague direction.

"She *was* over there," I said. "Then she was at the snack table."

He smirked. "Were you just pretending to pay attention to me?"

"Drake, she's my best friend. And this is kind of a big night for some people. People who, like, believe in this shit."

"Eloquent, as always."

I punched him in the arm. "Stop teasing me. I'm being serious."

"I know. I'm sorry. Listen, you go fulfill your Prom Court duties." He nodded to the cluster of girls in the center of the room. Naturally, devil-in-a-red-dress Kennedy had scored the best real estate in the place. "I'll look around for Lizzie," he said. "It's pretty warm in here anyway."

"We're not supposed to leave the ballroom."

"They're not even paying attention." Then, as if to settle the matter, he planted one on me.

"Thank you." I felt a spread of warmth as he left my side. Sure, he was a guy, but it was his prom too. He should've been mingling with his buddies and making lewd jokes about prom sex. Instead, he was searching the grounds for my friend.

Searching. And searching. Yeah, Drake ended up being gone for a long time. By the end of the first half hour, all my doubts had mutated, and I started to think about some more things. Things my heart hadn't let me see before.

I thought of that night in middle school when Lizzie described the attributes of her crush. Brown hair. Blue eyes. How many guys in our grade even had notably blue eyes?

I thought of that day in the Alternate Dimension Bathroom. Lizzie had looked so flustered after her talk with Drake. Her hair had been messed up. She'd immediately reglossed her lips. I had to have been an idiot to miss what those things meant.

They'd kissed!

Or he'd kissed her. God, had Drake wanted Lizzie all along? Had he merely settled for me? No wonder he hadn't minded that she'd come with us to prom.

She was the one he wanted to take.

I raced out of the ballroom. My heart couldn't even catch up with my feet, but damn it if it didn't try. It took practically no time at all to reach the hotel room. I remember thinking, even before I opened the door, that I'd gotten there too quickly. I wasn't ready for this, wasn't ready to be proven right. I'd never be ready.

But I opened the door anyway.

I opened the door and I heard Lizzie gasp.

It might've been a gasp of surprise. Looking back, that's what makes the most sense. But at the time, I heard it as a gasp of pleasure. And part of me died.

So much of me died.

*Lizzie.*

Yes, I looked at her first. I'd been close to her the longest. I'd trusted her the most. A part of me had always suspected Drake might break my heart. Hell, wasn't that why I'd been so afraid to get close to him?

But Lizzie? The sun to my moonlight? The girl I'd rocked to sleep when she had nightmares as a child. The girl who was always supposed to be a part of my life, whether boys came and went.

My forever friend.

The truth hit me so hard I could barely stand.

*Lizzie doesn't love me.*

My eyes turned to Drake then. Drake, crawling off her like an animal. He had a look in his eyes I'd never seen. Was it passion?

My heart cracked and spilled out inside of me.

Was it love?

Was this how he looked when he loved someone?

I looked him right in the eye and said, "Thanks for proving me right."

I tried, without turning, to back out of the room. But Lizzie called to me, and I looked. Stupidly, I looked.

Her eyes were bright. Her lips were red from kissing. I hated her in that moment, but only because I'd loved her so much. I hated her because she didn't love me, and hers was the only love I'd ever completely believed in.

*Why don't you love me?*

My eyes strayed to her hands as she pulled at the broken strap of her dress. Stumbling from the bed, she brushed past me, out of the room. But my eyes were stuck on Drake now, thinking: *You wanted her all along. She wanted you. You both fooled me.*

*Neither of you love me.*

I finally succeeded in backing out of the room. Halfway down the hall, I ran into the cheerleading squad. At the time, I thought they were worried about me.

Now I think they were just sniffing for a scandal.

It took three of them to lead me down the hallway. Ideally, they would've just locked me up in a hotel room, but hell, mine was already occupied. I remember Kennedy stroking my hair while the girls yelled obscenities in Drake's direction. We slipped into the ballroom through a door in the back (who knew?) and spent the next half hour taking pulls from Kennedy's flask. I don't remember much after that, though not really because of the alcohol.

What I do remember is this: Lizzie and Drake never returned to the dance, but their damage had been done. The entire ballroom was abuzz with whispers of my undoing. When the results for Prom Queen were announced, a quiet numbness overtook me. I climbed to the stage and looked out at the student body. They stared back at me, filled with sympathy. Filled with awe. And I realized something: I finally had the recognition I'd desired.

I had nothing.

# twenty

AT TWO IN the morning there's a knock on my window. Half-asleep, I'm convinced it's Lizzie's ghost. I'm scared shitless but I go to the window anyway.

I'm wrong. It's not a ghost. It's a flesh-and-blood person.

I open the window so he can climb in. I can see him perfectly in the moonlight. "Hey."

"Don't you answer your phone, girl?"

"My phone?" Yeah, my brain is still a little hazy. "Oh, I turned it off. Is everything okay?"

"It's fine," Jesse says. He's wearing all black like he's dressed for a spy mission. It takes me a minute to realize this is the mission. Me. My house. "I just got worried," he says.

*Worried about what?* I wonder. *Worried that the pain will become too great for me, or worried I'll bulldoze over someone who can't handle it?*

"I'm okay," I say as he sits on my bed. "I just needed a break."

"That's cool." His voice sounds a little wounded. He pulls off his hat and his hair is all matted. "I just couldn't sleep, and I remembered you were only a few blocks away. Sorry. Is that weird?"

*No, it's sweet.*

But I have to be cold. I sit on the bed, pulling my knees up to my chest. "Kind of. Look, Jesse—"

"I get it," he says. "I'm a stalker. I'll get out of here."

"No, wait."

"I can take a hint." Then, because he can't seem to go two minutes without teasing me, he sniffs. "I know when I'm not wanted."

"You're wanted," I say before I can stop myself. And since I've already started, I keep going. "You're wanted too much, that's the problem. I like you."

I can't believe I'm doing this. There's absolutely no reason to be telling him this. But he just looks at me with those dark brown eyes, taking it in.

"I like you," he says, poking my knee. "That's a good thing."

"No, that's not what I mean." I feel like a six-year-old when I say "I *like* you."

You know, *want to invite you under my covers* like.

I keep that one to myself.

"I see." He looks at the open window. "Do you want me to leave?"

"You probably should, yeah. I'm sorry."

"Hey, don't be." He stands. It happens so quickly, I feel panicked even though I told him to go. "It's okay."

"No, it isn't." I try to hide my face. Never in the history of the world has someone blushed like I'm blushing. Still, it's nothing compared to the tightness in my chest. "It's totally unfair of me. I'm so sorry for doing this."

"You're not doing anything." He hovers by the bed like he's wrestling with something. "It's just a feeling."

"I know, but . . ."

"It's not like you tried to maul me."

I laugh through my hands. "Yeah. That would've been bad."

"So don't worry about it." My hands are covering my face so I can't see him do it, but he swoops in and kisses my cheek. Except it's less like a swoop and more like slow motion and his hand goes to the side of my face. His lips linger long enough to rip a shudder through me.

He feels me shake. "You okay?"

I lift my head slowly as if waking from a dream. "I'm fine, I just— What are you doing?"

He shrugs, looking away. "Being friendly."

"Oh." I'm watching him intently. "Okay." My voice is very slow. Calm. But inside, my brain is bouncing off the walls . . .

*The way he finds excuses to touch me. The way he kissed my cheek just now, his lips lingering. That little winking smiley face at the bottom of his note. Like the one on the note someone gave to Lizzie. Along with a book of poems.*

Either I'm going crazy, or . . .

"You're not gay."

"Excuse me?" He steps back instantly, hands flying to his hips. But he doesn't look mad. He actually looks kind of scared.

"You're not—I mean . . . are you?"

He snorts. "Isn't that the straight-girl fantasy?" He's getting a bit of his attitude back. Still, his voice is trembling. "A guy who's well dressed, well mannered, *and* he's straight."

"You are *not* well mannered," I say, going for humor, but he doesn't seem to get that.

Already he's walking to the window. "I'm going to get out of your hair."

"Jesse, wait." I slide off the bed.

He doesn't slow down.

"Damn it, Jesse, you will come to my room *one time* without me chasing you away."

He stops, turns a little. I can tell he wants to smile but he can't. He looks completely defeated. "Shit."

I touch his arm.

I could swear the touch hurts him. He jerks away so fast. "I'm fine," he says.

"Yeah, seems like it."

He inhales slowly before sitting on the bed. He's looking at his hands, like maybe he wants to hide behind them. "For the record, I never told you I was gay."

My eyes are so wide my head doesn't feel big enough to hold them. I want to touch his arm again but I'm completely at a loss for what to do, or think, or say. Luckily, I'm quick on my feet, so I say the smartest thing possible. "Wait. What?"

He lifts his head. "You're right."

"I'm right?" I can't help it. The smile just creeps up on me. "Are you kidding me? That's crazy."

His eyes tell me I'm not helping. It's like he's drowning and I'm just pushing him down deeper.

"Okay, all right, it's not crazy," I say, sitting next to him. "It's fine, it's great. I mean, either way, it's—"

"Not like there's anything wrong with being *not* gay?"

"Don't make fun of me!" I punch him in the arm, lightly, just to touch him. If this is a dream, I'm making the best of it. Then again, that would involve a lot less clothing.

*Whoa there, Angie.*

"Are you sure?" I ask.

His eyes widen and I know I just sound ridiculous.

It only gets worse. "Are you straight?"

He shrugs.

"Jesse?"

"I really don't know." His head just drops. "For a long time I thought I was nothing." Then he falls silent. His hands are picking themselves apart.

I put my hand over them. "You already started," I say.

"What?" He looks over at me.

"You already started to tell me."

"Yeah?"

"So tell me."

He waits for a minute. Now he's wringing his hands. I slip my other hand beneath his so I'm holding both of them. It's harder for him to attack himself this way. "You want the long or the short of it?" he asks.

"Both. I want all of it." I don't even hesitate.

He exhales. I want to invite him farther onto the bed, to relax, but I don't want to scare him. So I crawl over to my side and pat the side where he's already sitting. I offer him half of my pillow.

"Thanks," he says, leaning into it.

"Mmm-hmm." I don't stare at him. I don't want to intimidate him with my gaze.

After a minute, he starts talking. "So, the short version? Well, I never once told anyone I was gay. But I've been dressing different since I was a kid so people just assumed it. I got beat up a lot in junior high." He looks at me like, *You sure you want to hear this?*

I just wait.

"Crazy thing is, when I denied being gay, they actually kicked my ass worse," he says, shifting on the bed.

I turn, stealing a glance at him. "They did? Why?"

His lips twist. "It was like, if I was different, they wanted me to be different all the way. But if I wasn't, well, then they got to ask themselves: If he likes girls and dresses like that, and I like girls too . . . It scares people to think that way."

"Like who you are might affect *them*."

"Exactly. Like stilettos were going to show up on their feet without their permission." He shakes his head. "Idiots."

"That's sad."

"That's life, baby."

I close my eyes at the sound of it.

*So . . . do you like girls?* I want to ask. But that's just a little too transparent, now, isn't it?

"What's the long version?" I say instead.

His gaze flicks to the ceiling. "A story for another day."

"Oh, come on!" I kick the mattress because I'm afraid to touch him. "If you leave me hanging like this, I'll scream. Then my dad will wake up and that'll give us a whole new set of problems."

"Not as relaxed as your mom?"

"Not nearly," I say, trying to force my body to relax. It's hard, with him lying so close.

"My mom's strict too."

"Tell me about her."

He doesn't respond. But his Adam's apple pulses as he swallows, revealing his nervousness.

"Is that part of the story?" I ask.

"Yeah," he says simply, still hesitating to tell me the rest. Part of me feels like I should let it go. But part of me thinks he wants me to push him, so that he can finally tell someone.

Guess which part I want to listen to?

I reach down, pulling the blanket over our feet. I could just shut the window but I don't want him to feel trapped. This way, he knows I'm looking out for him without forcing anything. "You're shivering," I explain.

He smiles at the gesture, pulling the blanket up to our waists. But he's still lying on his back, facing away from me. "My mom had me when she was fifteen," he says, very matter-of-factly, like: *Don't judge me and don't judge her either.*

I don't.

"Her parents made her give me up for adoption even though she didn't want to," he says more softly. "But it's not like in the movies. They throw us kids into a lottery. Couple of the cute, white babies get adopted. The rest of us go into foster hell."

"That's terrible."

"It's okay." He shrugs, and the blanket slides off me. I tug it back playfully, trying to keep things light. He smiles. "It's made me who I am."

"So when you said you were 'usually' the oldest kid in your house, that's what you were talking about?"

He nods. "I didn't get matched up with a family until I was six."

"What about before then?"

"Oh, you know. *Little Orphan Annie* shit. Minus the singing. And the optimism." I touch his hand. He takes it away. "By the time you get sent to a home, you think, *Finally, a family.*"

"But it wasn't?"

"It's more like a can of sardines. Even the well-meaning folks have, like, five to eight kids. I've changed enough diapers to last a lifetime." He laughs, but it dies off quickly. "You really do start to feel like one more mouth to feed. And I didn't want to take food from the kids who really needed it, so I started doing research, you know? Checking out my options. I got emancipated when I was sixteen."

"Where did you live?"

"Shit-hole apartment. I'd already been working a while. Then my mom came along." His smile widens. When he's happy, it's the most beautiful thing. "She'd been looking for a long time but my records were kept hidden until I was on my own. So I moved in with her and that was that. Happy ending."

"That's amazing."

"She's amazing," he says. "I have a brother I'd never even met."

I want to meet them. I honestly cannot express how much I want to meet them.

"How old is he?" I lean in just a bit.

"Four. He's, like, totally out of control." He laughs. "But really sweet."

"That's sweet."

"I love him so much."

"You sound like you're really happy."

"I am."

I wait a beat. "Then maybe I shouldn't ask what part you're hiding."

He sits up.

*Damn.*

He picks up his hat from the side of the bed. It's black with a blue *J* on it. I wonder if his mom knitted it for him. "It's nothing you couldn't guess," he says.

"You can tell me."

He speaks to the window. "I lived with five different foster families before I moved out on my own. I've seen the most messed-up shit you can imagine. Not to me," he adds, glancing back at me quickly. "But to the kids I lived with."

I feel like he's lying about that last part. Liars recognize lies. But I'm not going to call him on it. "I'm sorry," I say.

He runs a hand through his hair. He's holding his hat like a baby blanket and it's seriously the cutest thing I've ever seen. And yes, I realize I'm using these thoughts to distract me from what he's saying. I'm clearly no good at facing this stuff.

He says, "It just got to the point where I didn't want it, you know? I couldn't imagine being . . . close with someone without it being like that. Without it being bad."

I go to touch his arm but hesitate. I think about the way I've pulled at him, and cornered him. I think about how I figured those things were okay because he was a guy, like I didn't need to respect his space.

I think about where I get these ideas.

"I'm sorry," I say again.

He lifts his shoulders, a half shrug. "Don't be. I probably avoided a lot of bad stuff." He closes his eyes and I just look at him, dark hair blending with the shadows, hands clinging to his hat. "But it's pretty messed up, you know?" He turns, catching my eye. "I never even had a crush until high school. There was this guy at my old school. He was just, I don't know . . . He was nice to me. It made me feel good. But anytime I thought of anything more with him, I couldn't deal with it. I always connected it to the bad things."

He goes quiet.

*Come on, Jesse. Don't close off when you've finally started letting me in.*

"What happened?" I say after a minute.

"I moved." He laughs softly. "Not because of him. Because of my mom; I moved to be with her. But then it started happening again."

"With Gordy?"

"Nope."

I watch the side of his face. My spine prickles with heat. "Oh."

"Yeah."

"Oh, wow." I feel stupid for not seeing it. But how could I have seen it? "Lizzie?"

"Yeah." He turns a bit, to face me. "I felt like a real person around her. Like I could do normal things, and still be . . ."

*Safe*, I want to say, but I'm worried it might offend him. I know he's holding things back from me. But I'm not going to force it.

That would just prove him right about me.

"Lizzie was great about that," I say. "She made me feel normal too. She was the first person to get to know me before making up her mind. My life has been kind of weird. My mom has all this money, but my dad's . . . struggling."

He nods. "I heard something about that."

"Oh really?" I smile like it's funny that people gossip. Really I'm dreading what he'll tell me. "What do they say?"

He gives me this lopsided grin. "They call you white-trash royalty."

Wow. Ouch. But, also . . .

"Okay, that is kind of funny. I mean, that's the best they could come up with?"

"They just don't know how to deal if you don't fit into their neat little boxes." He bats his eyelashes, done up all prettily with liner. He's so beautiful I want to cry. And protect him. Possibly from me.

*He's too good for me.*

"Hey," he says. "Where did you go?" He reaches out like he's going to pinch me.

I squeal. Like I'm twelve. And I don't even care because now we're both laughing. I realize I want to kiss him, badly, and that stirs up all kinds of conflicting emotions.

*Damn it, Angie.*

I have to retreat, just for a minute. Everything's happening too fast. He just appeared out of nowhere, in my life and in my bedroom. On my bed.

"Hey!" I clamber to my knees. "You're on my bed."

"Yeah?" He tilts his head to the side. "So?"

"So"—I open my hands—"I'd never have let you in here so quickly if I thought you were . . . I mean . . ."

Jesse blushes. He flat-out *blushes* this gorgeous red. "Oh, yeah. Sorry." He scoots to the edge of the bed. "I can leave."

I catch his hand before he's moved too far. "You'd better not."

He smiles. After a minute, he pulls his hand away, holding it to his cheek. I bet he can feel the heat there. I want to feel it.

*Down, girl*—what is wrong with me? Now that I know it might not be wrong to like him, my mind is going wild. And my heart. My body.

Now I'm blushing. I'm pretty sure it's obvious.

"You sure this is okay?" He gestures to the space between us.

And I want to say: *No, let's shorten that space.* Instead, I shrug. "Yeah. I mean, it's not like you actually lied to me."

He slides a little closer. His hip touches mine.

"I trust you," I add. "Maybe I shouldn't, but I do."

"You can." He leans in, barely, like he wants to kiss me but he isn't sure if he should.

I pull back.

"Wait a second!" Yeah, I must be completely insane. But I really need to ask. "Is that why you call me Princess? Because of what people say about me?"

He puts his hand on my lips. Touching softly, but making a barrier between us.

It feels really, really nice.

"Nope," he says.

"Why then?" I talk through his fingers.

"There's just something about you. Like you're different from the rest of us. Not in a bad way. In an amazing way."

"Oh." I guide his hand to my cheek. My hand lingers over his, holding him. "Okay."

And then, because I'm suddenly feeling very comfortable, and very safe,

I

Kiss

Him.

# twenty-one

A WEEK BEFORE LIZZIE died, a group of senior girls decided to teach her a lesson about taking off her clothes at improper times. Each time they caught her alone in the halls, they attempted to snip off a piece of her outfit. In reality, very few girls managed to snag a decent piece of fabric, but it didn't matter much. By the end of the week, the mere snapping of scissors made Lizzie seize up in terror.

Sometimes the threat of something can be as scary as the thing itself.

Right now, the threat of entering the den of a child molester is all too real. I stand on the doorstep to Lizzie's house. I've already knocked and now I'm just counting the seconds as they pass. I don't even realize I'm holding my breath until Mr. Hart opens the door. It whooshes out in a rush.

He says "Angelina! This is a nice surprise," but all I can hear is Lizzie's voice in my head, warning of monsters. Telling me to run.

"Can I come in?" My voice is speaking in direct opposition to my brain, which is screaming, *Go, go, go!*

I tell it to shut up.

"Of course." He steps aside so I can pass over the threshold.

"I won't take up too much of your time." I sit in the rocking chair because it's facing the door. I need to be able to see through those big front windows into the house next door.

"Shouldn't you be getting to class?" asks Mr. Hart.

I glance at my purse. I've got my phone face-up in case I get a text from Jesse. The clock reads 6:38 a.m.

"Not just yet."

He shuffles into the kitchen. After a minute he returns with a little tray. "I don't know what I'd do without you," he says, handing me a teacup. "The drive was a big success."

"It was nothing." I watch him as he takes a drink. He looks like a drawing that's slowly being erased. The lines on his forehead bleed into his hairline. His eyes droop toward his cheeks.

"Tea okay?"

I take a baby sip. "It's great."

"Good. What can I do for you today?" he asks, like all he wants to do is help. I wonder how many kids he's tricked with that bit.

"There's something I wanted to ask you. Something that's been bugging me."

"Ask away."

"Earlier this year, Lizzie got cast in the school play."

"I recall that, yes."

"So she told you about it?"

He raises his cup. I get the feeling he's hiding behind it. "Can I ask why you're interested?"

"Lizzie was thrilled when she found out. She didn't think she'd get cast."

His frown lines deepen. Something about this is getting to him.

"She went on and on about it for weeks," I say. "I don't think I've ever seen her so happy. She seriously seemed like—"

"That play was an abomination!"

"Excuse me?"

His eyes have gone all shifty. He's splashing tea onto his fingers. "Teaching children about spirits and fornicating—they call themselves educators!"

Wow. He never used to talk like this. Now he's freaked out on me twice in one week. If I didn't know better, I'd think the loss of his daughter is to blame for his slipping so easily into psycho mode. But in light of Kennedy's and Marvin's testimonies, I have to wonder . . .

How often did he lash out at Lizzie when no one was watching?

"So you made her drop out of the play," I accuse. "Didn't you see how happy she was?"

I shouldn't have said it. But I'm done trying to protect him. He should have been protecting her from real danger. Not hypersexed Shakespearean fairies.

"Elizabeth never told me about the play."

"Then how did you find out?"

He falls silent. He's staring into his cup with ferocity. "I don't remember."

"I don't believe you."

He glares like I'm the devil incarnate. Then he sits bolt upright in his chair. "Just a minute."

"Where are you going?" I ask, my gaze flicking to the window. Up in Marvin's bedroom, the lights are still off. But he'll have to be getting up soon.

Lizzie's dad moves past me to the desk beneath the mantel and starts rifling through a drawer. "Here," he says. "Here it is."

He tosses a purple envelope in my lap. I pull out the decorated card. It's an invitation to *A Midsummer Night's Dream*. All the cast members send them to their friends and families. But inside the card is a hastily scribbled note:

*Depraved witchcraft and lurid sex. Your daughter: The Queen.*

"Ho-ly shit," I murmur.

"Excuse me?"

"Who gave this to you?"

I can tell he doesn't want to answer. He's scowling at my language. Unfortunately for him, I don't give a shit. Swearing is the least of his worries.

"I need to know," I tell him. "The person who sent this wanted to hurt Lizzie."

His eyes go wide. I wonder if he's thinking about how he treated her after reading the invitation. Did he scream at her behind the safety of closed doors? Did he threaten to teach her a lesson?

"The card wasn't signed," he says, and he's stuttering. "It came in the mail."

"Can I take this?"

"I have no use for it." He lowers his head.

I stand. "Hey, have you seen my jacket? I thought maybe I left it last time I was here."

He shakes his head, still avoiding my eyes.

"Can I check?" I gesture to the stairs. "It'll just take a minute."

"Of course." He looks up, and his eyes are red. He looks like a harmless old man. He *doesn't* look like a child molester. But God, does anybody? "Listen, Angie, I apologize—"

"Don't worry about it." I wave my hand. "I'll just be a sec."

I'm up the stairs before he can stop me. Lizzie's room smells like it always has, like lavender shampoo and a cake batter candle. I don't bother turning on the lights. I can see Marvin's window and his lights are still off.

*Damn, boy. Get up already.*

Time to improvise. I open the window and crouch down beneath it. This way I can see out but he can't see me. I take my phone out of my purse and call his landline. I can hear it ringing from here, which is a good sign.

Just when an adult voice answers, heavy with fatigue, I hang up.

*Ha-ha, just kidding! I didn't really want to talk to you.*

I crouch a little lower, waiting for several things to happen:

First, Marvin will roll over in bed, thinking: *What the hell?*

Next, he'll glance at his clock, ready to say: *Does the caller have any idea what time it is?*

Then, when he realizes it's time to get up for school, he'll . . .

The light turns on. Even from a distance, my eyes feel assaulted. But my heart is all aflutter, because Marvin's playing right into my hands. Now all that's left to do is hope he's not a modest sleeper.

*Jackpot!*

Marvin climbs out of bed in his underwear. That's when I activate the camera function on my phone. I lean out the window, capture his skinny body in the camera frame, and click.

Two minutes later, I'm jogging down the stairs.

Mr. Hart is nowhere to be seen. I should feel relieved, but it's more like a horror movie, where the killer can sneak up on you at any time. I don't want to look behind me, but I don't want to turn my back on him. After several seconds of quiet deliberation, I creak open the front door.

That's when he touches me.

A single finger grazes my arm and my entire body convulses.

I want to scream. I want to scrape the skin from my arm.

"What!?" I demand, spinning to face him.

He looks alarmed. I don't think anyone's ever spoken to him this way. "I'm sorry," he says, and suddenly he's meek Mr. Hart again. The guy I remember from my childhood. The guy who never hurt me. "I shouldn't have yelled like that."

"It's fine." I open the door further, that much closer to escaping. "I have to get to class . . ."

"The other day," he says, and he looks so pathetic I almost feel bad for him. "I shouldn't have blamed you for that boy. I lost my temper."

"Who? Drake?"

"Yes. *Drake.*" He spits the name. "That boy is not to be trusted. If I catch him here a third time, I'm calling the police."

"I don't blame you." I force a laugh. "It might do him good to— Wait. A *third* time?" My blood runs cold, and I was already cold to begin with.

He nods, teeth clenched. "I caught him rummaging through her things. In the middle of the night! I told him never to come back."

"Rummaging through her things? Are you sure he wasn't . . . they weren't . . ." I lean into the doorway. I'm falling. Always, I'm falling in this place.

When he says "She wasn't here," the bottom drops out beneath me. I can barely form the words: "When did this happen?"

"The night she . . . passed. I should have called the authorities, but I was too distraught to think properly. And the boy seemed distraught, and forgiveness is—"

"I have to go." I scramble to pull myself upright. But the doorframe is slippery. The whole world is slippery and I'm sinking into darkness. I try to tell myself Drake came back for something nostalgic. But to sneak into her room the night she died . . . it had to be something incriminating.

*What was it, Angie,* I wonder as I stumble to my car. *Was it a condom? A steamy letter? A picture of them wrapped up together in bed?*

Or was it Lizzie Hart's diary?

\* \* \*

AFTER SCHOOL, I track Shelby down in Busybody Corner. It's this cluster of rooms in the west wing where students hold their club meetings. She's the president of, like, eight of them. She's got so many extracurriculars, her transcript must look like a fake. It won't kill her to be late just this once.

I open with that as she reaches for the door to the journalism room.

"Sorry, doll," she says, smoothing a hair into place. She's got on these rolled-up jeans and a red halter top. Platform heels. "I've got to proof the final issue of *La Verité*."

Ah, Verity's little attempt at Breaking News. Presenting the illusion of a free press since 1968. If only we had a student club that actually prepared us for the real world. Something like Burger Flip 101, or Follow the Janitor Around for a Day.

"I'm glad I caught you, then," I tell Shelby. "I've got a story for the front page."

Several students are hurrying past us. She waves them into the room like she's directing traffic. "I'm serious, Angie, I just don't have time for this. We go to the printer at three o'clock *and* I've got to organize the graduation gowns by tomorrow night."

"They came in?"

"This morning. And no, you can't pick yours up early," she says. "You'll get yours, like everybody else, after I've put them in order. There's plenty of time between now and Saturday—"

"You agreed to alphabetize them?"

"Why not? I'm nice."

"You're ambitious."

*Keep talking, Shelby. I just might be able to use this information.*

"Fine," she says stubbornly. "I did it as a favor to Madame Swarsky. As you might imagine, considering our previous meeting, I don't want to do anything to invite suspicion on myself so close to graduation. Her recommendation helped get me into Juilliard. I'd hate for her to rescind it."

"Then you might not like this." I pull the purple envelope out of my bag. Shelby's face drains of blood when I show her the card.

"This doesn't prove anything," she says.

I snort. "Sounds like you just confessed."

"Well, I didn't."

"You know what I think?" I fan myself with the envelope, all nonchalance. "I think if I got a sample of your writing from Madame Swarsky, it'd match the writing in this invitation. I'm sure she has one of your character sketches lying around. Of course, to get that information, I'd have to tell her what her star pupil's been up to—"

"All right!" Shelby's eyes dart this way and that. For once in her life, she doesn't want to be seen. "I knew it was the wrong thing to do, okay? I knew it then and I know it more now. And I'm *sorry*."

"Not good enough."

"Hey, boss?" A voice breaks into our bubble. Marvin's head pokes out of the journalism room. He's got his sketchpad in hand. "You coming?"

"In a minute." Shelby waves him back inside.

"Marvin's on newspaper staff?" I ask.

"He does cartooning," she says, and shrugs. "He's a pretty good artist."

"I've heard." An idea is blossoming in my head, surrounded by spindly thorns. "So Shelby." I flash my prettiest smile. "How would you like help sorting those graduation gowns?"

She narrows her eyes. "Why would you help me?"

"You already guessed it. I want to take mine early."

*Mine and a few others.*

"Is it really that important?" she asks, curling her lips.

"Yes, it's really that important." I sigh, like I can't believe I'm about to tell her this. "It's not easy being bounced back and forth between my mom and dad. I spend a lot of time traveling." *You know, because I'm white-trash royalty?* I lower my eyes. "If I can pick up the gown after class, it's one less thing to worry about."

She raises her brows. Clearly, she's taken aback by my show of human emotion. Or maybe she just wants me out of her face. "All right, fine."

I smile, and just like that we're back to business. "I'll also be needing Marvin's email address."

"It's Marvin.Higgins@verity.edu. Same as yours or mine."

"I mean his personal email."

"Why?"

"I need to verify something."

"What?"

*The fact that he painted Lizzie without her permission.*

"None of your business," I snap. "Do you have it or not?"

"Not," she says.

"Well, maybe you should get it."

She knows it's a small price to pay to get off my shit list.

"Deal."


AFTER MY MEETING with Shelby, I stop off at the Drama room to practice my final monologue. I'm doing a scene from *The Children's Hour*, a scene that was supposed to be Lizzie's. After she died, I took it over to honor her memory. I used to sit in class, back turned to her, listening to the words roll off her tongue. We weren't speaking then, so it was nice to hear her voice.

I memorized the monologue before it was mine.

Now I know it too well. It takes me all of five minutes to realize I can't find distraction in this exercise, and I need it desperately. I can't allow myself time to think. Can't allow myself time to rest, to catch my breath, to obsessively look at my phone. Every time I look, my inbox is empty.

*Where is he?*

I haven't seen Jesse all day. He was gone when I woke up this morning. Normally, I'd see him in sixth period History, but since we're on a different schedule for finals, I won't have class with him until tomorrow. I keep telling myself not to worry.

*I'm not really a psycho. I just play one at parties.*

I need to give him time to gather his thoughts.

Still, as the seconds drag by, I begin to wonder. What if he's not just taking time to think? What if something's really wrong?

I glance at my phone.

Nothing. Nothing. Nothing.

If only I had some excuse to call him. Some reason unrelated to *us*. I catch a glimpse of Shelby across the room—not the real Shelby, but a picture of her hanging on the wall. She's dressed like Blanche DuBois from *A Streetcar Named Desire*.

It gives me an idea.

"I'm taking off," I call to Madame Swarsky. She's on the other side of the room, trying to keep some freshman from butchering *Dark of the Moon*. She nods, barely glancing my way, but I'm too busy to take offense. Already, I've hit the redial button on my phone.

Just when I've decided Jesse's the only person in the world without voice mail, he picks up. "Hello?"

"I've got a question," I say, crossing the parking lot. I'm not ready to go home yet, but I'm out of excuses for lingering at Verity.

"Okay."

"It's about the drawing of Lizzie. The one somebody sent you?"

"What about it?" He sounds impatient. Probably he just hates talking about this.

"Was it a forward or did it look like an original email?"

"Forward. I told you that."

"Oh." My little balloon wheezes air. "Right."

"But I saw who sent it originally."

"Do you remember the address?"

*Please say yes. Please say yes. Please say—*

"No. But I'd recognize it if I saw it. It was something idiotic like Big Daddy or Pimp Master. Pretty much what you'd expect."

"Thanks." *Okay, Angie, hang up now.* "Hey, I missed you today." Wow, that is not what I meant. I meant I missed seeing him at school. I meant he was literally missing. The longer he goes without saying "I missed you too," the more excuses I come up with.

Finally he answers. My heart is, like, in my knees by then.

"I know," he says. "I'm sorry. I needed to think about things."

*Told ya so.*

"It's finals week," I say meekly. I'm standing next to my car, trying to unlock the door with shaking hands.

"I took my finals," he says.

"Oh." He must've ducked out the minute he was finished. "I guess I'll let you go then."

*Don't let me. Do not let me hang up the phone.*

"Okay. I'll see you." He pauses. "Hey, Angie?"

"Yeah."

"I'm not trying to be a jerk."

"I know." I slip into my passenger seat. The door closes noiselessly, and then I'm contained.

"No, you don't. Listen . . ." *What the hell else am I going to do?* "Last night was amazing."

"Yeah?" If it was so amazing, why didn't he wake me up before sneaking out the bedroom window?

"You are amazing. And I'm just completely losing it and completely freaked out."

"Hey, it's okay. Welcome to my world."

"You don't understand," he says. "I've never done this before. And we just lost Lizzie, and . . ."

He doesn't need any more reasons. I understand. But he keeps going.

"The queer kids at this school look up to me. I'm the reason we have a Gay-Straight Alliance. They think I'm brave—"

"You are brave."

"I've shown them not to be afraid to express themselves."

"That's great."

"It is," he agrees. "It is. And it shouldn't matter at all, but if they find out I'm not who they thought I was, it's going to mess with them."

"So don't mess with them."

"I know, I just— Wait, what?"

"Don't mess with them."

"Do you mean that?"

"It sounds like they really need you. It's only natural you'd want to be there for them." Everything I'm saying, I'm saying about me. But he has no idea. I guess he doesn't know me that well.

"Angie, you're amazing."

"You said that." I laugh so as not to worry him. Inside, I feel like my heart is cracking and all the blood is oozing out. Really, there should be a limit to how many times that can happen in one life. "I just want you to be happy, Jesse. You're the best person I've ever met."

"I could kiss you," he says. *Yeah, but not in public.* "Can I see you tonight? We could just hang out . . ."

"I'm sorry." I tilt the rearview mirror down, so I can study my reflection. There's something fascinating about watching myself slip further into the darkness. "I've got plans. Maybe tomorrow?"

"Sure, yeah. You're really being great about this."

"That's me." I give a big fake smile. "Supergreat. I'll see you tomorrow."

"Have a good night, Princess."

"Mmm-hmm."

I hang up the phone and call Drake. He answers right away. It's like he was waiting by the phone. *Quite the opposite of Jesse's disappearing act*, I think.

"Hey, sweetie," he says in greeting.

"Hey, I've got a question." Seems to be the theme of the day, doesn't it?

"Sure."

"Did you read the diary pages you found in your locker last week?"

"Wh-what?"

"It's okay, Drake. I saw them in your hand."

He doesn't say anything. Maybe he knows anything he says can and will be used against him.

"I got some too." I'm using the sweetest possible voice. "And I read them. It's really okay. I just want to know what they were about."

"What were yours about?" he asks after a few seconds.

Ah, so he wants to play that game? Well, how does he like this:

"She wrote about the play. I guess she didn't really want to audition. Jesse Martinez convinced her," I lie.

But I'm not the only one. He says, "I got the same thing. That guy's a jerk."

*Liar. Liar. Pants on fire.*

"Listen, Angie?"

I hardly hear him. My thoughts are spinning too fast. "Uh-huh?" I manage.

"I really want to see you. Would you please come by later?"

This time when I smile, it's genuine. "I think I'd really enjoy that."

# twenty-two

DRAKE TAKES MY coat as I step into the house. The place feels like a furnace. His parents keep it at eighty degrees year-round. I guess it makes swimming in the indoor pool more pleasant.

"I'm so glad you came over tonight," he gushes.

"I figured I owed you a chance to explain," I say calmly, avoiding his gaze. I've walked through this doorway so many times. Seen the pristine, imported furniture and the wood-paneled walls. Through the door to the family room, that awful stag's head is staring me down.

"That's great." Drake leads me through the foyer. "You're great."

"People keep telling me that." Maybe I'm baiting him. But he's either too distracted or too clueless to notice.

"Did you bring your suit?" he asks. "Dad and Cynthia won't be home until late-late."

I hold up my purse. "Got my bikini."

His tongue just barely stays in his mouth. "Good. Great. Are you hungry?"

"Are you going to cook for me?"

"I thought I would."

I give him my wryest smile. "Seriously?"

"Come on, Angie, you act like I only think of myself." He pulls out a chair as I enter the kitchen.

"Okay, you're right," I say, sitting down. He pushes the chair in, to meet me. "Let's just get the bad stuff out of the way."

"Sure thing."

"So look." I cross my legs when I catch him looking at them. My jeans are so tight I can barely move. "I don't care if you go out with people. It only really bugs me when they're not conscious."

"No." He pulls up a chair right in front of me. His blue eyes are wide with concern. He looks innocent. The kind of guy you *want* to believe. "You got that all wrong. Cara came on to me and I told her I wasn't interested. But she was so wasted she wouldn't listen. I figured if I got her upstairs, she'd just pass out on the bed."

"That was smart of you."

"Right? But she got sick before we got to the bedroom. Then you showed up, and—"

"Oh no." I put a hand to my lips. "Oh Drake, I thought it was something totally different. I'm so sorry."

"No, *I'm* sorry." He tucks a hair behind my ear. My skin feels hot where he touches me, but it's not the heat of desire anymore. "I shouldn't have gone up there with her. What if she kissed me?"

"That would have been awful," I tease.

"Come on."

"Okay, say I believe you. What happens next?"

"We put it behind us." He puts his hand on my knee. "I make you dinner. I rub that place on your neck that always gets tense."

I giggle, leaning into him. "Then we swim?"

"Yeah. Totally. I mean, if you want to."

"I want to," I tell him. "I want to so bad, I could slip on my bikini right now."

He's choking on his Adam's apple. "Sure, do it."

"No. No, it's silly." I cover my face with my hand.

"I'll do it too," he insists.

"Okay, but there's just one thing . . ." I lower my head, like I'm hiding.

"What?"

"It's embarrassing."

"Come on, tell me."

I peek through my fingers. "I forgot to shave my legs."

"Oh." He frowns. He's glancing at my jeans like I'm Sasquatch underneath. "It's no big deal. You can use Cynthia's razor."

"Can I use your shower, though?"

"Only if I can come."

I lean back. "I need to know that I can trust you, Drake. If I can't trust you, I—"

He holds up his hands. "Hey, I was kidding. Use my shower. Take as long as you like." He makes a shooing motion.

"Thanks, sweetie." I smile, like the word just slipped out.

As I lean in, to give him a kiss on the cheek, he turns to try and catch my mouth. "This dinner is going to blow you away," he says.

"Can't wait."

I slink out of the room and up the stairs.

When I get up to his bedroom the first thing I do is lock the door. See, the bathroom doesn't have a lock. If I don't block him out somehow, he'll assume I want company.

Boys will be boys? No. But Drake will be Drake. Everything is a signal to him.

I start my search in the bathroom, turning on the water and going through the medicine cabinet. Nothing, nothing. Not even a questionable pill collection. The cupboard under the sink is filled with these perfectly folded towels. Tight-ass Drake has really outdone himself.

I return to the bedroom.

A peek under the bed uncovers socks and dirty T-shirts. The mattress is hiding your typical perv-o porn. Inside the closet, his clothes are arranged *by color.* His shoes sit in a row on the floor. I get down on my hands and knees and feel around inside them. I'm starting to get that pathetic feeling again but I've already come so far. And the instinct pushing me to search Drake's room is just *burning* in my chest, like a part of me knows I'm getting close. If I've learned anything from all this snooping around, it's that maybe the universe does have some kind of consciousness that's guiding me.

Or maybe I've gone completely insane.

Either way, I'm not going to give up until I've searched every inch of this room. I'll pull up the carpet and check under the floorboards if I have to.

A hand jiggles the doorknob.

*Drake.*

He's probably got a key. And I can't yell at him to stay out because then he'll know I'm not in the shower. I creep into the bathroom and wait.

After a minute the jiggling stops. I decide to take a chance. I shoot Drake a text to let him know I'm finishing up: "Almost done! I hope you're ready for this."

I figure it'll buy me another five minutes. With bikini paradise so close at hand, he'll have to be a good boy and wait.

Unfortunately, I'm starting to lose steam. I've searched everywhere I can except for that stupid antique bookshelf in the corner. I look up at the thick volumes. He's got *Walden* and *War and Peace* and a gazillion other books he'll never read. It's this big fat hoax, staring back at me.

Like a hollowed-out Bible with a flask inside.

I start pulling books off the shelf like a crazy person, only taking minimal care to make sure they don't crash to the ground. If I have to, I can tell Drake I fell in the shower. He'd totally believe it. He thinks I'm ditsy.

I let him think that.

The top row is clean. No secrets hiding behind any of the books. I start to pull off entire stacks, carrying them in my arms to the bed. The second row is also clean.

*Damn.*

I start to worry I'm going to find a big, fat pile of nothing before I even get to the bottom. For a second I think this feeling is defeat. But tiny fingers are creeping up my back and I realize it's something else entirely. It's intuition. I'm looking behind the books and under the books and I should be looking in the books.

I am, after all, looking for pages.

I find them slid neatly into his copy of *The Time Traveler's Wife*. Definitely ironic. Far be it from Drake to read a love story. I'm guessing the book was a gift from Cynthia. You know, a stepmother's sad little attempt to bond.

But never mind that. I've got the pages in my hand. Not photocopied, like the ones from school, but *real* pages. Pages torn out of Lizzie's diary. I can see where Drake ripped through the perforated edges.

I glance at the first page, my heart going crazy in my chest. A part of me wants to read them right now but I know I can't. I recognize the date on the top of the page: April nineteenth. Prom night. If I read them now, my heart will break, and I won't be able to hide my emotions from Drake.

I fold up the pages and slide them into my purse.

Drake knocks on the door just as I'm putting the last of his books on the shelf. I've tried to put them back in the right order but my brain isn't exactly at its best. All these books look the same and I have to get home—I need to get home—I have to get home right now. But I'm scared. I feel completely cold, like the blood has left my body. When I open the door for Drake the tears are already forming.

"Baby, you're in for a— What's wrong?"

"I'm sorry." I cover my face with my hands. "I'm such an idiot."

"Angie? What happened?"

I look at him like my heart is breaking. "I brought the wrong bikini!"

"What?"

"I just grabbed it out of my closet. One's blue and the other one's black. I can't believe I did this!"

"Whoa, wait. Did you just put the words *wrong* and *bikini* in the same sentence?"

I smile through my hand. "Stop."

"Come on, babe. You'll look amazing. Just get dressed and then we'll eat."

"I can't, Drake, it makes me look fat. And if I eat, it'll get worse, and—"

"You're not fat."

"I didn't say I was fat." I scowl at him. "I said it makes me *look* fat." Pushing past him, I head for the stairs. I'm clutching my purse to my chest like a baby. "It'll take me, like, two minutes to go get it."

"No way." He's plodding down the stairs after me. "Dinner's ready. You won't look fat."

"Yes, I will." My hand is on the doorknob and he can barely locate his brain to stop me. I can see those rusty gears trying to turn in his head. They're saying: She *is* a girl, after all. They do crazy things all the time.

*Eye roll.*

"I'll be right back." I breeze past the door, tossing it back in Drake's direction.

"Angie, wait."

It slams in his face.

I wish I could take back the times I spent alone with him. I wish a lot of things. But as I speed down the block to my house, with no intention of returning to Drake's for a late-night swim, I have no idea how good I've got it. Because once I read the entry Drake stole from Lizzie's diary, I'll never be able to go back to this moment.

Memory plays tricks on me. The more time passes, the less I'm able to get it right. I see the events leading up to my descent like movie stills hanging on a wall. Here, I'm perched on the edge of the bed. Here, he leans in to tell me something sweet. I'm not buying what he says, not completely. But part of me wants to believe.

I've had a best friend for as long as I can remember. I've had a father who looks out for my soul. But I've never been loved, not really. Never felt the warmth of it. At every turn, there has been doubt.

Maybe that's why things happened the way they did. Maybe, at least, that's why I invited him in. Like a vampire. Didn't I learn my lesson? Boys who come creeping into girls' bedrooms at night are only after one thing. First the KNOCK, then the tentative entering. I should have known better.

That phrase keeps replaying in my head.

I try to clear some static. This is how it looks inside of me:

I'm sitting on the edge of the bed. He's in the

chair, opposite me. I remember thinking, he's giving me space. He probably thinks I'll break. Everybody treats me this way.

Foolish me.

He talks about the dance, makes a joke about finals. I get the feeling he's trying to relate to me, the way a detective will invent commonality to get you to trust him. But I don't take offense at his manipulation. I think he's trying to make me comfortable. Maybe he wants my approval, since he's dating my best friend.

Better late than never, right?

Indeed.

His dark hair is slicked back, his jacket slung over the back of the chair. He looks like an old-time movie star, the kind that dies at twenty-five. That lifestyle gets under your skin, transforms you. I don't hear the change in his voice when he's about to transform for me, but I feel it. The air changes in the room.

I'm not sure what I say next. I remember paying him some sort of compliment. Maybe I say I like his tux. Maybe I tell him he'll ace his finals. I'm not saying anything deep. I'm just trying to make him comfortable like he is doing for me. My mouth feels dry. I'm nervous.

I have reason to be.

I can see him sitting there on the chair, several

feet away from me, and then he's crawling on the bed over me. I don't have time to think, or breathe. His mouth touches mine the instant the comforting words are out of my lips.

I realize, later, that he was waiting for them. I realize he took them as a signal I hadn't actually sent.

I don't stop him in that moment. In that moment, I don't even realize where I am. And for several seconds after, Elizabeth Hart goes spinning through space and time, her soul seeking a separate dimension in which this series of events would make sense.

Drake. Homecoming and soon-to-be Prom King. Reincarnated 1950s superstar kissing the most beautiful girl in school's forgettable best friend.

Me.

I need to think, to separate from him, to breathe. The need to breathe occurs to me last, but it's the best reason I can find to move back. There is something about the words "Get off me," "What are you doing?" or, the most vicious, "I don't want you," that seem utterly impossible to speak.

Clearly, there has been a misunderstanding, in which he believes I would ever, for any reason on earth, betray the trust of my best friend. Clearly, I need only to move away and remind him of this, and the miscommunication will be cleared up.

Oh Lizzie of the Past, foolish thing. I do and do not miss that girl. Certainly she looked on the world with brighter, more forgiving eyes, but she was an animal staring down the barrel of a gun. It was only a matter of time before

She

Got

Destroyed.

I duck away from Drake's suction-cup lips to tell him, "I need to breathe."

He takes this to mean: I need to take a shaky half breath and then you can go back to sucking my soul out through my mouth.

This is, of course, not what I mean. Neither of us is saying what we're thinking, but I'm the only one who'll suffer from it.

When I try to pull away, he holds on to me. He says, "You don't have to say anything."

What could I possibly say?

He says, "I know how you feel. How you've always felt. I know you're just afraid to hurt Angie."

That last part is true. I've spent much of my life trying not to "hurt Angie."

"But I've seen you looking at me," he whispers.

I say, "We're friends," or something equally stupid. It doesn't matter. It's like he doesn't hear me.

He says, "I've been looking at you too. You're so

beautiful." This, from the guy who's used to staring at perfection.

The universe has definitely turned on its head.

But here, for one time only, the confession:

There is a part of me that likes it. Not the kissing. Not the forcefulness, when I never so much as said "I like you," which is, I would think, the least possible prerequisite to this kind of coupling. We learned that in, what, kindergarten?

But I like the compliment. No one ever says that stuff to me.

And maybe I needed to hear it. Maybe we all do. In this world of models and popstar princesses, is it altogether shocking that I might respond to being physically appreciated for the first time in my life?

The most sought-after guy in school thinks I'm beautiful. I can't help it. I smile.

He takes that as a sign too.

Now his hands are tugging at my dress. I keep thinking: I just put it on. Why would I want to take it off?

Stupidity. Nonsense. But this is all my brain can process at the moment. It seems fixated on this simple contradiction, like, if I can figure that out, everything will make sense.

My first real words of protest are "I can't do this."

(As "I need to breathe" was apparently open to interpretation.)

And yes. I say "I can't do this" rather than "I don't want to do this." Seems clear-cut to me. But Drake's response indicates it isn't clear-cut at all; as if he too is working out an equation in his head, and if he can simply show that I can, in fact, do this (Look! It's happening! You're doing it!), I'll change my mind.

But I don't change my mind. I don't change it in the least, even as my brain tries to send messages to my heart that everything is completely fine.

It goes a little like this:

Everything's fine. No big deal. A kiss is just a kiss. And these may be the only kisses you'll ever get. Yes, by some celestial oversight, or rip in the space-time continuum, an actual human being has deigned to kiss you. That, in and of itself, should not be cause for panicking.

Never mind that my heart is panicking, regardless of the pretty lies my brain tries to tell. No butterfly fluttering in this chest of mine. My heart is all-out slamming against me. And heat, unbearable heat. The heat of fear, the heat of shame. I'm scared, and though I haven't even done anything wrong, I'm already sorry.

Relax, says my naïve brain. He'll stop if you

properly articulate yourself ("I can't do this" joining "I need to breathe" on the list of Improperly Articulated Feelings). He'll remember the rules any moment now, remember he belongs to someone else. Remember his decency.

He's just confused/overexcited/testing me. Probably some game boys play.

"I need to stop," I say.

I'm the one who needs to? asks my brain. As if my hands are barreling across his skin like territory I can't wait to claim. As if I've been doing anything but moving backward and pulling his hands away.

I suppose he takes my words to mean I need to stop doing that—resisting—because he doesn't stop anything. Not one thing.

Now his hands are visiting places I've never invited anyone, hidden places, places I keep secret for a reason.

Saving them for someone who loves me.

(And since no one ever will, you'll be untouched forever, taunts brain. And heart replies, Safe.)

At this point the conversation inside of me has taken precedence over anything going on outside. Maybe it's for the best. Drake is using his hand to dive into me. His face is close to mine, whispering how it feels to touch me. How it makes him feel.

That's what it should be about, right? How it makes him feel?

I start to choose my phrases at random. "Stop," I say. "I can't do this. You need to slow down. Seriously." I add the "seriously" when he rips my dress. He rips my dress, so that the moment this is over, I can't pretend it never happened. There is evidence for everyone to see.

Even you.

Oh God. What will you think of me? But I can't even focus on what this will do to other people because I'm too busy telling myself this can't be happening to me. It can't. It can't be. Everyone hears stories of these things. We all think of what we will do.

I would kick. I would scream. Bite, tear out hair, anything.

But I don't do any of those things because those things would prove something unspeakable is happening. Drake is my friend. He's my friend. He would never do anything to hurt me. I must not have made it clear to him—

My brain doesn't get to finish this time. My heart is fast at its heels and it is screaming:

You've said stop, you've said it a dozen times now. He knows what that means. Of course he knows what it means. He's not listening. He's not stopping. Look at him, he's—

Then, static.

The outside world goes quiet. I can hear no breathing. No voice speaking. My heart and my brain are at war and it completely takes over me. I don't have to think about the fact that my dress isn't the only thing he's ripping. I don't have to feel it, or anything. I'm having a conversation with myself, that's all.

I close my eyes so I'm the only one in the room I can see.

Time passes strangely. At least, that's how I feel after. But it doesn't matter because this war inside me stretches out into eternity. It is never-ending. My brain and my heart, mortal enemies. Neither will listen to the other ever again.

In the hours that follow, my heart speaks with a quieter voice.

All the while, my brain asks me things: If you wanted him to leave, why didn't you fight? Why didn't you scream?

All that time in that room while he was misunderstanding (must have been misunderstanding), I spoke softly: convincing, then pleading. I never once raised my voice.

Why?

Then finally, after hours and hours of hearing

this question on repeat in my brain, my heart
replies:

Because he wasn't a wild animal come to swallow
me. Because he wasn't a loathed enemy. He was a
friend. A friend of my best friend. A friend of all
of our families. Because it's so much easier to
believe I made a mistake than it is to admit someone
raped me.

Why didn't I raise my voice?

He could hear me perfectly.

# twenty-three

THE KNOCK ON my window comes at ten after one. My dad's sleeping soundly in the next room. Sure, I could have driven the five blocks from Drake's to my mom's place, but I needed the sound barrier created by Dad's snoring to hide my sobs. I don't know how I knew Lizzie's entry would pull all the anguish out of me, I just knew.

And I was right. Contrary to popular opinion, it does not feel good to let out what I've been holding in. It's been poison in my gut and when I let it out, it's all I can taste.

My eyes are dry when Jesse crawls through the window. I left it cracked so he could let himself in. I'm sitting on the bed like a statue, the book of poems he gave to Lizzie in my hands. Opened to the last page.

I start to read before he's all the way inside.

"Ericka Engleson has written twenty-two acclaimed titles in her lifetime, including *The Unofficial Guide to the Lesbian Love Nest* and fourteen books of erotic poetry. She lives in Vermont with her wife and their two beloved Yorkies."

He sits on the bed but keeps his distance. Yeah, he's scared.

"Tell me something, Jesse." I hold up the book, cocking my head to one side. "You gave Lizzie a book of erotic lesbian poetry. Whyever so?"

He fiddles with the zipper of his sweatshirt. "Where did you get that?"

Ooh. Big mistake. Answering a question with a question is a telltale sign of guilt.

"I got it in Lizzie's bedroom," I say. "When and why is none of your business."

He studies his palms like they'll give him the answers to the universe. His breath is coming out in little puffs. "I don't—I don't know anything . . ."

"Well, maybe you need more information." I lean over the bed. In one swift movement, I've switched the book of poems with the stack of pages I left sitting on my nightstand. The ones containing all of Lizzie's secrets, but only if you read carefully.

*"After this year, I might lose the chance to tell you how I feel,"* I quote from her September entry.

"I don't want to hear this."

"I didn't either," I say, fingers tracing the writing. "Not this way. Not from her diary. Not when she could've said it to my face."

"Angie."

"God, not even to my face." I shake my head. "She could've passed me a note in class. Stuck it in my locker and bolted—"

"Baby."

"Whispered it quietly, when she thought I was sleeping."

He reaches out. I jerk away, thinking he's going for the pages in my hand. But I should know better than that.

He's the only person in the world who doesn't want to read them.

"Tell me what I can do for you," he says, lips barely moving.

"You can listen. Listen to her story and understand. All she ever wanted was understanding—"

"I'll try." His voice is meek and broken.

"Thank you. Now, where was I?" I flip to the second page. "Here it is: *I used to sing for you all the time. Remember? At the park, when the three of us played trolls and fairies . . . Your eyes lit up at the sounds I could make.*"

I pause, smiling at the memory. Seeing it in an entirely new light.

"That's sweet," Jesse says.

"Isn't it? Lizzie really had a thing for old Drakey-boy." My body tenses at the mention of his name. But Jesse's still watching me, so I keep reading:

"*What if you could hear me sing again? Would your heart hear what your eyes refuse to see? Would you come running to me? Or even walking? Walking I would accept, at this point.*"

Jesse laughs softly. "Lizzie was funny."

"Lizzie was fucking hilarious. And nobody knew . . ."

"I knew." After a minute, he adds, "What else?" He says it casually, like we're discussing modern fashions, but he's tearing at his cuticles like he's trying to unravel himself from the outside.

"Here, she talks about auditioning for *Midsummer*: *You'll come to watch the play. The school's MVPs always do. Cheerleaders and football stars mingling with the artists . . . Then, maybe for one brief moment, you'll take my hand and feel what I still can't speak.*"

Jesse's gaze flicks to the windowsill. I know what he's thinking: *Two steps, and I'm out of this place. Two steps, and I never have to come back.*

"Just one more," I promise. "One more passage about Drake. That's who she loved, right? Drake, the football star. Drake, who turned into an ugly troll when we wanted to play fairies. And my God, to love him her entire life . . . that's dedication." I flip to

Lizzie's prom-night entry. My gut starts clenching, begging me to turn away.

"I'm really sorry about this," I say to Jesse, though he must know I'm not just talking to him. "I'm *really* sorry."

"Angie."

"*He rips my dress,*" I read quickly. "*He rips my dress, so that the moment this is over, I can't pretend it never happened. There is evidence for everyone to see. Even you.*"

His eyes are closed when I look up again.

"*You,*" I repeat, flipping from page to page. "You'll *come to watch the play.* You'll *take my hand. I might lose the chance to tell* you *how I feel . . .*" I return to the final page. "A different 'you' from who was in the room."

Jesse swallows audibly. He must know what I'm going to ask next. He turns away just as I speak the words, "Did you know?"

Still, my voice finds him. "She never told me," he says. "But we talked a lot during rehearsals. She thought I was gay . . ."

"*Why didn't you tell me?*" The pages slip from my hands.

He pulls his knees up to his chest. He's cradling himself, there on the corner of my bed. "I didn't know you then. I hardly knew Lizzie . . ."

I nod, but my heart is sinking. My entire body is sinking, and I don't think I'll ever climb out of this abyss. "All this time, I thought she was in love with *Drake.*"

*Brown hair. Blue eyes. Always a secret.*

He looks up at me. His eyes are wet, and I don't know if he's sad for me, or for Lizzie, or for both of us. For the future we'll never have in any capacity. "I don't think she wanted you to know," he says finally.

"She could've told me."

He nods but I can tell he doesn't believe me. He thinks I'm lying to myself.

*Why shouldn't I? I've lied to everyone else.*

"She was probably afraid," he says after a minute. "You meant the world to her." It's the absolute worst thing he can say. The numbness inside me ruptures. I have to fight to stop from breaking.

"And I let her down." I swallow over and over. I feel the poison rising again. But I refuse to let it out in front of Jesse. "How could I have missed this? How could I have thought she loved Drake? She didn't even *like* him . . ." I think of the prom-night entry, devoid of any romantic feelings. If Lizzie had loved Drake, she would've wanted to kiss him, even if she felt conflicted. She would've noticed the curve of his lips, the smell of his skin. She would've noticed *something*.

But she didn't.

Lifting Lizzie's pages from the ground, I slide them into my nightstand drawer. "You know what's really pathetic? I never would've figured it out without the missing entry. I would've spent my whole stupid life thinking—"

"Wait—what do you mean, *missing?*"

I stop, just watching him. "You really didn't read anything that was being passed around, did you?"

"Of course I didn't," Jesse says, and I have to believe him. He has no reason to lie about the thing I've been doing all along.

I inhale slowly. "The pages that got passed around were only from certain dates," I explain. "But the week of prom never showed up. So I figured either she didn't write about it or that part was missing."

"How did you find it, then?"

"I went over to Drake's tonight."

"Are you okay?" His body's inching toward mine. I don't think he even realizes he's doing it.

I curl in on myself. "I'm fine. He's the one who should be worried. I—" I freeze. My entire body crystallizes. "Wait a second."

"What?"

"Did you know about him?" I push myself to the edge of the bed. My teeth are so clenched it's a wonder the words can slip past my lips.

But he hears me. I can tell by the look on his face. "Know what?" he asks, trembling.

"Did you know what he did?"

"I don't . . ."

"You warned me about him," I say breathlessly. "You got my number that night he followed me after class. You said you were worried. Why were you worried, Jesse? Did you know the *entire time*?"

"I didn't!" His voice cracks. I wonder if he's going to break down right in front of me. I can't tell if that would be brave or weak, and suddenly it's very important, because I'm certain I'm going to cry in front of him. "I just suspected."

"Well, congratulations. You were right."

He's hiding his face between his knees. "No."

"Yes."

"It can't be what happened. It *can't* be."

"It is. And I let him go after her. I practically fucking orchestrated it." I close my eyes, trying to push away the memories. But behind my lids, the images of Lizzie in the hotel room are rearranging. Telling a different story from the one I chose to believe.

She's reaching out for me.

She's crying.

She's begging me to stop him.

This isn't how it happened, but every second since I read the missing entry I've seen it this way. I've seen myself abandoning her in her darkest moment.

I've seen myself pushing her into her grave.

"I believed something *ridiculous* about her because I didn't want to believe he'd hurt her this way." I turn away from Jesse. From everything. "I didn't want to hurt *myself,* so I let her suffer. I let her die."

"You didn't." His arms go around me. It happens so fast, it actually startles me, and I'm pushing him away before I can stop myself.

"Don't touch me!" I should lower my voice, but I can't calm down. "I don't deserve to be touched after what I did—I deserve to be punished. So does Drake."

"Sweetheart." His arms are scrambling to hold me, and it's the first time he's ever fought me this way.

I catch his eye, so he can see what a bad idea this is. "Don't you dare," I say. "Don't tell me not to hurt him."

"I don't . . ." Without me to hold on to, his hands go to his hair. "I think people should be warned about him. But whatever you're planning—"

"Don't worry your pretty little head."

"I'm worried about you. You're going to make yourself insane."

"Oh, baby, I'm so far beyond that."

"Angie."

"What? What can you say to defend the person who raped my best friend? What can you say to defend the people who killed her?"

He stares at me like I'm a stranger. And honest to God it makes me laugh.

I say, "They did. You know they did. If any one of us hadn't treated her like complete shit, she would still be here."

"I didn't treat her like shit."

"I guess you're special then."

"That's not what I meant." He's staring at me and staring at me but I can't *see* him. "I'm telling you I tried to be her friend. After that night. After . . ."

"What happened?"

"I pushed too hard. I knew something had happened that she wasn't saying. I thought if I could get to the truth, some of the tormenting would stop."

"It wouldn't have. They all love having someone to hate. It would've just made it worse when no one believed her."

"You would have believed her."

The words chill me deeper than I can say.

"But she never told you?" I ask. "Not about . . . him?"

He shakes his head. "She got mad when I wouldn't let it go. She said we were only friends during the play and pretty much told me to get lost."

"That doesn't sound like Lizzie at all."

"She wasn't herself at the end."

"No." I lower my head. The sadness is rising up in me, tearing my insides to shreds. "I can't handle this."

"Yes, you can."

"No, I can't." I pull my knees up to my chest. "I can't do this. I just want it to end."

"Please don't say that."

"I can't help it." I'm rocking back and forth and tears are soaking through to my pants.

He scoots closer to me.

My body goes rigid.

"I'm not going to do anything," he says, and it just makes me think of Drake.

I cry harder, trying to push him away without moving my hands from where they're wrapped around me. "I can't do this." I hug myself tighter. "I cannot live knowing what he did and I can't live with myself if I don't do anything."

"Angie."

"I can't live knowing what we did to her. I can't live knowing what I did."

"Listen to me." His face is close but it's not touching me. "You don't have to forgive them but you have to forgive yourself."

"I can't."

"Give yourself time."

"Time doesn't do anything."

"It will."

I don't answer, though I know it scares him. I can't even talk, there's so much poison pouring out of me. I want to swallow it down so I don't have to feel it. I want to swallow it down and sleep.

"Can I hold you?" he asks.

The thought of him holding me makes me feel trapped. Like I'm in a coffin. But I can't say no because he feels better than anyone I've ever met. "Please make this end."

His arms go around me so lightly, this time I could swear they're wings. "It's okay, baby," he whispers, and the words pour over me. "I love you."

I laugh at him. "Yeah, right."

"Look at me." He lifts my chin with his hand, though I keep trying to dodge his gaze. "I'm not saying *let's get married*." His breath is so close it makes me shiver. "I'm saying as a person, as a human being, I love you."

"You don't even know me."

"I do." He brushes the wet strands of hair from my face. "Everything's going to be okay." He looks so sincere I just want to make him feel better. To make up for the pain I've caused.

I kiss him.

He kisses me back. It's probably the last thing we should be doing but I don't care because I need to feel this right now. I need to feel his love so badly, I'm afraid I won't survive without it. He's being gentle so as not to hurt me, but I'm kissing him like I'm starving to death.

"Can I take this off you?" I whisper, sliding my fingers down his sweatshirt. He nods. When I pull it over his head, his T-shirt comes with it. But he doesn't seem to mind, and that's good, because I don't mind a bit.

Now I can see him, taste him, touch him. His skin looks beautiful in the moonlight. I've never had romantic thoughts like this. But it literally aches to look at him, and before I can stop myself I'm climbing on top of him, fingers stumbling over his chest. They slide up to his shoulders and down the muscles in his arms.

"Tell me if you want me to stop," I say into his lips.

He doesn't hesitate. "I don't."

I push him back, onto the bed. Lifting his arms over his head, I entwine my fingers with his, holding his hands against the mattress. But I start to worry that it's bad, like I have him pinned, so I let go and focus on his lips. He's kissing me more hungrily now, trailing his hands down my arms, to my waist. When he touches my stomach this wild electricity goes through me like I'm alive for the first time. Then I'm guiding his hands down, toward the waist of my pants. Just before he gets there he touches this rough patch on my skin, above my hip.

*Shit.*

He stops.

*Shit. Shit. Shit.*

I sit very still. Still is best. Still says: Not guilty.

"What is that?" he asks, breathing heavily.

"A birthmark." I lean back a little, out of his hands.

But his eyes are glued to the spot. My heart is beating so loudly I swear he can hear it.

"Come back," he says.

I shake my head. I start to climb off him but he stops me. Just gently, with his hands on my hips. I could push him away if I wanted.

"Baby, what's wrong?" he asks.

It's probably the last time he'll ever speak to me like that so I savor it, closing my eyes and letting myself feel warm. But the chill returns at full force when he lifts my waistband, just an inch, to see the word etched into my skin.

*KILLER*

"Did you do this?"

I can't breathe. I keep trying, but I can't. He tries to give me space by relaxing into the bed, but he's not relaxed, he's stiff as can be, and I can tell he's having trouble breathing too.

"I guess that proves it." I'm going for light and cheery, but I just sound tired. "You really didn't read her diary."

"What do you mean?"

"Lizzie carved *SLUT* into herself, just above her hip." I shrug, so casually. "We were best friends. Blood sisters, since first grade. I thought we should match."

"This is bad, Angie." He pulls his T-shirt over his head. He does it reflexively, like he can't stand the exposure now that we've stopped kissing.

"Everything I do is bad."

*Go ahead, ask me what I mean. I dare you.*

But he doesn't. He says, "You didn't kill her."

"Yes I did. I'm the reason they went after her." My eyes close, but it's too late. Tears are slipping past my lashes. "They did it *for me.*"

"You never asked them to," he says, brushing my cheek. His hands are so soft. I can't believe he's still touching me.

"It doesn't matter," I say, leaning into him. Taking what I can get. But his hand falls away. "If I'd stood up to them *one time*, they would've stopped."

He doesn't say anything. There's nothing he can say. My actions are unforgivable. My *inactions*.

"I thought she betrayed me," I say, unable to take his silence. "I thought she only pretended to love me all those years. But I was wrong. She loved me too much."

He nods but doesn't speak.

"You know what the worst thing is? It's not that her silence protected Drake. It's that even if she wanted to sleep with him, she wouldn't have deserved what we did. Even if she'd seduced him, she wouldn't have deserved it."

"Of course she wouldn't have," he agrees. His body is rocking a tiny bit, quickly, like it's vibrating. I wonder if he's sorry he kissed me. I'm clearly unstable.

*That's the nice way of putting it.*

"Everyone makes mistakes," I say. "But Lizzie never made one in her entire life. And the one time she does—the time I think she does—I turn my back on her completely." I look down at my scar. "That's why I did it."

"You shouldn't have done that to yourself," he says. "Let me look at it."

I would rather tear out my eyes, but I go very still and I let him. "I deserve worse," I say. "I abandoned her when she needed me most. I killed my best friend."

"Angelina." I wait for him to contradict me, but he's too busy staring at my skin. Running his fingers over the mark. "This scar is healed."

"So?"

"So, Lizzie's diary showed up at school last week. When did you do this?"

"I don't know. Sometime last week."

"When?" he asks, and his voice has gone cold. "Wednesday? Thursday? Pick a day, Angie."

"Why are you talking to me this way? We were just kissing." But maybe that's why he's angry. Maybe he's sorry he wasted those kisses on me. He was probably saving them.

He swallows thickly. "I need to know."

"I don't remember. Maybe Thursday." My whole body's shaking.

But that's okay. He's not looking at me anymore. He's looking at the space between us, like there'll never be enough of it. When he finally lifts his head, his eyes are red. "This couldn't have healed that quickly."

The world goes quiet. All I can hear is the ringing in my ears when I say "It did."

He shakes his head. He's staring at me and now I know he's sorry he kissed me. No, not sorry. Sick. "It was you."

He crawls off the bed like it's covered in insects. He's backing himself into the wall, desperate to get away from me. "*You* wrote SUICIDE SLUT on the lockers in Lizzie's writing. You brought copies of her diary to school."

I look at him. Just look. He's even more beautiful now that I'm going to lose him.

"Yes."

# twenty-four

FIVE ETERNAL SECONDS have passed since my darkest confession. The ringing in my ears is making me sick. I can barely breathe, but I open my mouth and I push out the words: "I found Lizzie's diary the night of her funeral. I went back home with her dad. You saw how he was at the service. He could hardly get his legs to function."

Jesse watches me from the windowsill. He's perched there in case he gets too disgusted and has to leave. Already the taste of him is gone from my lips.

Now it's just poison, and I deserve it.

"I knew she had a diary. Most of us saw her with it. I wish I could tell you I only read it to understand, but that would be another lie. I wanted to see if she knew who was harassing her."

"Did she?" he says, barely a whisper. I wish he would just yell at me and get it over with. Tell me how horrible I am. It's nothing I don't already know. It might even be comforting to hear it.

"Even in her diary, Lizzie was secretive. She mentioned Shelby, but not what Shelby did. Kennedy was tricky; it took some investigating to find out she was the girl Lizzie 'betrayed.' I have you to thank for that, spy-buddy," I add, but he doesn't smile. "The reference to Marvin was obvious—who else would be watching her through her windows?"

He lowers his head. His arms wrap around him protectively. I envy those arms, but it's too late to touch him.

"The only person she blamed outright was Drake," I say. "Even that, she had a hard time saying. But *rape* isn't an easy word. I find myself talking around it—"

His head snaps up. "Wait—you *knew* about him? And you went over there?"

I shake my head. "I didn't. I didn't know."

"I don't understand."

"Lizzie's diary was intact except for one thing. The part where she wrote about prom was torn out. At least, that's what I thought was missing. It made sense, because of the dates." I smile, covering my face with my hand. "I should have figured out how she felt about me based on the things she said. It should've been obvious, if I hadn't been *looking* for something else. But I was so focused on thinking she loved Drake because of the way she acted around him. Almost cold, like she was trying to keep us off her scent."

"She was."

"Yeah, but not in the way I thought. She never referred to her crush by name. Lizzie was smart. I spent a lot of time at her house."

"She thought you might read it?"

"I never would have, back then. I think she was just being careful, you know? It's sad, if you think about it. She let me think she was after my boyfriend rather than admit how she felt."

I sniff and try to hide it with a cough.

Jesse looks at the box of tissues on my nightstand like he's thinking of handing me one. He decides against it. I can tell he doesn't want to be nice to me anymore. Why would he?

*So much for loving me.*

Finally, he says, "Maybe it wasn't about hiding her feelings after what happened with Drake. Maybe she was just afraid of him."

"Maybe." I nod slowly.

"Or maybe she thought things would get worse if people knew how she felt about you."

I look over. He feels miles away from me. Still, when I ask "Could it have gotten worse?" I *see* the effect.

"Trust me, baby," he says, laughing into his hands. He's forcing a smile to hide his bitterness. "Just the *possibility* is enough to keep people quiet for years."

I lower my head. "I would've accepted her," I say, and I know it's true. The truth sounds different. It tastes different too. "I don't know if I could have felt . . . I don't know. But I loved her more than anything." I inhale slowly. "That's why I had to be punished for what I did. That's why we all did."

He stands, like he's either going to come to me or bolt. "That's why you wrote what you did at school? To punish them?"

"I did it so they couldn't forget. I could see them starting to move past it, treating other people like shit. Treating you like shit—"

"Don't make this about me."

"I'm not making it about you! I'm saying there's a connection. I'm saying that it's dangerous to *forget*." I close my eyes, pressing my fingers into my eyelids. "That week, after her funeral, I walked by her locker and all the words had been washed away. Painted over, like they never existed. Like *she* never existed. Like we didn't destroy her."

"So you wrote it again?"

"I didn't plan it. I just stood there, running my hands over the paint. If you got real close, you could still see the bumps where they'd etched it into the locker. They got smart after a while, you know? Once they realized marker would wash away."

He squeezes his eyes shut. "That's horrible."

"That's how I felt," I say, scooting closer to where he's standing. Sitting right in front of him. "It's exactly how I felt, and before I could stop myself, I was writing SUICIDE SLUT over the fresh coat of paint. It made everything sound different, didn't it? It made it obvious how stupid and cruel we'd been. SUICIDE SLUT. To me, it said we branded her a slut and now she's gone."

"Angie."

"And just like that, I knew something had to be done."

"The diary?" He's pacing a little. It would be cute if I weren't so scared right now. So scared and so sick with myself.

"I didn't copy all the pages. Just the ones about people who'd affected her final days. I wanted to smoke out the guilty parties, get everyone looking in their direction. I guess, in a way, I wanted them to know I was coming for them."

"So Shelby . . . ?" he asks, tearing a cuticle from his thumb. Blood springs up in its place.

"Shelby was tricky," I confess. "Marvin got to her pages before she did. Just like you did with Marvin's. Instant karma, I guess."

He slides his thumb between his lips. No doubt he's thinking of that day, of Troy and Zeke treating him like garbage. Maybe they would've done it anyway, without Lizzie's pages to provoke them.

But we'll never really know, and I'll never be able to make it up to him.

Suddenly he stops. He stares right through me. "You tricked me," he says, dropping his hand. "You tricked me into letting you write on the walls of the boys' bathroom."

"Jesse—"

"Don't say my name." He backs away. "Don't look at me. Don't talk to me."

I stand, though I don't dare touch him now. "Jesse, I'm sorry. It was wrong to do that to you. You have no idea how bad I felt."

He shakes his head. "You lie so easily."

"I'm not lying! I hated using you that way," I insist, and it's the truth. "I hated watching them read her words." I curl my hands into fists. "But I'd already set things in motion. I couldn't go back."

"You can always go back."

"God, I wish that were true. But I've tried to stop, Jesse. I can't."

He's holding his hair in his hands. Not long ago, my hands were holding him. How quickly everything slips from our grasp.

"I don't know how to deal with this," he says. "I don't know how to forgive you for . . . for *everything*."

"Good. You finally know how I feel."

"No. That's the difference between you and me. I'm not going to launch some psycho attack on you. You're out of my life."

"That's probably for the best."

"Listen to yourself!" He steps up to me, and I can't believe he can stand to be so close. "Listen to what you're saying."

"I hear myself perfectly." The words sound like an echo in my ears. They remind me of Lizzie, waiting for Drake to stop hurting her. Believing he would just because *she* wouldn't hurt anybody.

The numbness in my heart starts to spread.

"What are you going to do?" Jesse studies my eyes.

I dodge his gaze. "Nothing big."

"Please don't do this." He's switched from angry to pleading in an instant, as if darkness can't survive in his body. His hands slide over my arms. He's so fucking warm. "You have to let it go. I meant it when I said—"

"Just go, Jesse." I slip out of his grasp. "You're better than this. You've pretty much said so yourself." My voice is more tired than mean.

He's working out a battle inside him. I can see it in the way he shakes. "I really want to help you."

I open the window for him. "You can't."

"Just promise me one thing." He's staring at the glass. He's staring like he knows, once he leaves, he's never coming back. "Don't go after Drake by yourself." He looks over at me, still hopeful.

"Aw, honey. Don't you worry about that."

Jesse zips up his sweatshirt, bracing himself against the darkness. But me, I don't even feel it.

It's already so much a part of me.

# twenty-five

W‍EDNESDAY MORNING I manage to avoid Drake's many calls. His texts are getting angrier in my inbox. But the only one I care about comes in from a number I don't recognize. It says: DaddyMac6969.

Looks like Shelby came through on her end of the bargain.

I send her a quick response and head to the bleachers. I'm hoping to cut off a couple of Cheer Bears before they get to Cheer Central. I catch them halfway across the football field, arms linked, doing that faux-lesbian thing guys think is hot. Cara's whispering so close to Elliot's ear she's practically nibbling on it. Her dark hair blends with Elliot's red. A couple of runners have stopped to watch.

"Sexy ladies," I yell, jogging to catch up to them. "Hold up."

I put my arms around their shoulders and they part to let me in.

"Hey, babe," says Elliot.

*Ugh. Do not call me that.*

Cara says "I'm glad you're not mad about Drake," right off the bat.

"He's not worth it," I say with a snort. Cara may be on my shit list but she still deserves better than him. Everyone does. "If you know what I mean."

She grins. "Point taken."

"Good. So, last night I had the best idea," I say as the bleachers come into view. Kennedy's watching us from up above. No doubt she suspects I'm up to something. "You know how we decorated those T-shirts the first day of the year?" We wrote things like *Seniors Rule!* and *See Ya, Suckas!* "I thought we could do something on our graduation gowns. Something about the squad. Or even . . ." I glance at the bleachers, biting my lip tentatively. "About Kennedy?"

"To show her how much we love her?" Elliot gushes.

"That's so sweet!" Cara agrees. For an instant, I feel sorry for them. As beautiful as they are, either one would kill to be Kennedy. Both are going to Colorado State so they can be close to her.

"What should we say?" Elliot chews on a strand of hair.

"Something simple," I reply. "It has to be short, so it'll fit."

"Hey." Cara turns to me. I can tell by her widened eyes that she's falling right into my trap. "What if we each did one word? Like"—she points to each of us—"We. Love. Kennedy." Naturally, she assigns *Kennedy* to herself.

"That's brilliant." I clap my hands. "But we can't let her find out."

"We can keep a secret," Elliot promises.

"I know you can. We just have to find a way to get the gowns tonight instead of tomorrow."

"That Shelby girl's sorting them," Elliot says. "Isn't she in your Drama class?"

"Oh, yeah." I nod like the wheels in my head are turning. "Yeah, maybe I can get her to give them to me."

"Steal them if you have to!" Cara tugs my arm. "We *have* to do this."

"I agree," I say as we approach the bottom of the bleachers. "We have to."

Kennedy glares as we ascend. It's clear she's ready for a fight. All I have to do is point her in a different direction . . .

"Hello, darling." I practically sit in her lap.

She speaks casually but the words tickle my spine. "What are you girls cooking up?"

Cara and Elliot are guilty-conscience pale, but me? I'm cool as a cucumber. "Peace and love brownies?"

Kennedy chuckles. "Keep joking. I dare you."

"Okay, I'll level." I smile at the girls. "I needed their opinion. I heard something that might upset you."

"Oh really? And what's that?"

I glance at the other girls on the bleachers. They sprawl around her like a Royal Cheer Court. I wonder what they're going to do without their uniforms. "I think you'd appreciate discretion on this one."

Kennedy smiles at her subjects. "Like there's anything you can't say in front of my girls."

"All right, fine." I shrug. "Remember that story you told me? About the guy with the sketchpad who caught you in a—"

"Okay, let's walk." Kennedy jumps up faster than I can say "compromising position." Her arm slips around my shoulders like our chat will be friendly. "What did you hear?" she asks when we're a good distance away.

"It was Marvin Higgins."

"You serious? That little—"

I cut her off. "There's more. All signs point to him being the one who made that playing card of Lizzie. He's her neighbor, Kenn."

"Wasn't he into her?"

"Oh, yeah. He thought they were, like, soul mates."

"Then she chose Drake—"

"And it looks like Marvin flipped. But don't worry, I'm taking care of it."

"What exactly are you planning?" she asks, eyes narrowing. She really does look menacing, even with the ponytail. It's a talent.

"Nothing crazy," I say with a laugh. "Don't get your invisible panties in a twist. It's sort of an eye-for-an-eye–type scenario."

She watches me a minute. "Well, I'm not going to tell you to leave Marvin alone," she says finally. "That pervert made his own bed. But don't go after my girls."

I wave my hand, like that's *totally different.* "Don't be so paranoid. I was just warning Cara about Drake. You should've seen them at her party; he was totally taking advantage."

"Apparently that's his game."

"Funny how people hear things and no one talks about it."

"Just a rumor." She turns back to the bleachers. I expect her to flip that ponytail in my face.

But when she doesn't leave immediately, I step closer. "Have you given any thought to what I said? I mean, the other day . . ."

She tenses, keeping her back to me. Her hair is blowing in the wind. "Yes."

"Any thoughts?"

"Plenty."

"I'd go with you, you know. If you decided to talk to the police."

"Well, I appreciate that." She inhales. I can see it as much as I can hear it. "Give me a few more days."


TEN MINUTES LATER, I find Drake stationed in front of my sixth-period class. He's wearing his letterman jacket and rolled-up jeans. I smile like I'm happy to see him.

"Where have you been?" His voice is gruff.

"Extra-special busy," I say, tapping his chest. "But I haven't forgotten about you."

"Could've fooled me." He leans in. "What the hell happened?"

"My dad happened. He caught me leaving the house with my bikini in my hand. I guess I wasn't thinking about it. I'm so used to living with Mom." *Lie!* "He forbade me from going to your house."

"He forbade you?"

"He took away my phone!" *Mega lie!* "Hilarious, huh?"

"Why are you even staying with him?"

"He misses me."

Drake pouts like he thinks he's pretty. "I miss you."

"I miss you too." *Biggest lie of all!* "But I'm going back to Mom's soon." I play with his collar. It's like sticking my hand in a bucket of maggots.

"How soon?"

"Saturday. After graduation. I'll come over after and we can have a party in our graduation gowns. *Only* our gowns," I add.

He grins. "We can pick them up tomorrow, right?"

"I'm going to get mine tonight. I can get yours too if you want."

"How?"

"Don't ask questions. Just say yes."

"Yes."

"Good. I've got to go," I say, backing away. "I've got a final with Salinger the Sadist."

Drake laughs. "Guy's not so bad. You never gave him a chance."

"He thinks Columbus got a bad rap." I duck into the room before he can kiss me. I really don't need to vomit on the last day of class.

The first thing I see is Jesse. He's wearing a green thrift-store dress with black Converse. It's probably the cutest thing I've ever seen. I want to take my final in his lap. To counter this feeling I sit two rows in front of him. My teacher smirks, like, *too little too late*. Screw him. He just *loves* giving a final on the last day of school, doesn't he?

I must do an okay job on the test. I finish twenty minutes before the end of class. Old Sal barely looks up as I set it on his desk. He's too focused on his book. It's probably a manual on medieval torture practices.

I grab my stuff and excuse myself to the bathroom. Jesse's text comes in when I'm passing through the door.

"How'd you do?"

I reply, "Don't text during a test!"

"Aw, you really do care."

"I'm serious. He'll fail you."

"Small price to pay."

I don't respond. I want to but I can't. I run the water from the faucet over my hands until it gets too hot. Then I run it over my hands some more. My skin is turning red when his next message comes in.

"Just think of what you're giving up."

Can't respond. Can't.

"Think of lying in bed together," he says.

Why won't this water get any hotter? My hands are screaming, but the pain isn't enough. Nothing hurts like his words.

"Wrapped up together," he says.

Maybe he's done with his test. He has to be done with his test.

"I don't deserve it," I say.

He responds quickly. "What about me?"

"You deserve better."

"That's my decision," he says.

"I'm sorry. It isn't."

I turn off my phone. I almost throw it in a toilet. I cannot wait for this day to end. I do the hot-water thing one more time and then I leave the room.

In Drama class, I perform my monologue with a newfound understanding of why Lizzie chose it. Madame Swarsky gives me a standing ovation. Shelby applauds heartily beside her. I think she's afraid I'm going to bail on my side of our bargain. But when the bell rings I follow her to the auditorium like a good girl. We spend the next hour putting the boxes of graduation gowns in alphabetical order.

Around one thirty Shelby looks like she's going to pass out. Poor girl's run herself ragged this week. When I offer to finish up she looks at me like I'm crazy, but she's too tired to argue. Really, it's like taking candy—well, you know how the saying goes.

I'm done by two thirty and at the grocery store by three. I pick up some fresh chili peppers and a card with Jesus on the front. Inside the card I advise Mr. Hart to please disengage from activities that put him in contact with children. If he fails to comply, I write, I will be forced to share his secrets with the congregation.

I sign it "A Concerned Parent" and drop it off at the post office.

I'm back at Mom's house by four. I don't even think she noticed I stayed at Dad's a few extra days. But she does notice the smell of chili peppers as I set to work in the kitchen. It pulls her right out of her TV coma.

She holds her sleeve over her face, standing in the doorway. "What the hell are you making?"

I turn and smile. "It's a surprise."

"I'm not eating that."

"It's not for you." I push her playfully into the living room. "I can't bother with dinner tonight. I have too much work."

"I thought school ended today." She flumps back onto the couch.

"It did. But I'm planning something for graduation." I'm already disappearing into the kitchen again.

"Don't run yourself ragged, honey," she says.

*Good advice. A little late, but good.*

"I'll try."

It takes about half an hour to be satisfied with my witches' brew. From there, I head to my bedroom to work on Marvin's photograph.

Twenty minutes later, I'm emailing him the Photoshopped picture of himself in his underwear, complete with wizard's cap and magic wand. The caption reads: See You at Graduation.

I want him to know the photo's going to be passed around.

Now all that's left is to spin straw into gold. I want to add a little something extra to the graduation gowns I took home early. Shelby should have known better than to leave me alone with such precious cargo. She should, at least, have told Madame Swarsky I was giving her a hand. Now when a group of us show up with vandalized gowns, Shelby will be the number one suspect. From there, it's barely a leap in logic to assume she destroyed the costume Lizzie was supposed to wear, and I have to imagine that'll affect Swarsky's letter of recommendation.

I'm humming as I paint fat red letters on the back of three gowns. I cover the letters with glitter. Why not go all out? This is graduation after all. And Cara, Elliot, and I will be the belles of the ball.

Yeah. One of the gowns is mine.

Once my handiwork has dried I cut an old black skirt into squares. I pin the squares over the words I've painted. The gowns are black so the patches aren't too obvious. I don't want anyone seeing our message until the exact right time: after the ceremony is completed, the Cheer Bears have a tradition of rushing the stage and doing an impromptu routine in our gowns. You know, so everyone sees how fabulous we are one last time.

Egotistical? Yes. An important detail in my plan? Also, yes.

Once our routine is completed, Cara, Elliot, and I will turn around, showing the whole school one last message:

*WE KILLED LIZZIE*

I hang the gowns in the back of my closet before taking Drake's out of its box. The back is pristine, black and shining in the light. When I'm done with it, it will be branded, and that brand will seep into its owner, staining him for life. He'll never get away from it.

Whoever said there's no justice in the world wasn't trying hard enough.

# twenty-six

THURSDAY I GET a surprise visitor at Mom's door. Marvin shows up at eight in the morning. I answer the door in a tank top and sweats and I still look better than he must feel.

It's pretty obvious he's been crying.

"Yeah?" I've been doing the Ice Queen thing for so long it's starting to become second nature. But I step aside and let him sit on the couch because, well, I'm not heartless. I think I'd like to be, since it would make life easier, but, alas, I am not.

"We both know why you're here," I say, positioning myself on the arm of the couch. "I'm not deleting the photo."

He dabs at his nose. It's all red around the edges and I try not to notice. I can't afford to feel bad for him. "I don't care about that," he says.

"Yeah, right."

"I don't," he insists. "I just want you to understand. I want someone to understand."

I roll my eyes, but it's forced. "Understand what?"

"That I didn't do it on purpose."

I scoff and almost lose my balance in the process. "You're joking, right? You accidentally painted a naked picture of a girl behind her back and emailed it to the entire school? Gee, Marvin, you have worse luck than I do."

"I didn't mean to do that!" His hair is a rat's nest falling in his face. I want to offer him a comb.

"This is going to be rich," I say, repositioning myself. "Well? Out with it."

He's quiet a minute. When he speaks, all that forced bravado is gone. His voice sounds weak. "Lizzie didn't talk to me much. Art was the one thing we had in common." He smiles, remembering. "I liked to draw, she liked to make things. When she saw me trying to imitate one of my Alchemy cards, she got all animated. She said the woman on the card was the most beautiful she'd ever seen. So I thought . . . I could paint her on a card and then she'd see."

"See what? That you're a Peeping Tom?"

"That she was beautiful."

I wait a beat. "And you thought you would do that by *leering into her window*? When she wasn't looking?"

His face is red, but he doesn't lash out at me. I have to give him credit for that, at least. Or do I? It occurs to me that so many people I've trusted have turned out to be awful. My standards, as a result, are suffering.

So I don't give him credit. But I don't bite his head off either.

He says, "Lizzie had nightmares," and I can't help but counter with "I know that." It's like we're having this contest to see who was a better friend, which is ridiculous because we were both terrible to her.

But the fact that he might not be as evil as I thought scares me. When people are a hundred percent bad it's easier to hate them.

"She used to get up in the middle of the night," he says, and that I didn't know, before the diary. "She'd stand in front of her mirror, sometimes for hours, checking for something. I don't know what."

*Scars?* I wonder, thinking about the monster in her dreams. *Stains?*

"I shouldn't have watched her . . ."

"No, you shouldn't have."

"But sometimes I did. The blinds were open—"

"Don't blame her for choices you made."

"It was hard not to look in. I was in love with her."

"If you loved her, you would've thought about her feelings. You would've respected her privacy. And you never would've passed that picture around! Why did you do that?" My voice is rising. "Because of Drake—"

"No! I thought she was misguided," he says, and I want to slap him. Even if she'd loved Drake, it would've been her right to feel that way.

"But I did not mean to email that to everyone. I couldn't give it to her in person." He talks to the floor when he says "I feared she'd laugh at me—"

"She wouldn't have. She might've felt *horrified* and *violated*, but she wouldn't have been mean."

"So I chose to email it to her," he says as if I weren't speaking. "But even that seemed too much, so I dipped into my parents' liquor stores—"

"Ever heard of drinking responsibly?"

Now his eyes roll. "Angie, you really should learn when to speak."

"And you should stop treating girls like they're your fucking property!" I leap to my feet. "Lizzie's body didn't belong to you, and neither does my voice. Haven't you learned anything?"

His face just drops. I almost feel bad, but damn it, he makes me so angry. If he'd given the slightest bit of thought to Lizzie's feelings, he'd—

"Marvin? Oh, God, don't cry."

But it's too late. Big, sloppy tears are seeping out of his hands and now I do feel bad. "You're right," he's sobbing. "You're right. It's my fault she's gone."

"Oh, shit, that's not what I meant." I go to touch him, but I'm not sure where, or in what way. "I meant 'be more considerate.' I meant 'don't be a pervert.'"

*Shut up, Angie, you really think that's helping?*

"The point is, I wasn't saying it's your fault. Okay? We all worked together on this one, trust me."

He looks up from his blubbering. "I drank too much," he says. "I meant to send it to Elizabeth but I sent it to the Elizabethan Club."

My ears perk up. "Let me guess. Shelby's the president?"

He shakes his head. "She's head of the Shakespearean Club."

I almost laugh, the conversation is so ridiculous.

"The Elizabethan Club is mostly freshmen," he explains. "For those who don't make it into the Shakespearean Club."

I snort. "Junior varsity."

He peers at me like he's afraid he'll catch Cheerleader Disease. "I helped them with some sketches earlier this year. If I hadn't done that, I wouldn't have had their email address, and this never would've—"

"So it's the Elizabethan Club's fault?"

He inhales sharply. "I'm just trying to explain."

"I know. I get it." Again, I go to touch him, but I can't bring myself to do it. "Frankly, I'm not sure if I should be happy the email was an accident or horrified you thought it was acceptable to paint her without her permission."

The truth is, I'm leaning toward horrified, but I don't want to send him over the edge again. I'm not even sure I want to print out his picture now.

How screwed up is that?

A few minutes pass, and Marvin pulls himself together. I show him to the door, trying desperately to get my anger back. He's a pervert. He violated Lizzie's privacy and sense of freedom. And whether he meant to or not, he emailed a drawing of her naked body to a bunch of idiots. He deserves to be punished for that.

Still, hours after he's gone, I keep seeing that look on his face when he said he'd caused Lizzie's death. I know the look well. I see it every time I look in the mirror. It reminds me of the day I almost offered her my forgiveness.

THE DAY STARTED like any other post-prom-humiliation day. I dragged my ass out of bed, forcing myself to go through the motions: wash, dress, choke down breakfast. I'm not going to pretend my days were anywhere near as hard as Lizzie's. But I'm not going to pretend life was awesome either.

It sucked.

I was so lonely. I thought of approaching Lizzie so many times. I know that sounds like bullshit, like I'm rearranging the events after they happened, but it's the truth. The issue of forgiveness barely even came into play. If she had apologized to me, I would've taken her back. But she didn't, and I knew what that meant. She didn't want me in her life.

So I stayed away.

On that particular Monday, three weeks after prom, Lizzie was taking her books out of her locker. She wore jeans, a sweater, a sweatshirt, and a coat. Her hair was hanging in her face. These days, she used it as an extra layer of protection against the people who always followed her in swarms. They had to be careful, you know, with the administration watching, but how hard was it to knock into someone and blame clumsiness? How hard was it to whisper *"Stupid bitch"* in someone's ear? They could push her into the bathroom where all their friends were waiting. They could vandalize her locker when the tardy bell rang.

Case in point: the S-word now covered every inch of her locker door. The janitor couldn't wash the words away fast enough. They showed up in different sizes, some cursive, some printed, increasingly etched into the paint. People exaggerated the differences to make it clear her attackers were many.

I hovered halfway down the hall, waiting for her to finish gathering her books. Our lockers were still next to each other, in spite of several desperate pleas to the office to relocate me. And yeah, it made things incredibly difficult. But we had a system. We never approached when the other was there, and it had worked up until today.

*Why isn't she leaving?*

I needed my English book. Now. I couldn't afford another mishap after the Marvin-library fiasco. I had to be a good little student and come to class prepared. That meant going to my locker while Lizzie was still at hers.

It was probably the hardest thing I'd ever had to do, walking up to the girl who broke my heart. Still, it must've been a thousand times worse for her. She looked like she hadn't eaten or slept in days. In spite of everything that had happened, I wanted to lace my hand through hers and lend her my warmth. I wanted to summon that feeling of invincibility that came from knowing we'd never be alone as long as we had each other.

But I didn't do anything. I didn't reach for her. I didn't speak to her, even as the whispers reached a fever pitch. I opened my locker, making a wall between us, and pulled out my English book with hands that wouldn't stop shaking. My entire being wouldn't stop shaking, and I just stood there, not able to look at her, and cried right in the middle of the hallway, quietly, so she wouldn't hear.

Every move, a mistake.

Still, she waited. In retrospect, it's pretty obvious she was hoping I would say something. All I had to do was tell her I still loved her. All she had to do was tell me the same. If either of us had been brave enough to say something, everything would've been different. For the rest of my life, this ache wouldn't live inside me, reminding me of the emptiness Lizzie left behind. I wouldn't hate myself, and life, and want to leave this place. I wouldn't feel the desire to hurt everyone who took her life away, most of all me.

Neither of us spoke.

I zipped my backpack and wiped my eyes. I turned just so, closing my locker with my back to the crowd, so they wouldn't see that I'd been crying. And I walked away. I left Lizzie alone in the place that was destroying her. I left her to the mercy of Verity's vultures, when I could've stopped them from tearing her apart.

I did nothing.

# twenty-seven

Saturday morning I stop off at the police department to give Lizzie's diary to the detective who handled her case. I tell him I found the missing pages in Drake's bedroom, and if he doesn't believe me, he can check it for fingerprints. Then I tell him I've got to run. I have a graduation ceremony to get to.

My phone starts to ring as I cut through the school park. I answer it and say, "Meet me at the football field in five minutes," then hit the end button quickly.

Out on the field, Kennedy and the rest of the Cheer Bears are pretending to practice. Half of them have on their graduation gowns, unzipped, over their uniforms. I'm supposed to be in my uniform as well, but I really didn't feel like it.

I jog up to them, my heels squishing in the grass. Whoever thought they should water the lawn this morning was a moron. I've got four graduation gowns slung over my shoulder: mine, Cara's, Elliot's, and Drake's. I'm freezing my butt off but I can't put mine on in front of Kennedy. It'll spoil the surprise.

Cara and Elliot invite me into their circle like we're the best of friends. Elliot's already crying. I give her a cheek kiss and tell her it's going to be okay.

"No—it's not!" She's got the hiccups, bad. "Half—of us—are going—to different places—"

Kennedy wraps Elliot in her arms. "Knock it off," she says, but her tone is kind. She steers Elliot toward the bleachers. "I know what will cheer you up."

"Our surprise?" Elliot asks. Several girls perk up at the mention.

"Yep. Come on." Kennedy motions for us to follow.

"What surprise?" I ask, tagging along.

"It's for you." She holds out a hand for me. She's still got an arm around Elliot. "By the way, what the hell are you wearing?"

"A dress." Lizzie's dress, to be exact. The gold one her father pushed on me. I figured, whether Lizzie's looking down from some magical world, or giving life to daisies in the Fir Point Cemetery, seeing me in the dress would make her smile.

"You better have your uniform in that purse," says Kennedy.

I give her my best poker face.

"Okay, you do look hot," she concedes.

"Well, thank you." I clap my hands. "Now give me my surprise."

Kennedy digs through her giant purse. I check the position of the gowns on my arm. Right now I've got mine over the top, face-up, so it looks like I'm just carrying one. Still, the stack's a little bulky. Cara gives me a wink as I try to smooth them. Poor girl thinks we're in cahoots.

*Cahoots. Like we're spies.*

I'm not looking forward to seeing Jesse today. He's got that *I'm so disappointed in you* look down to an art. Plus, I miss him.

Okay, that's the real reason.

Kennedy pulls out a stack of photo sheets and some scissors to cut them into wallet-size prints. But she's not the subject.

"Oh my God," I say. "Is that—"

"Ew," several girls squeal at once.

"This is supposed to cheer me up?" Elliot asks, but she's wearing this deranged smile.

I take one of the sheets. The boy is dressed in tighty-whities and a wizard hat. He's holding a wand. It's Marvin.

But I didn't send it.

"Where did you get this?" I ask.

Kennedy grins mischievously. "Showed up in my email last night."

"That's impossible," I breathe, staring at my handiwork. "Who sent this to you?"

"Somebody named 'MacDaddy' something." She snickers while I cringe. "Sixty-nine—that's right. How could I forget? I thought it would be fun to print them out, like real school photos. See? We can cut them out and pass them around."

"Aren't you smart. Do I get to do the honors?" I hold out a hand.

She hands me the photos, eyeing me suspiciously. "Cut away, then."

I stare at the pictures. My eyes start to sting. With all these photos circulating the auditorium, everyone in the school will catch a glimpse of half-naked Marvin by the end of the day. He'll be a bigger joke than he already is. He'll know Lizzie's pain.

*Just like she would've wanted.*

Yeah.

Right.

Still, I can't steal all the pictures without the girls throwing a fit. And Marvin clearly wanted them to get out. Maybe the humiliation is supposed to assuage his guilt. I take the scissors and cut out a picture for each girl on the squad.

"That should be enough," I say with a shrug.

Kennedy smiles like she's my mommy. "Look at you, growing a heart."

"Whatever. I just don't want to alert the faculty to our dirty dealings." I slide the rest of the photos into my purse. "We should go."

"Fair enough," Kennedy says, still eyeing me. Elliot and Cara are sidling up to me but my attention is across the field. I can see Drake approaching from a distance. He's ambling along like he's got all the time in the world.

Or maybe he's scared.

I lean in to whisper in Cara's ear, "I have to deal with something. Meet me in the bathroom in five?"

"Upstairs?"

"Of course."

She skips ahead, taking Elliot with her. Kennedy glances back when she sees Drake coming. "You want me to stay?" she asks.

"I'll be okay."

She glances from him to me. "I'll do it, by the way."

"I just said you don't have to."

"No, I mean . . ." She rolls her eyes like I'm pathetically dim-witted. "I'll talk to the police."

"I'll come with you," I say, my chest burning as Drake reaches the fifty-yard line. Kennedy's words should make me feel triumphant, but all I can feel is my stomach turning and turning. I wish I could ask her to stay with me.

But I wave her along. She goes hesitantly, looking back like maybe I need her. Then it's just me, and Drake, and this big empty field between us. Soon, even the field is gone.

"What's with the scissors?" he says in greeting.

"What?" I look down. I've still got Kennedy's scissors in my hands. I'm clutching them like a weapon. I wonder if maybe I'll need them.

"Oh, just a project," I say. "Here, turn around."

He does so. I slip his graduation gown through his arms and over his shoulders. He turns again and lets me zip it up. "Thank God it fits," he says.

"I knew it would."

"Want me to help put yours on?" He steps closer.

I jerk away. "Not yet."

"What's going on with you?" he demands. God, he's hot and cold in an instant. I wonder if I should just go inside.

Instead, I say, "I've been thinking."

"About me?"

I nod. "There's something I can't figure out."

"What is it?" He's close now. He thinks he's about to kiss me. I swear, if he tries, I'll knock him out.

"If I committed a crime and someone documented it, wouldn't I destroy the documentation the first chance I got?"

He doesn't know what I'm getting at, not really. But a part of him responds to the accusation and he steps back. "What are you talking about?"

I pull some papers out of my purse. Some photocopies I made yesterday.

What, like I was going to sit around all day twiddling my thumbs?

Please.

I hand the copies to Drake. "I'm talking about this."

"Where did you get these?" He's making this shocked face, like he's never seen the pages before. It makes me so mad I want to scream.

But I won't give him the satisfaction.

I steady my hand as I point to him. "You lied to everyone about what happened. You lied to me—your girlfriend. The person you were supposed to love."

He holds up his hands. "I've never seen this before."

"Bullshit."

"Put down the scissors." He reaches for them. I yank my hand away.

*Time to regroup, asshole.*

It's almost like he hears me. "Angie, don't you see what's happening? Whoever wrote that stuff on our lockers is pretending to be her. It's not real."

"*I* wrote that stuff on our lockers."

He stammers, "You d-did not."

"I took Lizzie's diary from her bedroom. I brought those photocopies to school. But there were already pages missing, weren't there?"

"She was a friend of mine."

"'A friend of my best friend. A friend of all of our families,'" I say, quoting Lizzie.

His eyes are bugging out. "She *was* a friend of our families."

"That's not what I meant and you know it." I advance.

He looks behind his back. But nobody's there to help him. "This is crazy."

"You know what's crazy, Drake? Lizzie's father caught you in her bedroom the night she died." I'm close now and he's not backing away. "Why did you go over there that night? Did you know what she'd written? Tell me!"

I must look scary with the scissors and all, because he says, "I heard somebody tried to steal that book from her."

"That *diary*?"

"Yeah, that." He runs his hands through his hair. It doesn't hide him, though, even with strands falling into his eyes. He's still exposed. "I heard they went through her gym bag when they found out she had one. And she totally lost it. Started screaming until they gave it back. I knew there had to be something in it, for her to react like that."

His words are a weight on my chest. I've forgotten how to breathe. "When did this happen?"

"That week. The week before she . . ." He trails off. He can't say *died*, just like he can't say *raped*.

But I can. "So you knew it was a danger to you, and you had to get it back," I say. "Smart move, just taking the pages that incriminated you. I had to look really closely to know they were missing."

"I just wanted to see what she said."

"You wanted to cover your ass, in case the wrong person found out what you did. In case they found out you're the reason she's—"

"*Don't say it!*" he screams, and it actually scares me. I've never seen him like this. But the greatest dangers don't always come when people are the loudest. "Don't say I did that!"

"Oh, so it only matters because she's dead? Like if she wasn't, what you did wouldn't be vile and evil and disgusting—"

"I didn't do that! I didn't cause her death."

"But you *did* rape her."

He's shaking his head. I can't tell if he's somehow convinced himself of his innocence, or if he just can't live with the fact that there are consequences for doing *horrible* things.

"I don't believe you."

"You have to." He looks up at me, and those pale blue eyes are laced with red. Two weeks ago, I might've softened at the sight of them. Now I want to jab something into them and watch them bleed.

And yeah, it's scary how much this has darkened me. But I can't go back.

"Why should I believe you?" I ask, even though I'm very aware that there's danger here. "If you're so innocent, why did you keep those pages? Why didn't you destroy the *only evidence* against you?"

"I didn't understand it. Why did she invite me into her hotel room?"

"It was *our* hotel room, Drake. And you knocked on the door."

"Why did she kiss me?"

"You caught her off guard. For godsakes, Drake, it was a kiss! You can't be that mental."

*Can he?*

In a way, it's easier to believe he'd have to be insane to do what he did. But it's not that simple, is it? He chose to hurt her. He made that choice.

All of this is just a ploy to get me to believe him.

"You want to know what I think?" I move in closer. I'm shaking, but it just looks like I'm waving the scissors at him. "I think you kept those pages because you liked reading what she said. I think you got off on reading what you did, you sick, psycho—"

"Stop it!" He pushes me back.

I start laughing. I can't help it. "Nice, Drake." I pull my heel out of the grass. "Way to prove you're not violent."

"I didn't mean to do that." He's clenching his hands. "Just— please put those scissors away."

"Are you scared?" I snap them in his face. "Scared you're going to get hurt? That's ironic."

"Please." He reaches out. "It's me, Angie—your boyfriend. We've known each other our whole lives!"

He doesn't realize that just makes it worse. I slide the scissors into my purse. My fingers encircle the homemade pepper spray I brewed up at my mommy's house. "All right, Drake, I'll do what you say. If you stay back."

But he doesn't listen to that. He's too busy trying to get *me* to listen. Because that's what's important, right? Me behaving.

"Just listen to me." He steps closer.

"I said stay back."

His hand goes around my wrist. It happens so easily. It just slides over my skin, and then he's got me. "Why are you doing this?"

"See, that's your problem." I yank back my hand. Now he can see the pepper spray. "You don't listen—"

"Wait—"

"When people say—"

"Stop!"

"Exactly."

His hands go to his eyes but I'm already spraying.


THE INSIDE OF the school is packed. Students run around like decapitated chickens, posing for pictures and peeking through the stage curtain at their seated families. I refrain from the latter—I can only imagine Mom and Dad are situated at opposite ends of the room, *if* Mom remembered to come—but I do get caught in a hail of photo fire by various members of my class. Shelby pulls me into a Drama Club photo. A couple of girls from English make kissy faces on either side of me. By the time I make it to the stairs my cheeks are worn-out from fake smiling. I wonder how I'm going to make it through the ceremony without my face muscles collapsing.

I pull on my gown as I reach the second floor. This is a mistake. Jesse's standing between the boys' and girls' bathrooms.

*How did he know? How does he always know?*

I make sure the girls' gowns are positioned strategically as I approach. As long as I remain facing him I should be fine.

"Hi," he says, his voice quiet. His hair looks baby soft. He's got on his gown too and I wish I had a picture of us together.

"Hey." I peer at his gown like maybe I can see through it if I stare hard enough. At the very least, I can keep him from staring into *me*.

"Good luck," he says.

"What, are you naked under there?"

"Don't you wish."

I blush.

"How are you doing?" he asks after a minute.

"I'm doing okay." My brain keeps telling me to stop enjoying myself. But it's hard not to, with him. He's so damn easy to talk to.

"You look beautiful," he says.

"I look tired."

He shakes his head. "You could stay up for weeks and you'd still be the most beautiful girl I've ever seen."

That makes me want to cry. I back away. I'm feeling unsteady. "You don't have to say that."

"I don't have to say anything."

"Jesse."

"I want to tell you something." He steps up to me slowly. There's something ritualistic about it, like he's about to go down on one knee. It seriously gives me the chills.

He lowers his head so his forehead is touching mine. "I meant what I said."

"Yeah?"

"About loving you."

I should not have asked. I should not have stopped to talk to him.

"But you still think you have to hide it," I say. "I guess that's the story of my life." It's not a fair thing to say. Lizzie had reasons for hiding and so does he. But I want him to leave me alone. I need him to.

"That was wrong of me," he says, and it totally throws off my game. "I was just using that as an excuse." He touches a piece of my hair, following it down to my chin. "I was scared."

"Scared?" Behind me, the girls' bathroom door creaks open. I see Elliot peering out.

"Scared of us," Jesse says. His fingers linger on my chin. "Scared of you."

"Of me?" I wave Elliot back inside.

"Of how I feel about you," he says, searching my gaze. I look down. "Like I said, I've had crushes before. But that's not what this is."

"So you're going to tell your friends?" I ask. Then, because I've never actually seen them talking in the halls, I add, "The people in the Gay-Straight Alliance."

"I already did."

I look up. I didn't expect that. "What?"

He nods. "I announced it at our final meeting."

"And that went okay?"

"For the most part, yeah." He shrugs. "They weren't thrilled I hadn't been honest, but they want me to be able to be myself. That *is* what the club's about, you know?"

"Well, good. I'm glad it worked out for you."

"I didn't do it for me. I did it for us. I'd kiss you in front of everyone if you'd let me."

"I won't." It kills me to say it. But it must be worse for him to hear it. For a minute it's like he forgets how to breathe.

When he remembers, his breath comes out in a rush. "It's okay if you don't like me. I can deal with it. Just don't shut yourself off completely." His fingers are tangling in my hair. I don't even think he realizes it.

"What makes you think I am?"

"Open your eyes, Princess. You push all the good shit away until all you can feel is hate. I'm trying to touch you here and you keep backing up because you *know* you'll feel something."

"So touch me."

He does. His arms go around me in that soft way of theirs, but they're not wings this time. They're just arms. He's just a boy. And love isn't the answer to all my problems because this isn't a fucking fairy tale.

"I don't feel anything," I say, but of course I'm lying. I'm still living. I still have senses. He smells like shampoo and sweat and rain. Most of all he smells like *him:* that indefinable scent he left on my pillow and blanket. His skin is cool but it warms the moment our bodies touch. I can't stop myself from leaning into him. I can't stop myself from holding on.

His words drift into my ear. "I do love you," he says, so softly. "You know that, right? I want to be your friend. But if you go through with whatever you're planning, I can't be a part of your life."

"Your love knows no bounds."

"It doesn't," he says, and his voice sounds so familiar. How did I get so attached to him so quickly? "But I have to love myself first, you know? It's something that's taken me a long time to do."

"I want you to love yourself," I murmur, and he knows what I'm saying.

He starts to shake his head. I can feel his gut clenching, like his body's rejecting my words. "Baby, please," he says, lowering his lips to mine.

We kiss. His mouth parts to let me in. He's so warm, I could stay like this forever. Tasting him. Feeling the softness of his lips. Believing I deserve to be kissed.

But I don't.

I have to detangle myself from him. To push him so far away

he'll never get back. Teeth tugging on his bottom lip, I pull away.

"Good-bye, Jesse," I whisper in his ear.

His arms go slack. He backs away from me like I'm some angel of destruction. It feels good, in a way, to see him look at me like that. It proves I was right about myself.

Still, it takes far too much effort to push my way into the girls' bathroom, and when I do, I must look like a mess because Elliot's face falls at the sight of me.

"We need to talk to you," she says. Poor girl, she's already tearing up again. I can see where she wiped her cheeks clean of mascara stains, but she must've reapplied. When she blinks, little black dots appear beneath her eyes.

"There's not really time for that." I hold out their gowns.

They just look at me. Well, Cara won't meet my eyes, but her face is aimed in my general direction. I get that creepy-crawly feeling, like spiders are skittering over my skin. "It'll just take a minute," she says, clearly mesmerized by the wall behind me.

"We wanted to say we're sorry," Elliot says. She takes Cara's hand and I know it's not an act. She's being a good friend, like friends are meant to be. "About Lizzie."

*Please don't, please don't, please don't.*

"No worries," I say, which sounds absolutely idiotic. But what else can I say? I can't do this here and now. Can't have real feelings. Can't feel sympathy or sadness. Do they want me to dissolve into a sniveling mess in front of the entire student body? It's horrible enough when I do that alone.

"Not just her death," Elliot says, pushing the words out with obvious effort. "What we did to her. We shouldn't have been so mean. There was no reason for it."

*There must've been*, I think, but I don't say it. Why bait them? Why say anything at all?

"This whole thing is our fault," Elliot says.

"No, it's mine," I murmur. My hand goes to my lips. Why did I say that? Why am I doing anything but shoving their gowns in their direction and bolting? I don't need their forgiveness, and they're in no position to give it to me.

"What are you talking about?" Cara asks, still avoiding my gaze.

"It was my fault," I say. "Everyone tortured her for me."

"For you?" Elliot's face gets all scrunched. "Who did it for you?"

"Everybody. They hated her because of me." I pause, thinking of everything I've learned. "Most of them anyway . . ."

Elliot's shaking her head. They're both shaking their heads, looking at me like maybe I've gone a little crazy.

*Just a little? Please.*

"But everyone wrote the same thing," I insist. "Why would they do that, if not for me?"

"I don't know." Cara looks at me finally. "It was just easy. You call some other girl a slut, and nobody's looking at you anymore. Nobody was looking at Kennedy."

"Why would they be looking at Kennedy?"

But that's a stupid question, and she answers it quickly. "She dates more than anybody."

"*At least* dates," Elliot supplies, dabbing at her eyes. But she doesn't look bewitching anymore. She's more like a dime-store magician, performing emotional sleight of hand:

*Look this way, at the amazing slut-girl, Lizzie Hart!*

Meanwhile, Cara sneaks Miss Popularity out through a panel in the floor.

"You were protecting Kennedy?" I shift the gowns in my arms. They feel heavy. The whole world feels heavy, pressing into me. If the girls would just get dressed, we could get out of here, and my final act of vengeance would be completed. The karmic balance would be restored to the world.

That's how it works, right? You battle hate with hate, and things even out. That's why I can't look in the mirror. That's why I feel so fucking fabulous right now.

"We were trying to make things easier. But we're sorry," Cara says, reaching for me. I jerk away involuntarily. It's only after I've stepped back that I realize she was trying to comfort me.

"Really sorry," Elliot agrees. "But we don't expect you to forgive us."

"I'm the last person who needs to forgive you," I say, thinking immediately of Lizzie. I want to be able to choose the right memory of her, the one that will fit this moment, but it doesn't work that way. My mind jumps to the day I stood beside her locker, too afraid to talk to her. I was scared, so I did what was easy.

Over and over, I chose *easy* over *right*.

*Just give them the gowns and this will all be finished.*

But I can't. Their apology has ripped a hole in my anger and I feel myself inching toward the door . . .

Wondering if Jesse will still be waiting for me outside. His words circle around my head: *We can't do what they did. We'd become them.*

I push out of the bathroom and into the hallway. For a moment, it looks empty. Then I see his silhouette, lingering at the top of the stairs.

"Help!"

He turns around so quickly, my battered heart squeezes. He must think I'm in real danger. I've got to stop doing this to him.

"I need you to guard the boys' bathroom," I call before any more dark images can form in his mind. Hopefully, my words will amuse him long enough to abate the fear.

"Is this going to become a thing?" he asks, jogging toward me.

"Last time, I promise." I duck inside the boys' room before he can answer. Thank God the room is empty. My footsteps echo as I hurry to the sinks. I force myself to look in the mirror.

To see what I've become.

What I find there surprises me. It's just me. No monster or unrecognizable beast snarls back at me. I'm still Angie.

I'm still a human being.

I realize I can find a way back to myself. I can be the person Lizzie wanted me to be, the person I want to be. No matter what I've done I can still stop this cycle, because what does hate do but breed more hate? Destroying a person's life doesn't solve anything. It just keeps the circle going, making the world uglier and uglier.

And I have the power to stop it.

I spread the gowns over the stall doors. It takes about ten seconds to cut the words out of them; good thing I didn't leave Kennedy's scissors in one of Drake's extremities. When I've done all the damage I can do, I pin the black squares over the holes so the girls won't know what's missing until it's too late. Then I send Shelby a text thanking her for letting me sort the gowns.

She'll know what to do with it.

Jesse's the only one waiting for me when I come out of the bathroom. "I ushered them down the stairs," he says, looking worried, like maybe he helped me do evil.

"You did a good thing," I say as I take his arm. "I promise."

I savor the feeling of his arm against mine as we walk down the hall. I still expect him to say good-bye to me by the end of the day. But for now, as we approach the auditorium, I almost feel happy. No, not almost. I do feel happy.

It's kind of amazing.

I pass Cara and Elliot their gowns when we reach the auditorium. Kennedy gives me a look, but she's too far away to intervene. Then the music starts and we all look forward, mesmerized by the thought of getting out of this place alive.

Of course, that opportunity isn't afforded to everybody.

The ceremony starts out uneventfully. Principal Paisley welcomes us in this monotone that practically puts me to sleep. Valedictorian Shelby gives us one of her typical dramatic speeches. The highlight comes when Drake Alexander stumbles across the stage, still half-blinded by the pepper spray, to take his diploma.

As he exits, we get a perfect view of the back of his gown. The electric blue letters sparkle beautifully in the light:

RAPIST

# twenty-eight

DRAKE WASN'T THE first person to hurt someone this year. Two weeks prior to the start of winter break we all heard whispers about the girl who was abducted on Main Street. Two guys pulled over in broad daylight and dragged her into a van. The girl showed up three months later, but she was just a body then.

I'm not going to tell you what they did to her, but you can guess.

For several months afterward, everyone locked up their daughters like trophies in glass cases and pretended it would protect them from the evils of the world. Pretended it would protect *us*, even though the most common evils lurked behind our closed doors. Nobody said a word about the abuse already happening in those dark bedrooms. Nobody warned Lizzie that the worst moments of her life would be brought about by a family member and a friend.

Just like nobody warned Drake about whatever messed-up shit he must've endured growing up, because *good God*, you don't come out of your mother a monster.

No, monsters are made. We make them. And when we don't like what we've created, we play pretend.

Today, in the auditorium, I watch the senior class play pretend. I watch them stare at the word *RAPIST,* just like they stared at the word *SLUT* so many weeks before, and have the *exact opposite reaction.*

They're not gasping. They're not attacking Drake with hurtful names. They're laughing.

My classmates are laughing.

I close my eyes. Behind closed lids I witness the scene as if I were standing in the Alternate Dimension Bathroom—the way it should happen. I hear the cries, the outrage. I witness the mob of angry students rushing the stage. Maybe they lock Drake up and throw away the key. Maybe they draw and quarter him. It doesn't matter. All that matters is that he'll never hurt anybody again.

Yeah.

That's how it happens.

I open my eyes back to the real scene. The football team's bent over, slapping their knees and howling. Some of the girls are chuckling behind their hands. They're having a grand old time.

And I start to wonder, for the very first time, if Lizzie was right to want to leave this place.

I start to wonder if there's a way to see her again.

I stand, ready to leave this room, and maybe the world; I haven't decided yet. But as I turn, the auditorium doors open, bringing with them the light. I remember Lizzie's words then, when she caught sight of the clock tower in her dream:

*The light of God will fill me up.*

For a second, I actually wish for divine intervention. I'm starting to feel like it's the only thing that can help me. But it isn't God that enters the room in freshly pressed blue cotton and heavy black boots.

It's the fuzz.

And I've never been so happy to see the cops in my life.

I press my fingers into my eyes to stop the tears of relief. Two boys in blue are hovering at the top of the room. It's obvious they don't want to interrupt the ceremony, but they can't control the effect their arrival is having on us.

The laughter tapers off.

No, it *dies*. Invisible threads have wrapped themselves around the throat of every jerk who took Drake's innocence for granted. They can't laugh now. They can barely breathe. The possibility has finally dawned on them—not the realization, just the *possibility*—that Drake has had an ugly hand in things. And you know what else? Some of them are looking at me.

I inhale sharply, swallowing my fury, and give them my cheeriest smile. I wave, as if to say: *Yes, I did.*

They stare at me, mesmerized, like they're working out a math problem. The thought reminds me of Marvin, and suddenly I'm searching the crowd for his unruly head. All along the aisles, parents are taking stock of the Police Situation, gathering information and passing it down like they're playing a game of Telephone. Under different circumstances, it would be hilarious, but I can't focus on it.

I've located Marvin.

He's staring right at me. His face isn't red. He almost looks . . . impressed.

Same with Shelby: she's sitting much closer, in the Jesse/Kennedy cluster.

Kennedy gives me a nod. Even Cara and Elliot, whose gowns have suffered my scissors' wrath, are looking at me with a mixture of relief and awe.

They realize I've spared them.

And suddenly, the last people in the school who should come

to my defense start chanting for me, over and over again, until others join in:

"RAPIST," they murmur, softly at first, their voices heavy with the weight of the word.

"RAPIST," they shout to the red-faced, wide-eyed boy who's managed to exit the stage. He's cowering there, at the foot of the stairs. His graduation gown is balled up in his hands. Really, there's nowhere for him to go. Even if he manages to slip behind the curtains, the cops will eventually find him. It's not like he's going to make it to Mexico.

He might not even make it to his house.

I almost smile.

But I can't. The chant is getting louder, weaving its way into my brain. "RAPIST." It's ringing in my ears and making my heart pound. "RAPIST." I actually kind of wish they would stop. Even whispered quietly, that word has the power to turn your stomach. But maybe that's why it's important to say it out loud. Maybe we can't be afraid of talking about it if we ever want it to stop.

Maybe the first step to stomping out the world's ugliness is dragging it into the light.

Quietly, I start chanting the word, though I hate how it sounds and how it tastes. I'm not screaming—I'm barely speaking above a whisper—but it's enough to attract the attention of its target. Drake finds me in the crowd, eyes nervously settling on mine for one drawn-out second. His lips form the word "BITCH."

I mouth "RAPIST" back to him because, honestly, if bitch is the alternative, I'll be a bitch for the rest of my life.

I won't feel bad.

And Drake knows it. He knows he's lost his power over me. With one last, desperate glance at the cops, he bolts, disappearing behind the curtain. The chants turn to unintelligible screams. I stand, preparing to go after him.

Both Kennedy and Jesse hold me back.

The crowd swells forward. Now that Drake has broken loose, people feel like it's safe to follow. The cops are yelling at us to stop, one of them hurrying down the aisle while the other barks into his walkie-talkie and pushes out of the auditorium doors. Probably, he's calling for backup. I can only hope they were smart enough to position a third guy at the back door. I hope, too, that they catch Drake quickly, because chaos is starting to break out, and somebody could get hurt.

Somebody could get trampled, and their blood would be on my hands.

Not really thinking about what I'm doing, I break free from my captors' grasp. Jesse catches my wrist, but I'm able to slide out easily enough. He refuses to contain me, even to protect me.

I kind of love that about him.

I hear Kennedy's calm, condescending voice calling out, "You're an idiot," and Jesse saying, "Please . . ." and then I'm gone, into the chaos, the noise. People are elbowing me without even trying. My heart is thundering, telling me to return to safety. Anything could happen behind that curtain. Drake could resist arrest and get his arm twisted behind his back.

He could be shot.

I could be shot.

I push on. The red velvet curtain feels heavy in my hands as I slip behind it. The crowd in here isn't that hard to get by. There are maybe ten students, and they've formed a circle like they're watching a boxing match. But what's happening inside is no contest.

Drake is sprawled out on the floor.

Drake, the first boy I ever kissed.

Drake, who cradled me in his arms whenever I stayed the night.

Drake, who told me once, when he was wasted beyond oblivion, that he was terrified of becoming his parents, though he never told me why.

I know this boy.

I thought I did.

But when he looks at me, it's like we're strangers.

"You," he breathes. His cheeks are red, and I think maybe he's been crying. "She's lying," he snarls, as the cop struggles to contain him. "She's a lying bitch."

*Ouch, Drake. You kissed my best friend with that mouth?*

"She just wants attention."

Seriously, does he hear himself? Then he says something honest: "Wait till you hear what she did at school—"

My heart skips.

"She pretended to be a dead girl."

"N-no, I didn't." I take a step forward.

"Get back," the cop yells. I listen, but only because I don't want a bullet in the chest.

Still, I can't stop myself from asking, "What did I do, Drake?"

He sneers. He thinks he's got me in his crosshairs. "You stole the diary," he spits.

*See, that one I can use.*

"What diary?" I crouch a safe distance away. For one, brief moment, he's locked in my gaze. "No one said anything about a diary."

He freezes, unable to think of a response.

"You mean the one with your fingerprints all over it?" I lean in. The cop is *not* thrilled with me, but he can't intervene without taking his attention from Drake.

So I get in one last dig. "The diary that's already in police custody?"

Drake howls like an animal locked in a trap. I close my eyes and see visions of canines gnawing off their own limbs. Blood and bone. Such desperation. Back in the real world, Drake's scrabbling to catch me, but he can't go far with a knee in his back. "You set me up, you fucking bitch! I'll get you for this!"

"Oh, that one's damning, I bet." I step back. I'm waiting for the cuffs to go around his wrists. But he's resisting so badly, the cop goes for something else.

Oh, God.

I try to warn him: "Don't resist."

I try to look away.

Close my eyes.

Anything.

But I can't. I've come this far.

*I practically fucking orchestrated it.*

So I stay and watch. I watch the gun slide out of the man's holster. Freed of its bindings, it's ready to do its dirty work. I smell gunpowder and nothing has even *happened* yet.

The officer's finger curls around the trigger, soft, like he's caressing it. Bile rises in my throat.

"Harrison."

The voice comes from behind our backs. Together, we turn. Two cops are hurrying in, one with a gun, one gripping a Taser.

That's the one who kneels down beside Drake.

That's the one who detains him.

I close my eyes, relief flooding my body. But Drake's scream pulls me out of the darkness. I see his body trembling on the floor. I see his teeth cutting into his lips. Then I don't see anything except the dark, heavy curtain as I make my way toward it.

*I have to get out of here.*

I train my eyes on the space in front of me, not looking back. Still, I hear the cuffs clicking around his wrists. I hear the opening to the Miranda rights. I know that they've got him. And I realize, as

I pass through the crowded aisle and out into the light, that I'm the reason all of this happened the way it did.

I'm not powerless. I found a way to let everyone know how dangerous Drake is.

I did something.

# twenty-nine

THE QUIET OF Fir Point Cemetery is startling compared to the bustling auditorium. I can hear my heart beating in this kind of quiet. At the top of the hill, this great angelic beast looks down at the rest of the world. The most expensive plots are situated around it. It's nice to know that class distinctions don't die when we do.

*Right.*

Down below, skeleton trees take the place of fancy statues. The grass grows in patches around twisting stone paths. Maybe the seeder is a drunk. My heels squish in grass one minute and mud the next. You'd think I could just walk on the stones, but they don't actually lead to anything. They're just for decoration.

Lizzie's plot sits near the base of the hill, as if to say she had *some* money at least. There's a scattered bouquet of daisies rotting in the grass. I lay my graduation gown beside them and kneel on the fabric. And I just start talking.

"I always thought it was weird that people put flowers on graves. I mean, picked flowers are essentially dead, so you're bringing this decaying offering to an already . . ." I pause. "You know what I mean. Maybe the idea is to bring company. Like they say, misery loves company. Maybe the dead love company too . . . God, I'm rambling."

But I have to keep talking. The silence is too dangerous. Even though I know Lizzie is not here—she couldn't be—I still feel like her voice will chime in if I fall silent for too long.

She'll question me about not visiting since the day she was buried.

She'll ask me why I treated her the way I did.

She won't even be angry, she'll just look at me with those big, sad eyes. A little ghost girl, come to haunt me.

I can't allow it. So I just talk. I talk about the weather. I talk about graduation and my tentative plans for college. Then, when I've talked about every stupid, meaningless thing I can think of, I ask the one thing I've been terrified to ask.

"Lizzie . . . why didn't you tell me how you felt? I would've accepted you. I loved you. I—" I close my eyes, fiddling with the stems of the daisies. It's comforting, considering who brought them. "You could've trusted me. I could've trusted you too. And I'm sorry for that. I shouldn't have left you alone after . . ." I pause, curling my fingers into fists. "But I'm going to make sure he never hurts anyone again."

The voice comes at my back. "Calling the cops was a pretty good start."

I don't turn. After a minute he comes up beside me. He's still dressed in his gown, and he stands over me like he's God or something. And I wonder why I'm always thinking about gods and angels if I don't believe in that stuff. Maybe a part of me wants to. Maybe I need it right now.

"Do you think I'm a horrible person?" I ask.

Jesse looks at me. His eyes are dark to match the sky. I'm so sick of living in this perpetual winter. But I'm starting to fear that moving is just running away.

"No," he says.

"You sure?"

He shrugs. "I said I thought people should be warned about him."

"But you don't like how I went about it?"

"See, that's the thing." He runs his hand through his hair. "I've been thinking about it a lot. And I can't think of a good way to go about it. I mean, this is a really messed-up situation. So maybe it isn't about doing what's good. Maybe it's about doing what's necessary."

"To protect people."

"Right."

I catch his eye. "Do you think that's why I did it?"

"I think it was one of your reasons."

I want to tell him that he's wrong, that my reasons were selfish and vengeful. But he's right. He knows he's right. I exposed Drake because I didn't want him to hurt anyone else. Maybe my other reasons aren't as important as that.

"Are you mad?" I ask, my voice quiet against the wind.

"No."

"Okay, well . . ." I pat the ground beside me. "Sit down. You're making me nervous."

He hesitates. "I don't know."

"Are you worried about the gown?"

"It was expensive," he says without emotion, like he's just stating a fact. I'm fairly certain he came here to tell me good-bye. I don't even know why I assume he came here for me as well as for Lizzie. I just feel it.

I lift up the corner of my gown. Beneath the little patch of fabric, I can see the jagged edge where I attacked it with

Kennedy's scissors. "Hey, grass stains are nothing compared to this."

He stares at it with widened eyes. "You went after yourself too."

"Was there ever any doubt?"

He watches me a minute. I honestly have no idea what he's thinking. Then he unzips his gown and lays it beside mine.

"Oh my God." My smile catches me by surprise.

"Do *not* say anything." His arms go around himself.

"Oh, Jesse. You look—"

"Stop—"

"Amazing."

"Really?"

"Are you kidding? You're wearing a suit. A *suit.*"

He blushes as he sits down, folding his legs carefully so as not to wrinkle the pants. "It would look better on you."

"Don't be modest." I touch the collar of his jacket. "This is really nice."

"It was my grandfather's. My mom has all these old suits in the back of her closet."

"I love suits," I say. "I mean, on people who know how to wear them."

"Do I?"

"Oh, yeah. But you wear everything well."

He smiles, those cheeks round and rosy in the fading light. "I'm an asshole, by the way. I've been thinking about how beautiful you look in that dress since I got here but I haven't been able to put my tongue back in my mouth."

"We had more important things to say."

He nods like he knows compliments make me uncomfortable. That smile is still tugging at his lips. "It fits perfectly. She'd have been so happy—"

"She really did buy it for me? I always kind of wondered."

He's shaking his head. "She didn't buy it, Angie. She made it."

The words hit me in my gut. Another secret she kept from me. *No.* The words come from outside of me. *Another secret she didn't trust you with.*

"She was afraid of me," I say. "My best friend was afraid of me."

I wait for Jesse's hand on my back, his sweetness. I look up to find him grinning.

"I'm a little afraid of you," he says.

"What— Why?"

"You're not someone to cross. You might come after me with a blowtorch."

"I don't go after *everyone.*" I want to sound playful but that sorrow creeps in. I can't go five minutes without it finding me.

"No," he says. He's looking at the ground now, at the daisies I know he left for Lizzie. "But Drake wasn't your only target."

So he does want to talk about it. He almost had me fooled. "Nope," I say.

"What changed your mind?"

I don't really want to answer. No, I don't know *how.* Was it love that stopped me, or fear? Or was it the fact that, for the first time since Lizzie died, I felt hope brewing inside me?

I look up at him and he looks like hope embodied. At least, for the time being, I can pretend I did it for him. But even that feels wrong—another lie out of a million.

I tell him the only truth I can find. "I compromised."

He stares at me with that sweetness in his eyes. He hasn't touched me since he got here, not even my hand. I can feel him holding back.

Finally I just ask. I can't help it with him so close. "Is this over? I mean, are we . . ."

I wait for him to nod but he doesn't. He just sits there looking at me. I get the feeling he likes it. Maybe that will be reason enough to stay?

His lips part. I focus on them, in case his words hurt me. "I've thought about that a lot too. About you and me. I was willing to turn my whole world upside down for you. But I never got the feeling you would do that for me."

I shift focus to his eyes. *What world?* I want to ask. *I have nothing left.* But I think Lizzie would be mad if I said that. Like it's wrong to pretend my world revolved around her when I didn't act that way when she was alive.

"Go on," I say shakily.

"But that's probably not fair, and it's probably not true. You were going to turn your world upside down just to punish yourself."

I nod.

"And if I'm truly honest with myself, that's what bothered me," he says.

"What do you mean?"

"The truth is, I was way more scared of you hurting yourself than I was of you hurting others. I'd already lost Lizzie, and you and I had just started to be friends. I couldn't handle losing you too." He pauses, fingers playing with the grass. "There was even a part of me that wanted you to go after her dad. I just couldn't admit it. It made me sick to think I wanted you to hurt somebody because I couldn't."

"Jesse."

"But I couldn't," he says again. "I can't hurt people. Even if they hurt me."

"You shouldn't," I say. "You shouldn't lower yourself to their level."

"That's the thing. That's why I think we're good for each other. You can help me stand up for myself and I can help you choose love over hate."

It sounds beautiful. God, it sounds perfect. But nothing ever is. "You said before you couldn't be a part of my life."

"If you went through with your plans. But you compromised."

"Yeah?"

"So I can compromise too."

"What does that mean?"

He takes my hand. Finally. I feel warmth like I've never known. "It means I can't walk out of your life. I've tried to stop talking to you; I can't, Angie."

"But you're afraid?" I know it's true because I'm afraid too. I swear we can feel each other's emotions.

"Hell yeah." He smiles but it vanishes almost instantly. "I'm terrified. Every time I think about love, I think about losing. Especially with someone who pulls away so hard."

I lower my eyes.

"I'm sorry." His hand goes to my cheek, just for a second. "But it's true."

"So you just want to be friends with me." The words escape my mouth before my brain has fully realized them. They shouldn't hurt as much as they do. Before this moment, I was certain I'd lose him, but I want more than friendship. I want so much more.

"For now," he says. That vanishing smile returns. "I know it won't be easy."

"No, it won't," I agree, though it's not what I want to say. I want to tell him I've tried to pull away from him but I can't either. I want to tell him he's the only thing I want and that I'll fight for him. "We can just be friends," I say instead.

"We can?"

"Of course." I look at Lizzie's gravestone when I say "I need you."

*Please, please know what that means.*

"Just need?" he asks.

"I'm sorry, Jesse. I can't say it. Not when it's already clear I've lost you."

"You haven't." He scoots closer. I shiver. His jacket comes off so quickly, I barely see it before it slides over my shoulders.

I lean into him because I really can't help it. I can't feel angry and I can't feel alone. I'm tired of the darkness. "You promise?" I ask.

"I promise." His arm goes around my shoulders. "I just need to go slow with this. To know you're not going to hurt yourself."

"I won't make you save me," I say. "Just be here for me and I'll be here for you. Okay?"

"Okay." He kisses my cheek.

I keep my face straight ahead, no matter how much I want to turn. To look at him. "What do you think she would think of us? Do you think she'd be angry?"

He shakes his head. I can feel it. "I think she wanted you to be happy more than anything in the world."

"I should have been better to her," I say softly.

"You can be better to you."

"I want to be better for you."

"One thing at a time, Princess."

I close my eyes. I'm so warm now, I don't want him to move away from me. Maybe ever. But I lift my head from his shoulder. "Can you give me a minute?"

"Of course." His voice is soft like he's not at all annoyed with my request. I don't know why I expect people to get mad when I ask for what I want. "Take as long as you want. But I'm going to wait for you." He stands and heads down the hill. He follows the little stone pathways, leaping from one to another when the first one ends. I could watch him play this game all night but I turn back to Lizzie. To the place where they put her body.

I still have so much to say. *I miss you. I should have been the friend you deserved.* But only one thing matters now, for me or for her. For us.

"I love you forever." The daisies rustle like they're reaching out for me. I touch the petals with my fingers. I feel this electricity go through me, this warmth that is both outside and in. One of the petals breaks away in my hand.

*You love me,* I think, remembering the game Lizzie and I used to play with the daisies that grew in her yard. *You love me not?* I pull another petal but end up getting two by mistake. I feel like she's sending me a message from beyond. *Chase the love that is living,* I feel her say. *The love that warms you from inside and out.*

I look down the hill. I can barely see Jesse below, a dancing shadow angel in the blue light of dusk. "I love you too," I say, hoping the wind will carry my words along.

*Tell him,* says the voice that is and isn't me.

I rise on wings of my own and follow him down.

Final dress rehearsal. The energy in this room is indescribable. Jesse and I stayed up half the night putting finishing touches on costumes. Budgets being what they are, Madame Swarsky feared she'd have to use costumes from last year's spring production. But we came to the rescue and now not an actor passes by without a wink or a kiss blown our way. I feel for the first time like I'm a part of something.

I feel for the first time like I belong.

When it came time for my character's entrance, I swept across the room. I might have been walking on air. I might have been dancing. The whispers of my fellow cast members died in their throats as I emerged from a haze of gauze and moonlight. They held their breath as I sang my first note.

And then I was transformed. The Fairy Queen took me over until the last of my lines. As the stunned silence fell upon me I had a moment of doubt, a gripping moment where I feared I would be booed from the stage.

But there was no booing to be heard.

There was only wild applause.

The Players stepped out from their places to give me a standing ovation, the first I've ever had. (One of many, should I say? Should I be greedy? Should I feel hope?) I admit the moment was startling. I felt their acceptance as strongly as one feels an embrace. They cared for me. They wanted more.

I could do no wrong.

Tomorrow is opening night. My nerves are as frayed as a wire spitting electricity. Anyone who touches me will light up like the moon. (Oh, the moon! I shall dance in her light all the way home!) If I can contain this energy and pour it into my performance, maybe you'll see me as I am. A Queen, a wild thing, a creature worthy of being loved. And if this endeavor does not bring love to my door, at least I can say I tried.

I gave it my all, heart and soul.

My body is filled with possibility. It's filled with light and air. I am boundless, giddy, ecstatic. If I were to lift my arms right now, I might float to the ceiling and out into the night.

Honestly, I could fly.

# acknowledgments

THANKS TO MY superhero of an agent, Sandy Lu, for your intelligence, your optimism, and for believing in my work from the start. Without you, none of this would've happened.

Thanks to my amazing editor, Adam Wilson, whose wit and insight have made this a wonderful experience. You are the kind of editor a writer dreams of working with. To the brilliant Julia Fincher, for understanding what I'm trying to do even when I can't articulate it, and for referencing Brian Krakow in a professional correspondence—because you can't beat that. To everyone at Gallery Books, for your hard work and creativity. You've truly humbled me with your awesomeness.

Thanks to my family: John, Sheri, Sarah, and Jordan Pitcher for supporting me, encouraging me, and, let's be honest, entertaining me. If anyone asks where I got my sense of humor, I can always say "I learned it from watching you."

Thanks to the Hauths: Debbie and David for their never-ending support, and Crystal and Kiona for putting up with weird, random texts like "How many minutes do you have between classes?" and "Do people your age say 'filched'?"

Thanks to my readers Selene MacLeod and Brigid Kemmerer, for being the wizards who lent my characters heart when they needed it most.

Thanks to Rachel Schingler and Sunny Williams, for supporting my artistic endeavors from the start—even the melodramatic teen poetry. Sorry about that.

Thanks to Megan Pflum, Stephanie Garis, Ryan VanDordrecht, and Alex M., for being there when I needed a little help from my friends. Or a lot.

Thanks to Sarah Fairchild for telling me the story I couldn't get out of my head, and to Dan Ward for inviting me to the party in the first place.

Thanks to the mysterious Double E, Phoenix Sullivan, the Minions, Hellions, and Critters, for helping me spin straw into gold—or, at least, into straw that glitters in the right kind of light.

And massive, unending thanks to Chris Hauth, my common-law husband, my partner in crime, for *knowing* this would happen when I only ever believed.

Thank you.

GALLERY READERS GROUP GUIDE

# the
# s-word

## CHELSEA PITCHER

# summary

IN *THE S-WORD*, Chelsea Pitcher delivers an unflinchingly acute look at the world of high school students today. Seniors Angie and Lizzie have been friends since they were five, but when Angie walks in on Lizzie and Angie's boyfriend, Drake, together in a hotel room on prom night, their worlds fall apart. Shattered by betrayal, Angie stops speaking to her once best friend, and it seems the entire school is backing her up when they cast Lizzie as a "slut." When Lizzie then commits suicide, strange things start happening: incriminating pages from Lizzie's diary show up in the lockers of the students who harassed her, and the words SUICIDE SLUT show up on Lizzie's locker—in her own handwriting. Angie decides to punish the guilty parties and will stop at nothing, even when her vendetta threatens to consume her. With razor-sharp wit and keen sensibilities, Pitcher illuminates and explores some of the most pressing, deeply relevant issues for modern teenagers.

# questions and topics
# for discussion

1. Angie refers to getting a dose of "high school," a term Kennedy used, to justify why "SLUT" was first written on Lizzie's locker (p. 11). How does the high school environment portrayed in the story compare to your experience? In what ways is it less or more restrictive?

2. Labels at Verity High are powerful and prevalent: prude, slut, queerbait, easy, Drama Queen, Homecoming King, white-trash royalty. Angie contemplates, "I suppose it's hard to treat someone appropriately if you don't know what her classification is" (p. 54). Which characters seem to embrace their labels, and how are they treated by their fellow classmates? What happens to those who reject their assigned labels?

3. Early in the story Angie ponders the fallout from Drake and Lizzie's prom-night encounter, explaining, "while Drake got

off with a boys-will-be-boys slap on the wrist, Lizzie became the Harlot of Verity High" (p. 1). Why do you think some people are judged more harshly for their actions than others? Is it simply based on gender, or are there other factors? Have you ever been judged for things you've done by people who didn't know the full story?

4. Jesse explains that he's an outsider because "I'm Mexican and I'm wearing a skirt. The kids that *don't* want to beat the queer out of me want me deported" (p. 47). The students at Verity seem to feel entitled to condemn the sexuality of people like Jesse and Gordy, and then treat them badly because of it. Were you ever in a situation where you judged someone for his or her sexuality, even when it had nothing to do with you? Why do you think people feel the need to go from maybe being uncomfortable with something, like homosexuality, to outright attacking it?

5. In a conversation with Angie, Jesse says that when he was growing up, people treated him "like stilettos were going to show up on their feet without their permission" (p. 189), simply because *he* dressed differently. In your experience, has anyone ever challenged your idea of how people "should" dress? Have you ever used clothing in a way that challenged people's perceptions?

6. Angie dismisses her mother as "the parent who doesn't want me," while her father is "the one who can't support me"

(p. 157). How do her very different relationships with her parents affect her and inform her choices? Does she share any characteristics with either parent?

7. As her quest for justice progresses, Angie finds out there is more and more that she didn't know about Lizzie—things her own best friend didn't tell her. Angie thinks she would have accepted Lizzie if she had known the truth, but do you think she would have? Have you ever discovered something surprising about someone you thought you knew well? How did it affect your relationship? Were you able to be as understanding as you thought you'd be *before* you found that thing out?

8. When Angie begins to seek justice against those who wronged Lizzie, she feels righteous as a vigilante. Is Angie right to seek this type of justice, or is she merely sinking to the level of the bullies, as Jesse suggests? When bringing wrongdoers to justice, at what point do we cross the line? When, in your opinion, does Angie come near, or even cross, that line?

9. Throughout the course of her investigation, Angie uncovers many of her classmates' secrets. Kennedy's secret, in particular, seems to require further action. What is Angie's responsibility in this situation? Have you ever discovered something that made you feel like you had to intervene, even if you knew people would be angry with you? How would you have handled things if you were in Angie's shoes?

10. In her diary, Lizzie explored her feelings on being branded a "slut," writing, "Ask a hundred people the meaning of that word and you'll hear a hundred answers. It means absolutely nothing" (p. 89). While many of Angie's classmates used the word *slut* with relative ease, they seemed truly shaken when *suicide slut* appeared. What is the S-word? Chelsea Pitcher's website suggests the additional words *severed, silence, secret, shame, separate, shunned, shattered,* and *scorned*. Which word or words carry the most resonance for you in the story?

# taking it further

1. Lizzie, Jesse, and others in *The S-Word* are victims of bullying. If you are comfortable, discuss personal experiences with bullying, how it affected you when it happened, and whether it still affects you today.

2. Think of what you might do next time you see someone being bullied or singled out for ridicule. Planning out your actions ahead of time can help you know what to do when an actual situation arises and you're under pressure to act.

3. Read (or reread) *A Wrinkle in Time* by Madeleine L'Engle or Philip Pullman's *The Golden Compass*, two of the books on Lizzie's bookshelf. Consider the ways the stories address religion and science, and why that would have held significance for Lizzie.

# enhance your book club

CHELSEA PITCHER'S WEBSITE, www.ChelseaPitcher.com, includes information about her book and short stories, as well as links to her Facebook page, her Twitter handle, and her blog. Your group can reach out to her with questions about the story or share feedback from your book club experience.